W hat readers of the ebook edition of *A Death in Winter: 1963*, had to say:

Y ou can follow Jim's trials and tribulations as he writes the ⌐ ·· www.goodreads.com/au

GW00585660

A Death in Winter: 1963

Jim McGrath

ISBN-10: 1-91-260545-7

ISBN-13: 978-1-91-260545-3 (j-views Publishing)

Published by j-views Publishing, 2018

Body set in 11pt Brioso Pro, chapter titles and headings in Motorway

www.j-views.biz

publish@j-views.biz

j-views Publishing, 26 Lombard Street, Lichfield, UK, WS13 6DR

A DEATH IN
WINTER: 1963

A note on time and place

The winter of 1963 remains the coldest on record since 1740. The sea froze, and snow and ice covered Britain from the 26th December 1962 until late March 1963. Yet schools did not close, people continued to go to work and life went on as usual.

This book contains racist and sexist language. I don't wish to offend people by its use. However, just as smoking was a feature of life in the 1960s, and is depicted as such, so too was sexist and racist language.

The Black Country has no clearly defined borders, but it is usually defined as "the area where the coal seam comes to the surface". This includes Brierley Hill, West Bromwich, Oldbury, Blackheath, Cradley Heath, Old Hill, Bilston, Dudley, Tipton and Walsall. Using the above definition Wolverhampton is not part of the Black Country but try telling that to the locals and you may get a thick ear.

Each town has its own version of the Black Country dialect and none of them share any resemblance to the typical "Brummie" accent. The following few words are used by Clark and other characters throughout the book to give an impression of how a person from West Bromwich might sound.

Ain't = will not	Wi = we
Bostin = good/great	Wiek = week
Dain't = did not	Wem = we are
Kidda = friend	Yow = you
Sommut = something	Yowm = you are
Tarrar or tarrar a bit = goodbye	Yam Yam = person from the Black Country

Contents

Acknowledgements

Davidavid Brown was a police officer in the West Bromwich and Lichfield City Police Forces for several years during the 1960s and early 1970s before becoming a social worker. I think it's fair to say that without David's encouragement, help and support this book may never have been completed. He has acted as technical advisor, grammarian, critical friend and initial proof reader.

A man of many talents, David also painted the cover for this book, which I think you will agree is stunning. He also allowed me to adapt two stories from his unpublished short story collection *Brown in Blue* for this book, namely Three O'clock at the Swan and Death Message.

I would also like to thank Stephen McGrath, who was a police officer for over 20 years with the Staffordshire Police Service for the numerous anecdotes that he has provided from his time on the job. As the Collins and Clark books move beyond the 1960s much more use will be made of Stephen's insights into policing. Steve, it's a great shame that Tony is not with us to read the book. I'm sure he would be telling me where I got it wrong.

Hugh Ashton is an authority on Sherlock Holmes and has written several collections of Holmes stories which have been extremely well received. He has also written many thrillers. He is also the man who took the time and trouble to read my work and offer to publish it.

I'd also like to acknowledge the late Jo Lowe, CEO and editor. I only knew her for a very short space of time, but she was a constant source of encouragement and positivity. You'll be missed, Boss, by all your writers.

A DEATH IN WINTER: 1963

JIM McGRATH

A COLLINS & CLARK STORY

J-VIEWS PUBLISHING, LICHFIELD, ENGLAND

Part One: Earlies

Friday 8th February 1963.
Stratford-upon-Avon, 19.10hrs.

The phone rang twice before the Major picked it up.
'Yes?' he asked.

'It's me, Andrew.' The voice was high-pitched and panicked. 'She's dead.'

'Hang up,' he said calmly. 'I'll be over immediately.'

'Who was that, dear?' his wife asked from the sitting room, where she was watching *Take Your Pick*.

'Andrew. The silly fool has had an accident and skidded off the road. I'll take the Land Rover and pull him out.'

'Very well dear, but do be careful. It's so slippery underfoot. I really do think that this is the worst winter we've had since 1947.'

'Shan't be long, old thing,' he said, as he closed the front door. He could feel his anger rising. What a stupid, pathetic bugger Andy was. Would he never learn? Last time it was feeding sleeping pills to that Irish girl as if they were sweets, just so he could bugger her. Thank God the doc had been around to sort her out – and now this. Andrew was becoming a bloody liability to the group.

The Major brushed past Andrew and took the stairs two at a time and opened the bedroom door. His bulk blocking the entrance, he quickly surveyed the bedroom.

The girl lying face down on the bed was no more than fifteen. Her dark skin contrasted with the brilliant white of the Egyptian sheets and the bright yellow of her garter belt.

A pillow had been pushed under her hips, her legs partially opened. A long ribbon of purple velvet was wrapped around her neck. It had dug deep into the flesh when pulled tight. A wine glass and some pills lay on the carpet.

Probably knocked from the night table as she thrashed about, he thought, as he felt a familiar tightening in his groin.

Andrew began to snivel again. 'It wasn't my fault,' he cried. 'We've done it before. She liked it,' he whined like a spoilt child who had just broken a favourite toy.

'Well, I think we can safely say she didn't enjoy it this time, you stupid fucking moron.' Moving with surprising grace for his size, the Major crossed to the bed and flicked the sheet over the girl's body. He'd seen worse, much worse, than this in Berlin at the end of the War. When he spoke, his voice was calm and measured. It was the voice of a man who was used to dealing with problems. 'Where's she from?'

'Handsworth.'

'Good. That suits us. Call Phillip. Ask him to come over with a van. Then find something to wrap the body in. Make sure it can't be traced back to you or Stratford. Got it?'

'Yes.' Andrew ran the back of his hand across his dripping nose. For the first time in the last forty minutes, he felt better. With the Major in charge, everything would be all right.

'Good; then get along. You and Phillip can dump the stupid bitch back where she belongs tonight.'

With Andrew gone, the man locked the door and returned to the bed. He pulled the sheet aside and pushed the girl's legs wider apart. The vein in his right temple began to throb. His mouth had gone dry from the adrenalin coursing through his body. He felt his heart flutter as he undid his flies. *Just like old times*, he thought. Just like Berlin.

Sunday 10th February 1963.

Handsworth, 15.00hrs.

Collins stood near the gates of Handsworth Park and stamped his feet, thankful that he had decided to wear his police boots and not his black brogues. He rubbed his ears and shivered with the cold as he looked across to the boating lake, which was frozen solid. The weeping willows that edged the pond were covered in ice and a light dusting of snow. Every now and then the wind moved the stiff branches and small puffs of snow floated to the ground, adding to the three-foot drifts that had piled up against the frozen trunks.

He fumbled for the list of rooms to rent that the station sergeant had given him, his thick gloves catching in the lining of his pockets. There was just one to go. He was starting to feel dispirited. The first two on the list had displayed identical signs in their front window, "Room to let. No blacks, no dogs, no Irish". At the third house he'd been told, "The room's gone," as soon as he opened his mouth. He didn't take the rejections personally. *After all,* he thought, *it's their house. They can rent their rooms to who they like.*

Tucking a stray lock of chestnut-brown hair under his woollen hat, he trudged on looking for the "Mad Woman's house". The word in the station was that she was a religious maniac. *It'll be just my fecking luck if she turns out to hate Catholics,* he thought.

Underfoot, the compacted snow was as hard as iron and Collins regularly felt his foot slip. A half mile further on, he finally found the house. It was set back from the road and protected by eight-foot iron railings and matching gates. He pushed hard against the gates, dislodging two inches of snow that covered the top rail, and walked up the drive. The house was huge, with three double windows on each side of a solid oak front door, which looked as if it had been pillaged from a castle. The U-shaped drive had been cleared of snow and a grey Rover 100 was parked outside the garage doors. The whole place screamed money and position. Suppressing an urge to shine his boots on the back of his trouser legs and look for the tradesman's entrance, Collins grabbed the brass bell pull and, with a silent prayer to St Joseph, patron saint of the homeless, pulled.

He heard the click of Agnes Winter's heels on the parquet floor and steeled himself for the worst.

'Yes, can I help you?'

Collins was surprised at the sight that confronted him. This was not the religious lunatic he'd been expecting. Agnes was about an inch shorter than he, which would make her 5 foot 10. She had thick auburn hair cut short into a neat bob, with the odd grey hair starting to appear. Her mouth was full, with laughter lines at the corners. Her nose, long and slender. But it was her emerald green eyes that held him. They shone with a mixture of intelligence and toughness that he had rarely seen in any man or woman. Collins found it hard to look away and even harder to speak.

Finally, finding his voice, he said, 'I'm Constable Collins from Thornhill Road Police Station. The Desk Sergeant said you had a room to let.'

Agnes smiled, her eyes sparkling, and stepped back from the door. 'Indeed I do. Please come in, Constable Collins.' Her voice was deep and her accent proof of an expensive education.

After a brief inspection of the room and ground-floor kitchen, Collins found himself seated at a walnut table drinking tea from a bone china cup. He put his tea down and took another bite out of Agnes' homemade fruit cake. As he chewed, he decided that even if he was offered the room he'd never be able to afford it.

Agnes came in and he stood up. 'How do you like the room?'

'It's grand, but I don't think I can afford it.'

'Are you saying that your policeman's pay won't stretch to £2.10s a week. They really must be paying you a pittance.'

'I can manage that, but why would you let it go for next to nothing? It's easily worth £5 or £6 a week.'

'Didn't they tell you at the station? I'm a religious lunatic. I like to be charitable to deserving policemen.'

'That's very kind, but I don't take charity.'

'Oh, do stop it. I'm joking. I'm not a religious fanatic – at least I don't think I am. I've rented rooms to policemen for over ten years and it's proved to be a mutually beneficial arrangement. You see, my guests and I feel less vulnerable if there is a policeman living on the premises.'

'Guests?'

'Yes. From time to time I have women stay with me while they sort themselves out. They might be going through a divorce or separation and they need to get away from home for a while. Unfortunately, their husbands or boyfriends don't always like the idea. Some of them can become aggressive.'

'I see, and that's when a copper on the premises comes in handy.'

'Precisely. So for £2.10s a week, you not only get a roof over your head but a chance to improve your arrest record at no extra charge. So will you take it?'

'It's a lovely room, Mrs Winters. I'd be daft not to.'

'Good, but please call me Agnes. I don't believe in titles and I've no intention of calling you Constable Collins or Mr Collins. What's your first name?'

'Michael.'

'Any relation to *the* Michael Collins?'

'Yes, but you'd have to go back to when St Patrick was in short pants to find the link. Does that make a difference to your offer?'

She shook her head and, holding out her hand, said,

'Welcome Michael Collins. I think we're going to get on splendidly.'

—————

It took Collins all of two hours to move from the couch he'd been sleeping on in the Station House for the last two nights to his new digs. Everything he owned in the world fitted into a medium-sized brown leather suitcase, which looked as if it had seen service on the Titanic. Given that he'd never had a chance to unpack, most of his police kit was already stored in the case, along with an envelope containing the Birmingham City Police Stores voucher listing every item that had been issued to him and would have to be returned when he left the service. He spread out his police trousers, tunics and cape, then covered them with his one and only suit, two jumpers, a dark grey pair of trousers, sports coat, four shirts, underwear, a towel and shaving gear. He topped his packing off by adding his baton and handcuffs. The case was still barely three quarters full. *Best to travel light*, he thought, as he wrapped his eleven-stone frame into his father's old great coat, then picked up his case and the felt string bag that contained his helmet.

As he left the station, night was falling, along with the temperature. Somehow it didn't seem as cold as it had been a few hours earlier, nor the walk as long. From a nearby open window, he could hear someone playing the Beatles' latest record: *"Please Please Me"*. He had to admit they were good, but they'd never replace Elvis. He smiled at two young boys repairing a snowman in their front garden. Its head had fallen off and they were working to glue it back together using fresh snow, which would freeze overnight. He tried to remember the last time he'd built a snowman but couldn't. Maybe he would build one before the winter was over. For no reason he wondered when Agnes had last built a snowman. Perhaps they could build one together. He held that thought in his mind as he set out for Hamstead Road, his dark green eyes bright and alive. For the first time since he had left Dublin five months earlier, he felt truly happy.

Monday 11th February 1963.

Handsworth, 07.15hrs.

Collins had been told to report to the Superintendent at 9am sharp. The alarm sounded at 7.15, but he was already awake and quickly shut it off. *First day on the job,* he thought, and his heart missed a beat. Was it nerves he felt in his stomach or excitement? He couldn't be sure.

Pushing the bedclothes off, he swung his legs onto the floor and for an instant luxuriated in the feel of the carpet between his curled toes and the warmth of the bedroom. *Thank God for central heating!* he thought, grabbed his towel and shaving gear, and headed for the bathroom. Before stepping out onto the landing, he quickly checked that nothing was sticking out that shouldn't, while hoping that Agnes didn't have any guests. As he walked along the landing, he resolved to buy a dressing gown from his next wages.

Thirty minutes later, shaved, washed and dressed, he walked into the kitchen and stopped as if he had run into a plate glass window. Standing by the cooker was a woman who was no more than 5 foot tall, with bottle blonde hair, a red blouse and fishnet stockings. She had slim legs, upon which was balanced an enormous backside that was winning the fight with her short black skirt. It looked as if it would explode and make a run for freedom at any moment. She was standing lopsided as the heel on her right shoe was missing, and she seemed to be wearing some sort of turban. It was only when she turned around that Collins could see that it was a bandage secured by a large safety pin over her left eye, which was blue, black, red and swollen. It was impossible to guess how old she was. She had a face that had lived a thousand stories, none of them with a happy ending.

'Hello handsome. Come on in. I won't bite – unless yous

want me to.'

Just then, Agnes brushed past. 'Michael, I see you've met Gloria. She arrived at 3 this morning. What was it this time, Gloria? A disagreement with a rounders bat or a blackjack?'

'Christ, Agnes, you're going gaga. I told yous; he hit me with the pan.'

'Yes, yes you did, but it was the middle of the night and I only had one eye and half a brain cell working at the time.'

'Is he the new copper?' Gloria asked, as if Michael wasn't in the room.

'Yes.'

'Well yous better get over here then and cook yous breakfast fast. Unless we put a bit of meat on them bones, yous will be crap when Harry comes looking for me.'

'Harry?' asked Michael.

'Her pimp,' said Agnes.

'I'll see you later, gorgeous,' said Gloria, before limping out of the kitchen with a cup of tea in one hand and a bacon butty in the other.

'What happened to your heel?' Michael called after her.

'Oh that,' she said, looking down. 'The last time I saw it, it were buried in Harry's head.'

When Gloria was out of earshot, Michael turned to Agnes and said, 'When you said that you helped women who had been hurt by men I thought you meant married women. Not...' His voice trailed off.

Agnes' voice was curt and steely as she asked, 'Do you mean prostitutes?'

'Yes.'

'I help all women who are in need. No exceptions. Does that bother you, Constable?' Her voice was low and as cold as last night's freezing temperature.

Michael was conscious of her eyes boring into him. He felt a tremor run down his spine and knew with absolute certainty that if he said the wrong thing he'd find himself looking for new lodgings. Finally, he replied, 'No. No. Of course not. It's just that she caught me by surprise. I wasn't ready for...' he struggled to find the right words, before settling on, 'the sight that confronted me.'

He realised how stupid he sounded and, looking at Agnes, he started to laugh. Within seconds, Agnes was also laughing uncontrollably and had to resort to pushing a tea towel in her mouth to stop.

When the laughter finally subsided Agnes said, 'I'm not sure anyone is ever prepared for Gloria,' which set Michael off again.

———◆———

Sergeant Ridley marched Collins into the Superintendent's office at 9am on the dot. Collins halted in front of the Superintendent, came to attention and saluted.

'Probationary Constable Collins reporting for duty, Sir.'

'Thank you, Sergeant Ridley. I'll take it from here.' The Superintendent waited until Ridley had left, then said, 'Stand easy, Collins.'

Superintendent Hollis was a thick set man with broad shoulders that were pinned back as if an iron rod ran across the back of his neck, a powerful chest, and a large head. The left side of his face was pockmarked with shrapnel wounds and the little finger on his left hand was missing from the first knuckle. He stubbed out the cigarette he'd been smoking and lit another.

Collins decided that he was probably ex-army and, judging by the row of campaign medals, he'd had an eventful war. Everything in his bearing and posture exuded self-confidence. Clearly not a man to mess with, Collins decided.

'Sorry we couldn't put you up in the Station House, but as you know the water tank burst and flooded three rooms. God knows when we'll get it sorted out. Available plumbers are as rare as pools winners these days. Anyway, I hear you've got digs with Agnes Winter?'

'Yes, Sir.'

'A fine woman. A Quaker, you know. Friend of the Cadbury family, I believe. Everything all right on that front?'

'Oh yes, Sir. Grand, thanks.'

'From your file I see that your grandfather was in the Royal Irish Constabulary and that your uncle is a Chief Superintendent in the Met. Why didn't you join the Garda or the Met?'

'I didn't want people thinking I was trading on the family name. Nor did I want people comparing me to me grandfather or uncle.'

'Want to do it on your own, eh? Well, that's probably wise. Just one more thing before I bring your partner in. Your scores during training were uniformly high. One officer described you as possessing, and I quote, "a very high level of intelligence". But then I think you already know that you're brighter than most, don't you?'

Collins remained silent.

The Superintendent smiled. 'Good for you. You know when to keep your mouth shut, so you probably already know that you don't want to flaunt it in front of the men. Save it for your sergeant's and inspector's exams. Coppers don't trust bright sparks. They think they'll bottle out when things get rough. What the average copper wants is a mate they can rely on in a tight corner. Win their trust and you'll be in. Now I think it's time you met Constable Clark, who is a bit of a character but a bloody good copper.' Without expanding on what he meant, Hollis pressed the button on his intercom and said, 'Sergeant Ridley, send Constable Clark in please.'

Moments later, the door opened and Collins was confronted with the smallest policeman he'd ever seen. At just 5 feet 5 inches, and weighing around 9 stone, he looked more like a flat jockey than a policeman. His face was thin and his features were sharp and regular. Like so many thin people his eyes appeared deep-set, hidden in shadows. His nose had a distinct bump in the middle where it had been broken and reset in a hurry. Two rows of campaign ribbons adorned his chest and the crease in his trousers was sharp enough to cut the unwary. The toe caps of his boots had been bulled with dubbin and polished to a brilliant finish.

'Clark, this is Collins, our new probationer. I want you to teach him everything you know.'

'Yow must be joking Sir? What I knows would never fit in that tiny skull.'

'Ignore him, Collins. Clark believes that anyone born outside a one mile radius of the Hawthorns is mentally sub-normal. Isn't that right, Clark?'

'Damn right, Sir. In fact, I'm starting to think it should be half a mile.'

Collins had no idea what or where the Hawthorns was, but stepped forward and held out his hand. 'Pleased to meet you.'

'Oh sod me, Sir, not another bloody Paddy. Even a sodding Brummie is better than another Paddy.'

Collins was about to snap at the bait, but he resisted the temptation. Instead, he reeled his temper in and said, 'Is that right? Let's see if you feel the same after a month.' His eyes, locked on Clark's face, never wavered.

Clark looked at the Superintendent, who was trying hard not to laugh. 'I'll say one thing, Boss, this one has a pair of brass balls on him. Cocky bastard.' With that, Clark held out his hand.

Collins found the grip dry, honest and surprisingly strong. As he withdrew his hand, he felt the texture of Clark's skin. It was hard and abrasive, like pumice stone.

Outside, Clark said, 'Wait here, Paddy. I'll see if the Sergeant has anything for us. Then I'll start to learn you everything I know about police work.'

'Fine, but me name's not Paddy.'

'What?'

'You can call me Collins, Michael, Mike, even Mickey, but not Paddy. If you do, I'll just ignore you.'

'Strewth. Yowm a sensitive soul yow. Mickey it is then. With those ears, yow look like a bleeding mouse anyway.'

Before Collins could think of a reply, Clark had gone. He returned minutes later with a piece of paper. 'Well, Mickey, it's our lucky day. We're off to see Mrs Ashcroft. She's complaining about fly tippers – again.'

'Fly tipping? Shouldn't the council look after that?'

'Normally they would, but she's got contacts. Her old man used to be Chairman of the Watch Committee so she gets our silver service. One thing. We don't ever go in her house.'

'Why not?'

'Yow'll see. And while we're laying down a few rules: yow can call me Clark, Clarkee or Chipper. Only me mother and father ever call me Clive. Clive makes me sound like a right ponce, OK?'

'Fine.'

'The only other thing yow have to remember is: if we ever get in a punch up, get behind me and watch me back. Leave the rest to me. Do that and I'll get yow through your month's attachment, and yow might learn enough to survive the remaining twenty-three months of yowr probation.'

For a moment Collins thought about protesting that he could look after himself, but there was something in Clark's slate grey eyes that didn't allow for disagreement.

Clark set off at a brisk 2.5 miles an hour, which Collins found hard to keep up with, given the conditions. The roads were passable, but the pavements hadn't been cleared, and conditions under foot were treacherous.

'I'd normally cut through the park, but yow'd need bleeding snow shoes after last night. I'm afraid it's the long way round for us, Mickey. Come on; keep up.'

As they walked down Holly Road and along Grove Lane, Clark kept up a running commentary on the occupants of various houses and streets that they passed. Wife beater, tea leafs, slags, Toms, pimps, burglars, hard bastards, Teddy Boys, receivers. Nothing big.

Collins broke into the monologue and asked, 'What about Birmingham? Anything bigger there?'

'There's a few bigger firms. One or two that go in for armed robbery and the like, but nothing like the London gangs.'

'Why's that? I would have thought they'd be in here like pigs at a trough.'

'Bloody hell, yow ask a lot of questions. Training to be a detective, are yow? Brum has this thing called the Watch Committee. They enforce the licencing laws and everything is closed by 11 pm, so there are no nightclubs worth the name. Nowhere for the Krays and their mates to put their money and have a good time. There's also the Welcome Wagon.'

'The Welcome Wagon?'

'Yeah, whenever one of the London boys is spotted, a DCI and a couple of the boys pay him a visit and explain why he should piss off back to London before something nasty happens to him and his mates.'

'And it works?'

'Oh yeah. It's amazing how co-operative these guys can be when hanging upside down outside a sixth-floor window.'

'Does that really happen?'

'Last time I were on the Welcome Wagon, I was holding some guy by the balls for fifteen minutes while the Inspector explained why he should leave and go home that night. It were really painful.'

'I bet.'

'Yeah, I got terrible cramp in me fingers, but he were very attentive.'

At the top of Grove Lane, Clark slowed down as he approached a row of newly built semi-detached houses set well back from the road. At the third house, a dark-haired woman in her early thirties was cleaning the inside of the lounge window. Clark stopped and waved to attract her attention. She eventually caught sight of him and waved back. He gave one final wave and walked on with a smile on his face.

It was the first time Collins had seen him smile and it

transformed his face to that of a child's on Christmas morning. Collins said nothing but began to turn over the various possibilities of who the woman was in his mind. Wife? Unlikely, as she was ten or fifteen years younger than Clark. Girlfriend? Unlikely. Sister? No, he'd been too glad to see her. Fancy woman? Maybe.

———

Even before he pushed open Mrs Ashcroft's gate, Collins could smell it. Cat pee. The pungent smell of ammonia stung his nostrils. It came in waves from the house and surrounding garden, which had an unnaturally high percentage of yellow snow. Even ten yards from the house, and in the middle of winter, the smell was overpowering. Hell knows what it was like in summer.

Clark knocked on the door, then took two steps back and three to the side. Collins remained in line with the door. That was a mistake. As the door opened the full force of the stench hit him like a brick in a sock. An old woman with one stocking around her ankle, and cats' hairs covering her skirt and jumper, looked at Clark and said, 'Well, I must say you took your time, Sergeant Clark. I phoned on Saturday morning.'

'Sorry, Mrs. Ashcroft. I only got your message today,' he said loudly, as he backed off even further. 'I can only apologise.'

Collins followed suit and moved back.

'I should think so. In my husband's day, when he was Chairman of the Watch Committee, such tardiness would not have been tolerated.'

'You're right, Mrs Ashcroft, standards have fallen since the war.'

'Quite right. They have. It's a pleasure to find another who sees the decline so clearly.'

Collins suppressed a smile. Clark had changed his accent, agreed with everything the old lady had said and had in a matter of seconds placated the old dear. Maybe there were some things he could learn from the little man after all.

'Would you and your man like to come in for a cup of tea?'

Clark was prepared for the invitation. 'That's very kind of you, Mrs Ashcroft, but we have a burglary to go to on Rookery Road as soon as we finish up here,' he lied. 'So if you can just tell us where you saw the man drop the rubbish.'

'It's over there in the ditch between the road and the allotments. If you find an address, I do hope you'll prosecute.'

Collins looked in the direction she was pointing and moved towards the ditch. Anything to get away from the stench. The weekend's snow had covered whatever had been dumped. Using his truncheon Collins started to prod his way along the ditch.

'It's further up the lane, young man,' cried Mrs Ashcroft.

Collins moved to his right and almost immediately saw the flaps of a cardboard box. Clearing the top snow, he could see some clothes and a roll of felt inside. He grabbed the edges of the box and pulled hard. The box came out as if it were a sled and Collins fell backwards arse over tip. As he lay on the hard snow, he started to laugh. Looking towards Clark he expected to see the same reaction, but Clark was running towards him ashen-faced. Only when he sat up did Collins see the girl's head, arm and naked shoulder protruding from her felt shroud.

———

Detective Inspector Hicks had taken charge. He was new to the station, but came with the reputation of being honest and fair. The word was that he'd cocked up his last case at the Met and had decided that his future lay away from the bright lights of London.

Breaking away from the pathologist, he walked over to Collins who was seated on a low brick wall, writing up his notebook and drinking a cup of tea provided by Mrs Ashcroft's neighbour.

'You all right, Collins?'

'Fine, Sir.'

'Good man. Hell of a way to start your first day on the job. Why don't you and Clark do a house-to-house for the rest of the road and check if anyone saw anything. If you find anything, tell Sergeant York. He'll take the statement. Then piss off to the station and get a bite to eat.'

'Yes, Sir. Thank you, Sir.'

Hicks re-joined the huddle of officers that were organising a search of the ditch and adjoining ground, and Collins went looking for Clark. He found him in the neighbour's kitchen with a cup of tea and a round of buttered toast in front of him. Collins looked at him accusingly.

'Perks of seniority, Mickey boy. Yow get a cup of tea and a cold wall to sit on and possibly piles while I get the honoured visitor's treatment. What can I say?'

'Well, now we both get the honoured job of canvassing the rest of the neighbours courtesy of Inspector Hicks.'

Clark started to reply when the neighbour, Mrs Wilcox, came in. She was in her sixties and had a cheerful red face and twinkling blue eyes. Collins guessed that she would have been a handful in her youth. The centre of attention wherever she went.

'Another cup of tea, officer?'

'No thanks, Mrs Wilcox. That were bostin. The Inspector wants Constable Clark here and me to check if anyone in the road saw anything on Friday night. Would yow mind answering a few questions?'

'Not at all. I know I shouldn't say it, but this is the most excitement we've had around here since the ack-ack guns on Hill Top shot down the German bomber in 1942 – or was that '43?'

Clark pulled out his notebook. 'I'll keep the notes.'

Collins was surprised. He'd expected Clark to take the lead with the questioning. *Maybe he's testing me*, he thought.

The three of them sat down at the kitchen table and Collins tried to remember what he'd been taught about interviewing a witness.

'Were you in on Friday night?'

'Oh yes. Me and my husband normally go to the Uplands for a drink with our friends, Harry and Maud, on a Friday, but it was much too cold to go out last Friday. Blooming perishing, it was. So we stopped in and watched *Take your Pick.*'

'What time did you go to bed?'

'About 11.'

'And your bedroom is at the front of the house?'

'Yes.'

'After that, did you see or hear anything?'

'No. I fell asleep as soon as my head touched the pillow. You really need to speak to my hubby, Bert. He's up and down to the toilet five or six times a night. He might have seen something.'

'When will he be in?'

'He's normally back from work by 5.30, but give him time to have his dinner. He's always in a foul mood until he's had his dinner. So, say 6.30.'

'Well, that seems to be...'

'Just one last question, Mrs Wilcox,' said Clark. Have yow seen any cars or men hanging around the Avenue recently?'

'No, it's too cold for that sort of thing.'

'What sort of thing?' asked Collins.'

'You know, canoodling and such like. In the summer we get a lot of couples parking by the ditch and walking up the hill. Did you know that Hill Top is the second highest point in Birmingham? At night you can see all the lights in Birmingham spread out beneath you, winking like diamonds and rubies.' She paused before adding, 'Not that those who go up the hill are interested in the view. I know I never was.'

As they left the house, Collins said, 'I should have asked her about cars and strangers.'

'No worry. Yow did OK. It ain't easy to remember everything when yow know some sod like me is watching yow. Just try to relax.'

'OK.'

The remaining six houses in the Lane produced no new information. The two men sat on the wall that Collins had vacated an hour earlier and made up their notebooks, careful to ensure that they both recorded the same information and times. They knew how defence barristers loved to exploit even the most minor details in an officer's notebook in an attempt to plant the seed of reasonable doubt in the mind of jurors. Finished, they reported to Inspector Hicks and then headed back to the station for some snap.

———

Both men had eggs, beans, sausages and chips. They then proceeded to argue if what they had eaten was either a British or Irish breakfast, Michael claimed that the Brits had pinched it from Ireland in the 19th century – but Clark was having none of it. Their dispute was still going on when they sat down to write their statements.

Clark finished writing at 4 pm, waved tarrar and went home. Collins couldn't resist the opportunity to see what Clark had written. He wanted to see what was considered an acceptable standard and reckoned that Clark's report would be around the minimum required. Retrieving the report from the Inspector's in-tray, Collins was surprised to find that it was a superb example of how to write a report using simple, clear, accurate English that highlighted all the main points and left no room for ambiguity or confusion. Even the handwriting was elegant and precise. It was the second time that day that the little man had surprised him and he wondered what other surprises Clark might have up his sleeve.

Collins returned to his desk, ripped up his draft and started again. He continued to write and rewrite his statement like an author polishing a piece of prose. It was his first day, his first murder and his first statement. He wanted it to be perfect. But no matter how hard he tried it didn't match Clark's work. Making a promise to himself that he would improve, he finally signed and handed in his report at 5.45.

Stepping outside, he suddenly felt exhausted. The excitement of the day, the adrenalin rush that had followed finding the body, even the mundane experience of talking to the neighbours had left him drained. *I'm going to sleep the sleep of the dead tonight*, he thought.

At the Park Gates Stores, he picked up a loaf of bread, a bottle of milk, a packet of Brook Bond tea, sugar, bacon, eggs and a packet of Walls sausages. Another fry-up and bed were calling him.

He was about to turn right on Holly Road and head for home when he remembered Bert Wilcox. It was just gone 6 pm. Bert would be home. With a resigned sigh, he turned left and headed for Ashcroft Avenue.

B ert was enjoying an after-dinner cup of tea when Mrs Wilcox showed Collins into the snug dining room. The coals of the open fire were glowing red and barely a string of smoke escaped up the chimney.

'You get warm, love, and I'll get you a cuppa and a sandwich. You look like you could use both.'

Mr Wilcox turned the telly off and said, 'Mavis tells me you want to talk about Friday night last. Ask me if I saw anything. Well, happens I did.' His accent was different to those Collins had been hearing all day. More like those used in old George Formby films.

'You did?' said Collins, his tiredness washed away by a flood of excitement.

'Didn't I just say so, lad? It was 2.20. I know 'cos I looked at the clock when I got up to go to the lavatory, like I always do. I heard a car on the road. The curtains weren't full drawn so I went over to close them. That's when I saw them lifting a cardboard box out the back of an Austin A35 van.'

Collins felt his pulse quicken and worked hard to keep his voice level. 'Did you get a registration number?'

'No. It were parked sideways onto the house. But it were green, if that's any help.'

'Oh yes, it is. Are you sure it was a green A35 van? I mean it was dark?'

Leaning forward, Mr Wilcox fixed Collins with a stare. 'I'd been working with cars for twenty years before you were even an itch in your father's pants. So if I say it were a green Austin A35 van, you can be bloody sure it were.'

'Yes, of course. I'm sorry. I didn't mean to question your knowledge. I just wanted to be certain. What about the man? Can you tell me anything about him?'

'Men, lad, not man. There were two of them.'

'Mrs Ashcroft only saw one man.'

'She also thinks that she still owns the land that the rest of the houses in the road are built on, but she's wrong about that an' all. Stuck up snob. Puts on all sorts of airs and graces because her husband was a bloody alderman. Treats us like we're skivvies living in her bloody garden.'

'The men, Mr Wilcox?'

'One were tall. Six foot or more and skinny. I'd guess he was around twenty, and he had long, light-coloured hair like them Beatle characters.'

'Sounds like you got a good look at him.'

'I did. I remember thinking he were a right prat wearing no hat with the temperature below freezing. Besides, he were standing in front of the sidelights. I could see him plain.'

'And the other?'

'He were a bit older. Thicker set. Muffled up well against the cold. He seemed to be giving the orders and it were him that were driving.'

'Would you recognise either man again if you saw them?'

'The young one for sure. Not the other.'

Between chomping on his sandwich, Collins went over the details twice more with Mr Wilcox and jotted them down in his notebook before he left. He'd never sleep now. He was too excited. He'd found a clue.

In his rush to get back to the station and report this important information to the Duty Detective, he'd half run, half trotted 400 yards before he realised that he'd left his shopping at the Wilcox's and had to retrace his steps.

—————•—————

Collins arrived at the station and headed for the CID Room. Sergeant O'Driscoll was sitting behind his desk, feet up, reading through a pile of crime reports. His hair, grey and thinning, was uncombed, his tie askew, shirt tail flapping in the wind and his beer belly overlapping his worn brown belt, he looked every inch of an Irish farmer. Looking up, he squinted and asked, 'Collins?'

'Yes, Sergeant.'

'Come in and shut the door. This place is bloody freezing at night.' His accent was unmistakably from the north side of Dublin.

'How did you guess?'

'You're new and I know every other bugger in the station. Here,' he said waving his cup in the air, 'the kettle's just boiled. Make me a cuppa and have one yourself.'

Collins brewed up and carried both cups over to the Sergeant. As O'Driscoll removed his feet from the desk, Collins noticed that there was a hole in his left sole. 'So, what's brought you back this time of night?'

Collins quickly outlined the contents of his conversation with Mr Wilcox.

'Well, me fine lad, not only do you find a body on your first day, but a clue as well. They'll be making you Sergeant before you know it.'

'Do you think we should call the Inspector in?'

'Now if I go doing that, then neither he nor, more importantly, you are going to get out of here before midnight – which means that you'll be knackered in the morning after less than five hours' sleep. No, me fine friend. This is good stuff, but it will still be good stuff in the morning. So write up your notes and get off home to bed. I'll brief the boss in the morning. I'm sure he'll want to see you.'

'OK. Thanks, Sergeant.'

'Use York's desk.'

Collins moved to the bombsite that was Sergeant York's desk and carefully cleared the papers that covered the ink blotter. Searching in the top drawer, he found an officer's statement form and started to fill in the details of his conversation with Wilcox. He took his time double-checking everything he wrote with the contents of his notebook. It was nearly 10 by the time he'd finished.

Looking up, he saw that O'Driscoll had fallen asleep over an unopened file. Collins sighed. It looked like there was more than tea in O'Driscoll's cup. Standing up he pushed the chair back with maximum noise.

O'Driscoll sat up and grinned. 'I'm at an age when I need me beauty sleep,' he said, by way of explanation. 'Are you finished?'

Collins nodded.

'Good. Give it to me and I'll put it in the Inspector's hand first thing in the morning.'

Collins handed over his report, picked up his shopping and had his hand on the door handle when O'Driscoll asked, 'Do you know where Wilcox works, laddie?'

'No, I never asked. Is it important?'

'No, not that important, but Hicks will want York to take a full statement and he won't want to wait until Wilcox comes home. Don't worry, York can get the details from the wife.'

Collins opened the door and stepped into the corridor. He should have thought of that. He should have asked Wilcox where he worked. Sod it. Well, that was another mistake he'd never make again.

Tuesday 12th February 1963.

Handsworth, 05.45hrs.

Collins was first to arrive for Parade. He'd hardly slept the night before, tossing and turning in bed trying to work out what Mr Wilcox's information meant to the investigation. One thing was sure: more than one man was involved in the girl's death. He just had time to brief Clark on what he'd discovered before they went on Parade, handcuffs and truncheon at the ready to show the Sergeant when required.

At 6am sharp, Collins and Clark left the station. Walking the beat for the first time was an unusual experience. Collins quickly realised that the uniform set him apart from the rest of the crowd on Soho Road. Some nodded good morning or waved as they hurried to the early shift at work; others gave way to him and Clark as they passed; and a few, those with a guilty conscience, seemed to sigh with relief as he passed by.

Shopkeepers were keen to invite them in for a cuppa and a biscuit, hoping that such hospitality would be rewarded when they were next on night duty by giving their premises more than just the usual cursory glance.

Clark had the beat timed to perfection. Without stopping for a chat or having to deal with a problem, it took exactly two and half hours to do a complete circuit – which ran from the Palladium Cinema in Hockley to the boundary line between Birmingham and West Bromwich.

As they approached the border, Clark asked, 'Have yow been up this far yet?'

Collins shook his head.

'Well, yow are now entering holy ground. See that blue brick wall? That's the Hawthorns, the home of West Bromwich Albion. Make sure you genuflect when you pass or whatever you lefthanders do. Me, I always touch the wall for good luck.'

All Collins could see was the curved corrugated steel roof of a stand that had no sides and was in need of painting. The turnstiles were closed and litter had accumulated by each entrance. Everything was dirty and grime-encrusted.

'It could do with a clean and a lick of paint don't you think?' said Collins.

Clark stared at him with disgust. 'This is the highest football ground in the Football League, which means it's about as near to God as yow'll ever get. It is also home to the biggest pitch in England – and that includes Wembley. Yow do know what Wembley is, don't yow?'

Collins decided to wind Clark up. 'Of course I do. It's where England play cricket.'

'God give me strength! How the hell did yow get through selection? Wembley is where football is played, not cricket. And the Hawthorns on a Saturday afternoon is where great football is played – except when they have an off day. And then them crap. But on a good day, it's the best place in the world to be with 30,000 other Baggies fans – especially when wi stuff the Villa.'

'I'll take your word for it.'

'No need to. When this snow finally clears, yow can come to a match with me.'

'OK,' said Collins, doubtfully.

'Now, come on, I need to report in.'

The familiar police pillar was on the other side of the road. Standing five feet tall, and surmounted by an orange light that flashed whenever the station wanted to contact the beat bobby it contained a locked telephone box for the exclusive use of police officers and a separate phone that could be used by the public to summon police assistance. Clark spoke briefly to Thornhill Road, confirmed that they were heading back to the station and hung up.

'See that row of bus stops just before you get to the Hawthorns?' asked Clark. 'That marks the boundary between Birmingham and the Black Country. If you ever go to Dudley Zoo to visit yowr relatives, you'll pay one bus fare to the boundary and another to the zoo.'

'That sounds like a bit of a palaver.'

'If I had my way, yow'd have to show your passport before yow could get into God's blessed Black Country. Now, opposite the Albion, and officially in the Black Country, is *The Boundary Café* – or, as its regulars call it, *The Shit Hole*. Great tea and bacon butties. But always remember: never step in any puddles when yow goes in, especially on a Sunday.'

'Puddles?'

'Yeah, puddles. Yow see when wi go to an away game, the coach drops us off at the café. It's usually late when wi get back and there's no buses, so before wi start walking, the lads take a piss. Most pee against the wall of the cafe or see how high up the windows they can reach. But one or two, those who've had a run in with Sid, piss through his letterbox – and someone has always had a row with Sid that wiek.'

B ack at the station, Collins was wiping up the last of the egg yolk with his fried bread when DS York sidled up to the table.

'Collins? The Inspector wants to see you in his office.'

Collins looked at Clark, pushed his plate away and stood up. He felt a mixture of nerves and excitement as he knocked on the Inspector's door. He knew what it was about; he just hoped his report had been clear.

'Ah, Collins. Come in. I read your report. Well done. You showed a bit of initiative going round there last night. Sergeant York will follow it up and take Wilcox's statement.'

'Thank you, Sir.'

In stark contrast to the clear, freezing air outside, the office was stifling hot and blue cigarette smoke filled the air. It was those swanky French Gauloises, which smelt like rotten cheese, that Hicks was smoking. Collins could feel a cough forming in his throat and fought it down.

'I thought you might like to spend the rest of the day with me. See how the CID do things. I've cleared it with your gaffer. OK?'

'Fine, Sir,' said Collins trying to sound casual.

'Let's hope you feel the same way tonight. We've identified the girl. Simone Winston. Her mother reported her missing on Saturday morning. We'll see her first. Then, it's a trip to the pathologist. He's new and from what I saw of him yesterday a real delight. I hope you're not the fainting type?'

'No, Sir, I'm not.'

'OK then. Grab your coat and let's get going. Can you drive?'

<hr>

Collins drew up outside 211a Holly Road. Mrs Winston lived in a second-floor flat that overlooked the tennis courts in Handsworth Park. The view would have added £250 to the value of the house pre-war, but now it was worthless. The neighbourhood had changed. The professional classes, who had once boasted of an address in Handsworth, had moved to Sutton Coldfield – well away from the common riff-raff of Handsworth, and the Irish and coloureds that seemed to breed like rabbits.

The houses were now occupied by Irish immigrants and children of the Empire from the Caribbean, India and Pakistan. Those from the dominions had expected to be welcomed by the Motherland, who had called on them to be doctors, nurses, bus conductors, hospital orderlies and factory workers. But, like the Irish before them, they had quickly found that they were wanted and despised in equal measure. To pay the mortgage, they rented out spare rooms. The result was that the desirability of living in Handsworth had quickly spiralled downward and would never recover. Mrs Winston led Hicks and Collins into a tidy living room with a cooker and sink in one corner. Against the longest wall stood a glass display cabinet with a mixture of pottery and souvenirs from day trips around England.

Hicks settled into a small two-seater settee and Collins remained standing by the door.

Collins watched as Mrs Winston eased herself into a chair next to a two-bar electric fire. She had a blanket draped across her shoulders, but was still shaking. Collins guessed that she was probably only in her early forties, yet she looked sixty. Her jet-black skin was grey with shock and grief. Her eyes, red-rimmed from crying, stared into the distance.

'I need to ask you a few questions,' Hicks said slowly, in a low voice. 'Constable Collins will take some notes. If that's all right with you?'

'If it will help...' Her voice trailed off.

'How long have you lived In England?'

'I came after the war. I was one of the first. I'm a nurse at Dudley Road.'

'And your husband?'

A grim smile played around the corners of her mouth. 'Him? He's long gone. When I arrived, I thought all Englishmen were gentlemen – but when I fell pregnant he disappeared quicker than the mist on a summer morning.'

'I'm sorry.'

'I'm not,' she said, her voice animated for the first time. 'Simone and I are doing... I mean, *were* doing fine. She was a good girl. Went to church. Didn't hang around with boys. Worked hard at school. I don't understand how this happened to her.'

'Where did she go to school?'

'St Martin's in Hockley.'

'And you say that on Friday she told you she was visiting a friend and would be back around 10.30?'

'That's right. Whoever did this must have took her as she came back from Carol's house.'

'Carol?'

'Carol Midgley; she lives at 26 Prince Albert Road.

They often spent Friday night together listening to Radio Luxemburg.'

'And that's what they were doing last Friday?'

'Yes.'

'Weren't you concerned when she didn't return on Friday night?'

'No, I was working. I do nights every two weeks. It gives me a bit extra. We're saving... sorry, we *were* saving for a holiday back home in Jamaica.'

'What time did you get home from work on Saturday morning?'

'I got in at about 8.30. I made a cup of tea and looked in on Simone before I went to bed. That was about 9.15.'

'And that's when you found her missing and rang the police?'

'No, I didn't ring the police. I went to the station and reported it straightaway. I knew my girl wouldn't stay out all night. Something had to be wrong. I could feel it.'

'She'd never stayed out all night before?'

'No, sir. Never,' she almost shouted. 'Simone was a good girl.'

'I'm sure she was. Do you mind if I take a look at Simone's room while I'm here?'

'Of course not. It's the next room along on the landing. I need a cuppa. Would you like one?'

'That would be very nice, Mrs Winston.'

On the landing, Hicks asked, 'Well, what do you think, lad?'

'I think she's telling the truth as far as she knows it. But if she's working nights every fortnight, she can't know what her kid's doing.'

'Exactly, but I bet Carol Midgley does.'

Simone's bedroom was not what Collins had expected from a teenager. It was immaculate. The bed made. Books and magazines stored neatly in a white, painted bookcase. A new Dansette record player resting on a pine chair by the bed with half a dozen or so singles on the floor beside it. Her white ice skates hanging on a hook behind the door. Not a single pin-up of Beatles, Elvis, Billy Fury or even Cliff Richard adorned the wall.

'You take a look at the dressing table,' Hicks said, as he started to go through the bookcase. Working from the top down, he carefully inspected each book and magazine in turn for any hidden papers or photos.

Collins remembered his training and kept his hands in his pockets as he surveyed the white dressing table. Every item was arranged precisely, as if the layout had been planned and precisely measured. A hairbrush and comb lay side by side, with a single bottle of red nail varnish, two lipsticks and a bottle of perfume lined up close by. At the back, aligned precisely with the corner of the dressing table, was a wooden jewellery box.

Collins slipped on his leather gloves before he picked up the perfume bottle. The label said Chanel and although he didn't know much about perfumes, it looked expensive. He put it to one side. Next, he opened the jewellery box. It was the usual assortment of cheap costume jewellery. Typical tat made from plated metal and decorated with either glass or wooden beads. He poked about the contents with his finger and was closing the lid when he spotted what looked like an old brooch. He fished it out and was surprised by its weight. It was shaped like a bird, but the wings had been broken off and several pieces of glass were missing from the tail and eyes. Turning it over, Collins saw that the clasp was missing. *What a pity*, he thought. *It would have been a nice piece if it were undamaged.* Then, he saw the hallmark.

'Sir, I think you need to have a look at this.' He handed Hicks the brooch.

The Inspector felt its weight. It certainly wasn't made of cheap metal. He turned it over in his gloved hand and examined the hallmark. 'Interesting,' he said. 'What's a fourteen-year-old girl doing with a broken brooch made of gold and diamonds, and hallmarked "Birmingham 1912"?'

'Is it worth much?'

'Not a lot. Maybe a fiver. She probably picked it up at a jumble sale. If you find any more like this, it might be worth looking into. Anything else?'

'I haven't finished looking yet, but the perfume seems expensive.'

Hicks picked up the bottle. 'Chanel. Definitely not a perfume that a kid can afford. See what else you can find that is expensively out of place.'

Fifteen minutes later, they had found a London-made dress and skirt hidden at the back of the wardrobe, along with two silk blouses. Collins also found a stash of bras, knickers, suspender belts, slips and a corset in the space between the bottom drawer of the dressing table and the floor. The underwear was both gaudy and expensive. It was definitely not the type of thing a mother would buy her young daughter. The list of suspect items was completed by the new record player.

'Are you thinking what I'm thinking, lad?'

'I think she had a sugar daddy, Sir.'

'Damn right she did. We need to ask Mrs Winston if she knows anything about these. It's possible she was pimping the girl herself.'

The thought hadn't entered Collins' head and he was sure the Inspector was wrong, but he stayed quiet.

Collins watched as the look on Mrs Winston's face turned from surprise to shock to horror, then anger as she realised the implications of what she was seeing. Eyes blazing, she flung the black corset with the white stain on the front panel against the wall, stumbled to the bed and collapsed. Head in hands, she rocked backwards and forwards crying dry tears and heaving on an already empty stomach. It was clear to Collins that either she was a world class actress or she knew nothing about this collection.

Only the Dansette and the jewellery were innocent. She'd given the record player to Simone last Christmas, along with the top five singles. As for the jewellery, Simone had shown

it to her and said she'd found it in a snow bank between the
road and the footpath in the middle of January.

Still fighting for composure, Mrs Winston looked Hicks
in the eye and said, 'You catch this bastard. Promise. I want
him to hang for what he done to my child.'

'I promise I'll do everything I can, Mrs Winston. You have
my word on that.'

Straightening her back, she took a deep breath and, with all
the dignity she could muster, said, 'I believe you.'

Collins watched on helplessly. He wanted to comfort this
poor woman on the worst day of her life. A mother, who in
the space of forty-eight hours had lost her daughter and then
discovered that she had been living with a person she barely
knew. It was obvious that she would forever blame herself
for failing to protect her only child against the evil bastard
that had corrupted, exploited and killed her. Collins could do
nothing but stand there and promise himself that he would
catch whoever was responsible. No matter how long it took.

As he followed Hicks onto the landing, Mrs Winston
handed Collins a snapshot of Simone. 'I want you to have
it, so you don't forget my girl.' Collins didn't know what to
say. He squeezed the woman's hand and carefully placed the
photo in his breast pocket.

Hicks and Collins left the car on Holly Road, crossed
Grove Lane by the chemist's and walked down Prince
Albert Road, looking for number 26. Carol wasn't at home.
She'd been upset by the death of her friend, but her mother,
thinking that it would help if she kept busy, had sent her to
school.

Mrs Midgley had an abundance of pasty white skin, which
hung in folds from her neck and arms. Despite the liberal
use of Lifebuoy Soap, personal hygiene remained a problem
for the big woman. She confirmed that Simone regularly visited Carol, but had not been there the previous Friday. She

expressed the view that "Simone was a nice enough girl for a half-caste", but there was something in her tone that implied Carol was better off not mixing with Simone's sort.

Turning from the door, Hicks waited until it had closed and said, 'There's a woman overflowing with the milk of human kindness. Not a single mention of Mrs Winston and how she was. Come on, lad. We'll give Carol a visit on the way to the pathologists.'

St Martin's Secondary Modern School was located at the bottom of Hockley Hill. It was almost exactly halfway between Handsworth Park and Birmingham City Centre. Nestled in its own valley, it was surrounded by factories and workshops. Just a short walk away, on Soho Hill, Robert Stephenson had erected the first purpose built factory in the world and at a stroke revolutionised manufacturing in Britain. The smell of chemicals infused everything, skin, clothes, wood and brick. There was no escaping it. It stung eyes, irritated throats and slowly destroyed lungs. Even on this bright, cold day, a yellow-and-blue haze hung over the valley and dimmed the sunlight.

St Martin's was run by a formidable nun, whose chosen name, Sister Etna, described her perfectly. More than one city education officer had been on the wrong end of an explosive tongue lashing from this formidable woman when she thought her "kids" were being treated unfairly.

Inspector Hicks explained that Sergeant York would arrange to take statements from Simone's friends and teachers later in the week. For now he just wanted to speak to Carol Midgley and clarify a few things, and, if it wasn't too much trouble, have a look at Simone's desk.

Looking at the office clock, Sister Etna said, 'Lunch ends at 1.30. The classroom will be empty for the next hour.'

'That sounds ideal. Thank you, Sister.'

'If you'll come with me.'

For Collins, walking into the classroom was like taking a step back in time to Synge Street School, Dublin. The same scuffed oak desks arranged in six rows of eight. The walls covered in pictures from the bible, along with scenes showing the prairies of America and the Industrial Revolution, all capped off by a large crucifix over the blackboard. Not only was the Church's teaching universally consistent, so too, it seemed, were its classrooms.

'One thing I do insist upon, Inspector, is that I be present as an observer when you interview Carol.'

'Of course.'

'Good.' Sister Etna indicated Simone's desk and left to find Carol. The contents of the desk were as neat and tidy as Simone's bedroom, with her copy books neatly covered in wallpaper, numbered and stacked according to size. All pens, pencils and rubbers were neatly stored in a roll-top pencil case with a picture of the Beatles glued to the bottom of it.

Working methodically, both men went through the copy books. All of the subject books were spotless. The only marks were the red pen of the teacher's comments – all of which appeared to be positive. It might only have been a Secondary Modern but Simone seemed brighter than the average fourteen-year-old. It was obvious to Collins that whatever else might have been going on in Simone's life, it hadn't affected her schoolwork.

It was only when he started to flick though her two rough workbooks that he said, 'Sir, what do you make of this?'

Hicks examined the books. Along with the outlines for essays, maths formulas, doodles and notes to herself, there were seven strings of meaningless numbers. Each string circled in red biro. The shortest string ran to five numbers and each number was separated by a neat slash.

12/1/14/24/3

'What do you think it is. Collins?'

'I'm not sure, Sir. Maybe it's a code of some kind,' he replied, thinking that his suggestion was both daft and amateurish even as he said it.

'That's what I was thinking. A bit melodramatic, but we're

dealing with a child and a code could be her way of keeping secrets from Mom and teachers. Take all her copy books and we'll have a closer look back at the station.'

As Collins started to empty the desk, there was a knock at the door.

'Come in,' Hicks said.

Carol Midgley and Sister Etna entered. Carol had the same dark hair as her mother, but the likeness ended there. She was tall and thin with sharp, almost hard, features. Her eyes were puffy and red, and she looked very nervous.

Hicks tried to put her at her ease immediately. 'Thank you for talking to us, Carol. You're not in any trouble. I know this is very hard for you, but if we're to catch the man who killed your friend, we need your help. OK?'

'Yes.'

'Speak up, child, so the Inspector can hear you.'

'Yes,' she repeated at Sister Etna's urging.

'Good. Come and sit down.'

'Ta.'

'We know that Simone used her meetings with you as cover to go and see her boyfriend.' Hicks looked at Carol for confirmation and she nodded. 'Now, nothing is going to happen to you. You've done nothing wrong. You were just helping out a friend, but we need you to tell us everything you know about this boyfriend. No matter how small the detail is, it could be important. Understand?'

'Yes.'

'Good. So when did it start?'

'Just after Christmas. There were a kid's dance at The Palms, just off Rookery Road, one afternoon in the holidays. But I got tonsillitis and had to stay in bed, so Simone went by herself. She said it were really good. There was a new DJ and the music was great. All the latest stuff, straight off Radio Luxemburg. Anyway, she met this guy who was with the DJ. He had his own car and loads of money.'

'Did she ever tell you his name or anything about him?'

'Na, but she had a pet name for him. She called him Bucky.'

'Did she say why she'd chosen that name?'

'No.'

'It all sounds very secretive. Weren't you annoyed that your best friend was keeping secrets from you?'

'Na. You see, he'd made her promise. He said that because she were only fourteen, he didn't want people to think he was a baby snatcher. Said people wouldn't understand that they were in love, like Romeo and Juliet, and if they found out she'd be sent to borstal and he'd go to prison.'

'Anything else?'

'He promised her that she'd get a reward if she stayed quiet.'

'What did he mean by that?'

'Well, at first he gave her money, then he started buying her clothes and things. She showed me one dress – it were lovely – and some smashing underwear.'

Hicks exchanged a look with Collins before asking, 'How often did they meet?'

'Every Friday that Mrs Winston was working nights, and sometimes on a Saturday afternoon or evening. He even turned up at school once.'

'When was that?' Hicks tried to keep the excitement out of his voice, but Collins could see it in how his body had stiffened at the news.

'It was one Tuesday about a month ago.'

'Did you see him or his car?'

'I never seen him, but I saw his car. He parked just up the road from the school and Simone got in.'

'What make was it?'

'I don't know much about cars.'

'Was it a small green van with a sort of wing on the front of the bonnet?'

'No, nothing like that. It was a big black car and had a tiger – you know, like in the advert for petrol – in the back window.'

'Had Simone told you that she was being picked up?'

'No, but I remember she looked nice that day. She had a new white jumper on, so she probably knew he were coming. She told me later that he took her to some restaurant near Stratford and they went to this really nice hotel afterwards.'

'For sex?'

Carol looked at Sister Etna, whose face was pinched and white. Her eyes reflecting the anger she felt. Finally, Carol replied, 'Yes. She said she loved him and that when she was old enough, they were going to get married.'

'Did she ever say how old he was or describe him?'

'The way she talked, I thought he were in his twenties...' She hesitated, wondering if she should continue.

'What is it, Carol? What have you remembered?'

Again, she looked at Sister Etna. The girl seemed both embarrassed and afraid about what she was going to say. 'I think he had blond hair.'

'Did Simone tell you that he had blond hair?'

'No, but we were messing about talking about boys and she said that what she found really odd was that Bucky had blond hairs around his... you know.'

'His penis.'

'Yeah,' she said, blushing violently and bowing her head to avoid having to look at Sister Etna. 'That would mean he had blond hair, wouldn't it?'

'Yes, it would. OK, you've been very good. We'll need to take a statement from you and we'd like to search your room just in case Simone left a note or anything that might help us. I'll call my Sergeant and he'll pick you up from school. I'm sure Sister Etna will excuse you from lessons this afternoon given the circumstances.'

Sister Etna nodded in agreement and started to lead Carol out. At the door, Carol turned and asked, 'Did you find Simone's diary? I bet the answers to all your questions are in that.'

Dumfounded, Hicks looked at Collins and said, 'Come back a sec, Carol. What's this about a diary?'

'Simone wanted to be a writer when she left school. She read somewhere that writers kept diaries and use what's in 'em for their stories, so she started to keep a diary.'

'When was this?'

'About last July. It's just a big, black foolscap book.'

'Mrs Winston never mentioned any diary.'

'I don't think she knows about it. Simone didn't want her reading it.'

'Do you know where she kept it?'

'Sorry,' she said, shaking her head.

'That's OK. You've been a great help.'

Hicks said nothing until they were by the car. 'What's that saying? Out of the mouths of children shall come wisdom?'

'Something like that, Sir,' said Collins and slid in behind the wheel.

'We have to find that bloody diary. I'll get a search team over to the house tomorrow. They can check with her mates and the school, too. What do you make of the rest of it?'

'I think he's done this before. I don't mean killing young girls, but picking them up. He had his story and excuses down pat. We should find out when this youth dance was at The Palms. If we can trace the DJ, maybe he can tell us who the boyfriend is or at least confirm what he looks like,' said Collins.

'What about the money and gifts?'

'He did it to impress a chit of a girl who had no money and probably saw a drive in a nice car as an adventure – but he was clever enough to keep her quiet. After all, the girl was underage. He spun her a cock-and-bull story about the danger they faced if people found out.'

'Which is one reason why Simone hid the clothes,' said Hicks. 'You'll be back on the beat tomorrow with Clark?'

'Yes, Sir.'

'Well pop into The Palms, it's on your patch, and see what you can find out. I'll clear it with your gaffer, OK?'

'Yes, Sir.'

'Good. Let's go and see Dr McEwan and find out exactly what killed the girl.'

L ike any visitor unused to attending a mortuary, the first thing Collins noticed was the smell. Everything smelt of disinfectant. The second was the smell of death. Not the gut-churning stench of a ripe body in the summer heat, but the taste of low-level decay that clings to the back of the throat and impregnates everything. A strange mixture of stale sweat, human waste and rotting flesh, which has been doused in disinfectant but not eradicated.

The mortuary had been built around 1880. Its white tiled walls and floors, scrubbed regularly, were spotless. The cold steel examination tables, neatly laid out in a row of four, gave Collins a nervous feeling in the pit of his stomach. The unbidden thought that he'd end up there one day popped into his mind – and once there, he couldn't shrug it off. *Bloody Irish. Half Catholic, half Celtic pagan; we're a superstitious lot,* he thought.

Dr McEwan entered from the glass office at the far end of the room. 'You're late, Inspector,' he said, as he shook hands with Hicks.

Collins didn't even rate a glance. He was clearly unworthy of the good doctor's attention. It didn't bother him though, and he took out his pen and notebook. The guy looked too young for the job of Chief Pathologist. Maybe that's why he wore a waistcoat, watch fob and sported a bright yellow bow tie. He was trying to impress by looking like the young brilliant eccentric medic of so many American TV programmes, but his short stature and bulging belly made it a hard act to pull off. He just didn't have the looks of Dr Kildare. Collins hoped that he was competent and had something for them.

'Well, I'm here now, so let's get on with it.'

'There's nothing to get on with. It's already done.'

'What do you mean already done?' Hicks asked, astonished.

'I said that the post mortem would take place on Tuesday morning. It's now nearly 2. I can't wait around for you. I've got a mortuary to run.'

'You'll be in the fucking mortuary if you ever start a PM on one of my bodies again without me present. Do you hear me?'

Collins was amazed at the change in Hicks. The Inspector was bent forward as if ready to lunge at McEwan. His face purple with rage, voice hard and vicious. His eyes blazed with a mixture of anger and contempt.

'How dare you speak to me like that? I'll report you to the Chief Constable and I have a witness,' he said, nodding in the direction of Collins.

Hicks strengthened up and took a deep breath. When he spoke his voice was calm, but a vein still throbbed purple in his temple. 'What did you see, Constable Collins?'

'Nothing, Sir, except that the Doctor swore at you for being late without giving you any chance to explain why we had been delayed.'

'You were saying, Dr McEwan?'

McEwan knew he was beaten – if only he hadn't allowed the orderly to go to lunch. Still attempting to show his superiority he said, 'My title is Mr McEwan, not Doctor.'

'Sorry about that, *Mr McEwan*,' said Hicks. 'Personally, I've always thought that the title "Doctor" meant more to the common man than "Mr".'

Collins suppressed a smile. *Two nil to Hicks.*

'Quite so, common being the operative word. Anyway, as I said, I've completed the autopsy on the girl, Simone Winston. As you rightly suspected, she died from strangulation. I found some fibres in her hair that may have come from the cloth that was used to strangle her. I'll be able to tell you what type of material after the lab get back to me. She

was strangled from behind and, although this is part supposition, I think she may have been on her hands and knees at
the time of death.'

'Why do you say that? She could have been standing up.'

'Doubtful, Inspector. You see, her hyoid bone was broken.
If she had been standing up, the body would have slumped
forward immediately and that would have caused more
widespread bruising and abrasions to the neck as the ligature
slipped over the skin.'

'I see,' said Hicks.

*The Doc might be an irritating, pompous, fat git but he seems to
know his stuff*, conceded Collins.

'The vaginal sex that she had prior to death appears to have
been consensual. There is no evidence of bruising around the
thighs or vagina to imply otherwise – although I can't rule it
out until the lab confirms what drugs she'd taken. She may
just have been unconscious so didn't struggle and...'

'Therefore no bruising,' said Hicks.

Annoyed that he'd had his speech interrupted, McEwan
continued, 'At this stage, if I were a betting man, I'd say that
the death was probably an accident. A bit of rough fun gone
wrong, but what happened afterwards wasn't.'

'What do you mean?'

'She was violently buggered post mortem. There are sub-
stantial tears and bruising to the rectum and lower colon.'

'So it's all lovey-dovey until she dies, then the guy fulfils his
fantasy. Is that it?'

'Yes and no. There was a second person involved.'

Collins had to concede that McEwan had a talent for the
dramatic. Both men were now listening intently to the che-
rubic pathologist.

'Loverboy 1 is AB; Bugger 2 is O Res. Negative.'

'How do you know this?'

'The mortuary assistant noticed the bruising as he un-
dressed her before filing her away last night. I took swabs
and sent them to the lab. I asked them to rush as I needed

them first thing Tuesday morning, as that was when I was expecting you. I knew you'd be interested.'

There was silence for a few moments as McEwan savoured salvaging a point. Then, he continued, 'She was also in the very early stages of pregnancy – and no, I don't know if Loverboy 1 or Bugger 2 was the father. You'll have to wait for the lab results.'

'Would she have known she was pregnant?'

'Unlikely, as I say it was very early.'

Collins was too busy taking notes to look up, but he could imagine the look of satisfaction that was spreading across McEwan's face as he revealed the mysteries of science to two ignorant coppers.

'You said there were signs that she'd taken drugs?'

'Yes. There were the remains of undigested pills in her stomach. My guess is that they were amphetamines, but I won't know for sure until I have the toxicology report. I should be able to let you have the results tomorrow.'

McEwan somehow managed to make it sound as if he were doing them a favour.

⸻

They drove back to the station in silence. Collins was so busy thinking about what they had just learnt that he had to swerve to avoid a bus that emerged from the Hockley Bus Station without warning. *Bloody sods think they own the road.* The only new information they had picked up was that Simone had been pregnant and had probably taken drugs prior to her death. But if she didn't know she was pregnant, then the father wouldn't have known and it couldn't be considered as a motive for her death.

As for Bugger 2, they'd already known that there was a second man involved. The older, chunkier guy who had helped Blondie/Bucky dump the body – but now it sounded like he had buggered Simone. Did that mean that they operated as a pair to pick up girls and use them? Or was he just a friend who had been given the chance to indulge in a fantasy that he would never get the opportunity to try again? But would a friend, no matter how close, be willing to get involved in a murder? Collins didn't think so.

It was only as they were pulling into the station that Collins gave voice to something that was bothering him. 'Sir?'

'Yes.'

'I was thinking; what if Bugger 2 and the second guy who dumped her are not the same person? What if there were three of them involved?'

'I was thinking along similar lines. But spread your net further. What if we're dealing with a group of men and not just two or three? I've seen it before in London.'

As they walked into the station, Hicks said, 'Don't forget to check out The Palms tomorrow. And make sure you take Clark with you. I'm starting to smell something very rotten.'

Collins deposited all the evidence that they had collected at both Mrs Winston's and St Martin's on Sergeant York's empty chair. Simone's rough workbooks were on top. He opened them on impulse and scribbled down the seven series of numbers on a scrap of paper, before shoving it in his pocket, and heading home.

———

Collins was sitting in the kitchen, digging into 1/3d worth of fish and chips and staring at the list of numbers he'd written down before leaving the station. The Home Service's 6 pm news was just ending when he heard the front door open. Moments later, Agnes entered the kitchen.

'You look frozen,' he said. 'Will I make you a cup of tea?'

'That would be lovely,' Agnes replied and slumped into the chair nearest the radiator.

'How was your day?' Collins asked.

'Meetings followed by more meetings. I don't suppose you've ever been to a Quaker Meeting?'

Collins shook his head.

'Well, we have two types. Meetings for Worship and Business Meetings. I love the quiet and serenity of Meetings for Worship, but Business Meetings can drag on for ages. They make Civil Service meetings seem the epitome of efficiency. And today, I had two very long meetings to chair. Still, I think we arrived at the right decisions eventually.'

'So it was worth your while then?'

'Yes, it was.' As she took the offered cup from Collins, she glanced down and noticed the list of numbers that Collins had been struggling with. 'What's this?'

'What?'

'These number sets,' she said, picking up Collins hastily scribbled note.

'Oh them. We were at the murdered girl's school today and found these strings of numbers in her copy books. The Inspector thinks that they're some kind of code. He's going to send them to Steelhouse Lane tomorrow.'

'He's right. It is a code, or to be exact, a cypher.'

'Are you sure?' Collins asked, surprised that Agnes knew anything about codes.

'Definitely. It's what I call a reverse substitution code with one shift. Fairly basic really.'

'You lost me with reverse. Can you read what it says?'

'Yes, this five number set says "BUCKY".'

'Bucky, you say. Wait here. I'll be back in no time.' Collins rushed from the room, took the stairs two at a time and returned seconds later with a pen and pad of paper. 'Show me how it works.'

Agnes took the pad and spent a few seconds sketching out a grid, before listing the letters of the alphabet and the numbers from one to twenty-six. She then showed Collins her schedule.

1	2	3	4	5	6	7	8	9	10	11	12	13
A	Z	Y	X	W	V	U	T	S	T	Q	P	O
14	15	16	17	18	19	20	21	22	23	24	25	26
N	M	L	K	J	I	H	G	F	E	D	C	B

26	7	25	17	3
B	U	C	K	Y

'That's brilliant! Where did you learn to do that?' Collins asked in astonishment.

'Just a little party trick of mine. It's a very basic code; exactly the type a schoolgirl would use. Although the shift adds a bit of twist to it.'

'Yes. But where did you learn to do it?'

'I was a translator in the Signal Corps during the war. I picked up the basics from typing reports and such like. Besides, I've always been good at crossword puzzles.'

'Amazing – a whole station full of coppers and no ejit can break it! You take one look and hey presto, it's done.'

'Well, as I say, it's very basic.'

'So, if I go through all the strings of numbers...'

'They're called sets of numbers,' Agnes corrected him.

'OK, so if I go through all the sets, I'll be able to translate everything she's written.' Collins still couldn't believe how quickly Agnes had solved the problem.

'That's how codes work. Find the key and they're easy to read,' said Agnes, amused at how excited Collins was about her discovery.

The fish and chips forgotten, the two of them spent the next few minutes translating the seven sets of numbers. Agnes rose even higher in Collins' estimation when she proceeded to translate each set without reference to the written key. The only difficulty she had was resolved when she realised that actual numbers weren't encoded. So, for example, 17 meant seventeen.

With all seven sets translated, Collins picked up the pad and read:

- *Bucky.*
- *The Other Queen's Head.*
- *Club on 17.*
- *Pan Cottage*
- <u>*Durex*</u> *(underlined three times).*
- *Meet Bucky 4. 22/1. School.*
- *Friday 8/2. 6.*

'All right, now that you've whet my appetite, you have to tell me more about this case,' said Agnes.

Collins realised that he would have to return, yet again, to the station with what he had just learned, but as he finished his lukewarm fish and chips, he briefly outlined what the police knew. Agnes was particularly interested in how Simone had died and the fact that she had been violated after death. Collins finished by saying, 'We think she was being played along by this fella Bucky. He might just have liked young girls or maybe he planned to put her on the game. It's even possible she may have been killed by accident.'

'That's one possibility, certainly, but if this boyfriend of hers likes to play rough, you should talk to the working girls. Find out if any of them has a customer who likes to strangle them.'

'That's a good idea, but I wouldn't know where to start. I don't know any prostitutes.'

'You do.'

'Who?'

'Gloria, of course. She was looking for you this morning. I think she has a crush on you,' Agnes teased.

'God, keep her at bay! I'll do anything, but just don't leave me alone with her.'

'You're not afraid of little Gloria, are you?'

'No, I'm terrified,' he joked.

'You'll never make a policeman if you don't get to know at least some of the working girls in Birmingham. They know more about what's going on in Birmingham than any other group of people. Their list of customers includes everyone from factory workers to judges. And a great many customers like to talk – to impress the girls. The girls are told things that no one else ever hears.'

'Not even a priest in confessional?'

'No, and I bet the girls could tell you about one or two priests, and Quakers, I don't doubt – although we don't wear dog collars and are therefore harder to spot. Tell you what; I'll call Mary tomorrow. She's an old friend and can tell you who's who in the game in and around Birmingham. Now, you look like you could use a good night's sleep. Why don't you have an early night and I'll tidy up?'

'Not a chance. I have to get back to the station and tell the CID Duty Officer what you found.'

'Can't you just ring him?'

'No, I need to show him.'

Collins arrived at the station and headed for the CID Room. Sergeant O'Driscoll was on the phone taking notes when Collins arrived. Waving him into a seat, O'Driscoll continued to listen and jot down the odd word for the next five minutes, only occasionally asking a question to clarify what the person on the other end of the line had said. It seemed to Collins that he had enormous patience and a sharp, analytical mind. He asked probing questions and then gave the person on the other end of the line plenty of time to respond.

After some time, O'Driscoll finally hung up and said, 'So what's brought you back to this wonderful shrine to justice for the second time in two nights, me fine Dub friend?'

Collins quickly explained about Simone's code. Then, taking from his pocket the decoded list of words, he explained how Agnes had cracked the code.

'She sounds a bright woman, this Agnes of yours. Still, we

Irish have always known that women are as good, if not better than us poor ejits. Why, if it wasn't for the mothers, I don't think any Irish family would survive.' O'Driscoll sounded even more maudlin than the previous night.

Collins ignored the comments and asked, 'Do you think we should call the Inspector in?'

'As I said last night, all we'll be doing is ruining the Inspector's night. If he was willing to wait until tomorrow before sending the code to Steelhouse Lane, he'll be happy to wait until tomorrow for your translation. Do me a brief note and attach it to the grids, and then get off home to bed.'

'OK.' As on the previous night, Collins found a space on the shambles that passed for York's desk and briefly outlined what the seven sets of numbers meant. As he stood up to leave, the older man asked, 'Would you mind if I gave you a piece of advice, Michael Collins? One Irish man to another?

'No, Sergeant, of course not.'

'You've started well. Hicks was impressed with what you did over Wilcox. You need to keep it up. If an Irishman is to progress in this force – Christ, what am I talking about, in this country – then he has to be miles better than the nearest Englishman. Either that or he needs to be a Mason with friends in high places. Remember that.'

'I will, Sergeant. Thanks.'

Stepping out of the station, Collins turned over in his mind what O'Driscoll had said. *It may or may not be true,* he thought, *but one thing it did confirm was that the Sergeant was not alone in the CID room.* He had a bottle or two to keep him and his regrets company through the long, dark night. Even so, Collins realised he'd taken an immediate liking to the rumpled scarecrow of a man. It would be interesting to get to know him better.

Wednesday 13th February 1963.

Handsworth, 06.00hrs.

As Parade came to an end, Sergeant Ridley fixed Clark and Collins with a stare. 'I've got a little job for you pair. Stop off at Linwood Road during your beat and interview Mrs Susan Jones. She's reported an incident of indecent exposure.'

'Do wi know where it happened?' asked Clark.

'She says the corner of Rookery and Soho Road.'

'I could'a guessed. Is Upright Freddie back on the streets?'

'Yep. Got out of Winson Green last week.'

'Well, it's a pound to a penny he's back there next week. Come on, Mickey, my lad, you're about to meet the biggest wanker on the patch and I mean that literally. This guy can wank-off up to twenty times a day, no bother.'

'Now, don't get jumping to conclusions. It may not be Upright,' said Ridley.

Clark gave Ridley a mocking stare.

'All I'm saying is talk to Mrs Jones before you pick the bastard up.'

As they began to walk the beat, Clark gave Collins a quick resumé of Upright Freddie's criminal record. He'd been in and out of prison since he was eighteen and, despite "numerous attempts to cure him of his tendencies", he was still on the streets at the age of thirty-one. 'Mind you,' said Clark, 'Freddie is very selective about who he flashes. It has to be a female. Age don't matter, nor looks, size, black or white. As long as it's female it will do.'

'But why would anyone expose themselves in weather like this? It's flaming perishing,' said Collins.

'Upright's a real professional – come hail, sleet, rain or snow, he'll be out there knocking one off the wrist. He's mental, but basically harmless. He'd never dream of speaking to any of the girls or women he scares – let alone touch them.'

'It must be awful for the women, though?'

'For the youngsters, it is. They can get right upset. But he doesn't get it all his own way. A few months back, one old girl walked up to him, grabbed his prick and nearly ripped it off. Then, for good measure, she punched him in the balls. The judge said she were a fine example to all right-thinking people everywhere and awarded her ten quid from public funds. Upright got three months, it must be that stretch which he finished last week.'

———

It was just gone 9 when Mrs Jones let Collins and Clark into a house that was overcrowded with both furniture and people. Judging by the family photo on the mantelpiece, there were five kids living alongside the parents in a two-bedroom house; with a recently built extension off the kitchen, which boasted a bath and toilet.

Mrs Jones poured three cups of tea and handed the fig rolls around. She didn't wait to be asked a question before she launched into her story.

'That pervert, Upright Freddie, is at it again. He's only been out of clink for a week and there he is pulling on his dick in broad daylight. When are you going to lock him up for good and throw away the key? Dirty bastard.'

Clark jumped in with a question when Mrs Jones stopped to take a breath. 'Where and when did yow see him?'

'Last night at about ten past five. I'd just finished a bit of shopping and was walking home, when Upright stepped out of an alley and opened his coat. His flies were open and his cock sticking out.'

'What did yow do?'

'I gave him a right slap around the ear. I bet it's still buzzing.

Dirty little shit.'

'Did he threaten yow in any other way?'

'No. He just stood there. I mean, it were bloody freezing.'

'And yowr sure that the man in question was Freddie Bartholomew, also known as Upright Freddie?'

'Of course I'm bloody sure. I've known him since he was in nappies. Come to think of it, he were always playing with his dick then and all. Look, I know he wouldn't attack anyone – he's too afraid of women to do that – but he scares the youngsters when he does it. They shouldn't have to look at the likes of him. Get him off the streets for everyone's sake will yow?'

'And yow'd be willing to repeat what you have just said in court.'

'Yes.'

'OK, we'll take your statement; then go round and pick Freddie up. Collins, yow can write it.'

It took thirty-five minutes and another cup of tea and a piece of toast to finish the statement and sign it.

Outside, Clark looked up and down the road.

'What are you thinking?' asked Collins.

'I'm thinking we could save a bit of shoe leather if we go to The Palms first and then pick up Freddie on the way back to the station. What do yow think?'

'Fine by me, if it will save traipsing all the way back here.'

The cleaners were just leaving as Collins and Clark arrived at The Palms, and asked for directions to the manager's office on the first floor. Mr Spencer was everyone's idea of a dance hall manager. Over 6 feet tall, he was brash, confident and immaculately turned out. All that tarnished his image was his ever-expanding beer belly, which even the best cummerbund could not disguise. He seemed eager to answer Collins questions.

'Yes, we had a back-to-school dance on Friday 28th

December from 2 till 5. 1/6d entrance fee. It was my idea, and, if I do say so myself, it was a great success.'

'Did you notice a young man in his twenties at the dance? He has blond hair, is over six feet and on the skinny side?' asked Collins.

'No, I can't say I did. It was very crowded and I was running the snacks and soft drinks. Peggy had failed to turn up. A bomb could have gone off and I wouldn't have noticed.'

'This guy would have stood out. Tall, blond, skinny. He were friends with the DJ,' repeated Clark.

'Sorry. Like I say, I didn't notice anyone like that.'

'What about a young half-caste girl. Very pretty. Did you notice her?'

'Not a chance. There were lots of good-looking teenagers. White, black, blue – after a bit, they all blend into one another.'

'Maybe the DJ remembers the bloke. We've been told they were friends. What's his name?' asked Clark

'Ravenal. Jimmy Ravenal.'

'Is he the guy off Radio Luxemburg?' asked Collins.

'That's him. Now, he does have blond hair but he's not in his twenties.'

'Where can we find him?' asked Clark.

'Sorry, I have no idea. He travels from gig to gig in a caravan. You could probably chase him down by contacting his mother, but he'll be here next week if you want to speak to him. He's DJ here next Tuesday, Wednesday and Thursday.'

'OK. Tell him we'll see him on Tuesday.'

'Certainly.'

On the way out, Clark turned to Collins and asked, 'Why were that an interesting conversation?'

'Not once did he ask us what it was all about. Either he's the least curious man in the world or he already knew.'

'So yow were awake. Hard to tell with yow at times. I think Hicks will be interested in our Mr Spencer.'

Spencer watched the two men leave the building before he followed them. Crossing the road he made a beeline for the phone box outside Rookery Road School. He dialled a Leeds number from memory and waited. On the second ring, the phone was answered. 'Hello.'

Spencer pushed the change into the box, waited until the line cleared and said, 'Could I speak to Jimmy please, Mrs Ravenal? This is Colin Spencer.'

'Ah, hello, Mr Spencer. I'll just get him for you.'

After a short pause Ravenal picked up the phone. 'Hello Colin, me old mukka. What can I do you for?'

'Jimmy, I thought you'd want to know that I just had the coppers around. They wanted to know about Andy and the half-caste girl. They know she came to the dance and that she's been going out with a thin, blond guy in his twenties.'

'What did you tell them?'

'Nothing. Played a straight bat all the way. But they also asked about you. They said that you knew Andy.'

'Christ. What did you say?'

'I told you, nothing. They want to speak to you. I said that you were travelling around in that caravan of yours and that their best bet was to see you at The Palms next week.'

'You'd better tell the Major about this.'

'That's what I was going to do.'

'Good man.'

⸺

Agnes waited until she had finished breakfast, completed *The Times* crossword and tidied up before ringing Mary. On the fourth ring, a woman answered. 'This is Karla speaking. How can I help you?' The voice was low and sensuous. Almost an exact imitation of the black-haired comic vamp Fenella Fielding, who seemed to be on every TV quiz and variety show at the moment.

'You can stop trying to seduce me with your husky purr, Mary, and do me a favour.'

The voice rose several octaves and there was genuine pleasure as Mary said, 'Agnes! How are you?'

'I'm well, and you?'

'Oh, you know. The same. The game gets harder as you get older, but I'm doing OK.'

'That's good.'

'Anyway, what's up? You've not decided to become a lesbian after all these years, have you?'

'No. The sisterhood will have to get by without me. I assume you've heard about the young girl found near Hill Top.'

'Yeah, poor little sod.'

'My latest private policeman is on the case. He needs to speak to someone who knows the game in Birmingham and can point him in the right direction.'

'For you, Agnes, anything. Send him over and I'll enlighten him.'

'Well, don't enlighten him too much. He's only just arrived from Ireland and I think he's a bit innocent.'

'You mean a virgin?'

'No. I don't know. Just don't embarrass the poor lad.'

'You sound very protective. Fancy him a little bit, do we?' Mary teased.

'Don't be ridiculous. I'm old enough to be his mother.'

'That didn't stop Jocasta from bedding Oedipus, did it?'

'You should be walking the corridors of academia not—'

'The streets. I know, but my chosen career pays better. Besides, I only read what I want to, not what I'm supposed to, so I'd be a useless academic. Anyway, send him over tomorrow and I'll talk to him. Get him to give me a ring first, OK?'

'That sounds fine.'

When she hung up, Agnes smiled. For all her banter, Agnes knew that Mary would want to help. She was happy to entertain transvestites, slaves, mackintosh and gas mask lovers and a whole range of other tastes, but she hated anyone who hurt children.

It didn't take Collins and Clark long to track Upright Freddie down. He was at home in his flat; a one-room hovel that consisted of a single bed, a chest of drawers and a two ring gas stove. He'd managed to pinch a 17-inch TV from somewhere, which sat on an upturned orange box at the end of the bed. Strewn around the floor were a fine collection of glamour magazines. His favourite appeared to be *Spick and Span*, which featured well-endowed young women showing off their knickers and stocking tops, with just the occasional breast on view.

For someone who indulged in such tiring work, Freddie was remarkably sprightly. As soon as he heard the knock and the word "Police", he was out of bed and yanking the window open.

'He's making a run for it,' Collins shouted and hit the door with his shoulder. The lock wasn't strong enough to withstand a two-year-old and the door crashed open just in time for Collins to see Freddie drop from the window into the yard below. 'He's in the yard. Cut him off.'

Clark turned and ran down the stairs. Collins went out of the window. Dropping onto the lean-to coal bunker, he landed in the yard just as Freddie tried to disappear over the back fence. Lunging, he caught hold of Freddie's jumper and pulled him back. Freddie tried to wriggle out of the jumper, but with the arrival of Clark he was never going to get away.

'OK, you got me,' he said as he slid down the fence.

Neither Collins nor Clark were prepared for what happened next. Freddie screamed. Not the sort of scream you hear in a horror movie or at the fun fair. This was the real thing. A howl of anguish that the damned must make as they are finally dragged into hell. It started from the very bottom of his soul, passed into his stomach and grew louder and more shrill as it worked its way through his lungs and out of his throat.

'What the fuck is up?' asked Clark.

Freddie could hardly speak. His face was the colour of old

dough. Between gasps of air, he finally said, 'I'm stuck.'

'What do you mean you're stuck?'

'I'm stuck on a nail.'

'Well, unstick yourself,' said Collins.

'I can't,' he said, sobbing. 'I'm caught by me balls.'

'Hoist by your own petard,' said Clark and giggled.

'Don't mock me,' whined Freddie. This was too much for Clark and he dissolved into convulsive laughter, which quickly spread to Collins.

As Freddie hung by his balls, trying not to move, the occasional muffled groan escaped his lips. Collins and Clark were bent double. Tears streaming down their cheeks. They were laughing so much that they could barely breathe and their stomach muscles screamed for relief. After several unsuccessful attempts, they managed to regain some composure and eased a block of wood from the coal bunker under Freddie's feet. This took some of the strain off his torn scrotum, but the rusted nail still held him.

Clark suggested that Freddie looked as if he was trying to hump the fence, which was enough to set Collins off again.

Clark left Collins laughing and went in search of a phone, finding one in the butcher's around the corner. He phoned for an ambulance and the fire brigade. As an afterthought, he rang the Duty Sergeant at Thornhill Road to report what had happened.

When the ambulance arrived, the men had to fight their way through seven police officers who had crowded into the back yard. All of them, at one time or another, had nicked Freddie and wanted to be present on the day that divine justice was meted out to the greatest wanker on the patch. Two had even managed to find their Box Brownies and were happily snapping away, recording the event for posterity. All of them wanted to be able to claim that they had been present on the day that Freddie's sack had been shredded.

Despite their best efforts to ease Freddie off the nail, the ambulance men had to concede defeat and let the fire brigade take over. To much cheering from their colleagues in the police, they were eventually able to cut through the nail – although the vibrations caused by the hacksaw's grinding passage across the nail had led to a series of screams from Freddie that sounded like a banshee's death cries.

Finally freed, to a chorus of cheers from the ever-sympathetic police, Freddie was taken to hospital with four inches of nail still imbedded in his scrotum. On the toss of a coin, it was agreed that Collins would go with the ambulance and Clark would return to the station.

Clark's return was triumphant, but he was modest in taking the credit. He insisted that it had been Collins who actually pulled Freddie down the fence and onto the nail. He'd only leant on Upright to make sure that he was firmly impaled.

By the time Collins got back to the station, Freddie was all tucked up in a nice clean hospital bed. His scrotum had nineteen stitches in it and one testicle. The amount of damage done to the remaining testicle was unclear, but it would certainly be out of working order for a prolonged period.

On entering the canteen, Clark stood up and introduced Constable Collins to the assembled throng as the Ball Buster in Chief. A cheer went up from the near-full canteen and a chant of "BBC, BBC," could be heard throughout the station.

As Collins got stuck into a plate of mashed potatoes, sausages and peas, all liberally covered in dark brown gravy, Clark brought him up to date. 'I spoke to Hicks about Spencer. He wants us to sweat him a bit. Maybe call him in for questioning early next week. He also wants to join us next week when we speak to Ravenal.'

'OK. Anything else?'

'He said that he wants to see you before you clock off.'

'Damn.'

❧

Collins knocked on the Inspector's door and waited to be called in. Hicks was at his desk, his shirt sleeves rolled up. Another of those stinking French cigarettes hanging from the corner of his mouth, meaning that Collins came to attention and saluted in a cloud of blue smoke.

'Sit yourself down, lad. I imagine you're knackered after the day you've had, but not as knackered as Upright Freddie,' said Hicks, laughing.

'I think I'd agree with you on that, Sir, but I'm not sure what to make of this BBC stuff.'

'Take it as a compliment. You're one of the lads now. Besides, it's always useful to have a nickname that implies a certain proclivity for violence. The villains on the patch will think twice before mixing with you.'

'Yes, Sir.'

'Anyway, I didn't ask to see you to talk about balls. Tell me how you broke the code?'

'I didn't, Sir. My landlady did.'

'You shared police information with your landlady?' asked Hicks, his voice rising.

'No, Sir – not on purpose, that is,' replied Collins, and quickly outlined the events of the previous evening.

'I see. I hope you didn't share any other police information with her?'

'No, Sir,' lied Collins.

'Well, no harm done then. In fact, some good was done. The Queen's Other Head is a pub in Stratford-upon-Avon. Odd thing is, it has a reputation as a hangout for queers. The Manor is a hotel not far from Stratford and the "Meet Bucky" message confirms what Carol Midgley said about the boyfriend picking Simone up from the school. And of course the final entry seems to indicate that she had a meeting planned with this Bucky character on Friday 8th February.'

'Well at least we have a date for when he picked Simone up at school. Maybe that will help the kids remember something.'

'York's already on it. You know, Collins, you've been like a rat up a drainpipe with this enquiry. I'm impressed. Keep it up. Now, get the hell out of here and get some sleep.'

'Thank you, Sir. Good night.'

Collins was almost out the door when Hicks said, 'By the way, you can thank your landlady from me for her help. Unofficially, of course.'

Collins smiled and shut the door without reply.

Thursday 14th February 1963.

Handsworth, 08.00hrs.

It was 8.15 when Mr Mitchell of Mitchell's Greengrocers waved at Clark and Collins from across the road.

'Morning, Clarkee. Who's this then?'

'Hello Bert, meet Probationary Constable Collins. Another bloody Paddy. I'm supposed to break him in.'

'Pay him no attention, lad. He's always been a cheery git. Yow should see him after we've lost a game. Fit to slit his wrists, he is. Anyhow, I've got a problem for yow.'

'For us?'

'Yeah. Come on.' Mitchell led them down the alley to the rear of the shop to a locked storeroom. 'Here,' he said, giving them the key, 'I found him in the shed this morning. He can't be any more than fourteen. He's in a hell of a state and I don't think being locked up will help, but I'm buggered if I know what to do with him.'

'OK, let's have a look,' said Clark.

Collins unlocked the door, which was suddenly flung open and a ball of fury came charging out. Clark sidestepped the youth, but left his leg trailing. The boy hit the outstretched leg and skidded on his hands and knees across the backyard.

Clark pulled him up by the scruff of the neck and shook him. 'Calm down, lad, or I'm going to thump you.'

The boy was about 5 feet 8 inches, of slim build and wearing a pair of jeans, a shirt and a jumper. He had no coat and his face and hands were chapped and red with the cold. He stood beside Clark, shaking with the type of cold that burns its way into your bones and that once endured is never forgotten. Despite that, however, there was still fight in his eyes. The world may have given him a good kicking, but he was ready for round two.

'Come on, lad, calm down. Yow look froze. Let's go and have a cuppa in Mr Mitchell's nice warm backroom. Then yow can tell me why yow were sleeping in his shed on the coldest fucking night of the year.'

It was only after the lad had drank two mugs of tea and demolished both a bacon sandwich and, moments later, an egg sandwich that Clark asked him, 'What's yowr name, lad?'

Colour was returning to the kid's face and he'd stopped shaking. 'Jamie O'Conner.'

'And how old are you, Jamie?'

The boy hesitated before answering, 'I'm sixteen,' he said.

'You don't look it,' said Collins.

'I've always looked young for my age. It's because of me fair hair.'

'Well, we'll leave that for a minute,' said Clark. 'Where do yow live?'

'Nowhere. Me old man threw me out last Tuesday.'

'Where have yow been staying since then?'

'The first night I stayed with this friend of mine, but his wife came home on Wednesday and there wasn't room for me. He gave me a few bob to get something to eat, but there weren't enough for a room. So I reckoned that there would be somewhere to sleep behind the shops.'

'And where does this mate of yours live?'

'Over on Hagley Road. I'm not sure of the address. I know where it is like, but I don't know the address.'

'Any chance yow can go home?'

'Na. None.'

'Well, if you're sixteen, there's nothing we can do for yow. If Mr Mitchell here presses charges, we could lock yow up for the night. Do you want that?'

Jamie's answer was just about audible, 'No.'

Collins caught Clark's eye and beckoned him outside.

'You don't believe that bullshit that he's sixteen, do you?'

'No,' said Clark.

'Then we should call the council and get him into a

children's home.'

'Maybe, but there's more going on here than he's letting on.'

'What do you mean?'

'It takes one hell of a hard bastard to throw his own son out of the house in the middle of winter. Whatever the reason it must be summut serious. Secondly, how many married men do yow know have a young lad as a friend? A friend that they don't want their wife to know about?'

'You mean he's queer?'

'Possibly, but if he goes into care and gets labelled as a poofter he's going to have a hard time. Let's try and find him some place to stay for a few days until we get the full story.'

Collins looked at Clark and a smile slowly formed at the corners of his mouth.

'What? What yow grinning at, you Irish fuck?'

'You. The hard man with a gooey soft centre. Who'd have guessed?'

'Yow'll find out how soft I am when I put me foot so far up yowr arse that my toes tickle yowr tonsils. Yow cheeky git. C'mon, let's sort this out.'

'Wait, I have an idea.'

One telephone call and twenty minutes later, Agnes turned into the alleyway next to the greengrocers and parked up. At first, Jamie had been suspicious of the suggestion that he stay with a woman in Handsworth Wood. He was sure it was a con and that he would be taken to a council home, but five minutes with Agnes and he was pleading to stay with her.

Back on the street, Collins asked, 'So what are we going to write this up as?'

'Exactly like it were. Young man by the name of Jamie O'Conner of no fixed abode found sleeping rough in the storeroom of Mitchell's Greengrocers. Mr Mitchell did not want to press charges and, after a stern warning, the young man was allowed to go.'

'Fair enough.'

Jamie said nothing on the short journey home. Agnes could see that he was exhausted and suggested that he have a hot bath and go to bed. They could talk later. While he slept, she washed his clothes and hung them over a radiator to dry. When she looked in on him mid-afternoon he was still asleep – the eiderdown tucked under his chin.

⸺

Collins waited until he could change out of his uniform before he visited Mary. He surveyed the street furtively. Embarrassed that someone might see him go in and think he was a regular customer. Satisfied that there was no one watching, he rang Mary's doorbell.

'Who is it?' asked a voice from behind the plain blue door.

'Collins, I called earlier.' He heard a bolt being drawn back and the click of the lock as it was released.

A mop of blonde hair, piled high in a beehive, blue eyes and a pert nose looked around the door jam. Collins was aware of being inspected and tried to appear relaxed and confident, as if calling on a prostitute was something he'd spent his entire life doing. Inspection over, Mary stepped back and opened the door just far enough for him to squeeze past. She was wearing a pale blue candlewick dressing gown, which had been selected for comfort rather than sex appeal and matching slippers.

Inside, Collins found himself in a short corridor with red walls and black ceiling and doors. The effect was like walking into a small hot cave.

'It's the second door on the left,' Mary said, 'unless I can interest you in a session with Mistress Karla in her dungeon of pain before we start. I do special discounts for the police.'

Collins felt the blood rush to his face and mumbled, 'No I don't. I...'

Taking pity on him, Mary relented and said, 'It's all right, I'm just kidding. Agnes told me what you wanted and I'll help if I can. Would you like a cuppa?'

'That would be grand.'

As Mary busied herself boiling the kettle and finding some biscuits in the cupboard, Collins inspected the room. It was small, maybe nine by ten, with no windows and a connecting door to Mary's dungeon. The only furniture in the room consisted of a small folding table, two wooden chairs and a rocking chair pulled close to the gas fire, which was blasting away on full power. Heaped against the chimney breast was a pile of paperbacks. The top one was Graham Greene's *The Power and the Glory. She has decent taste in books*, thought Collins, as he removed his coat.

Handing Collins his drink Mary said, 'This is where I reside when I'm not humiliating, beating, bossing around and generally insulting some poor punter for £3 an hour or £2/10s if they're a regular. So, tell me Constable Collins, what do you want to know?'

'The girl that was murdered was strangled by a ribbon of cloth or something similar. We think she was having sex when she died, but there were no bruises or signs that she fought back. So it probably started out as just ordinary sex and then the guy got overexcited and strangled her.'

'You mean a sex game gone wrong?'

'Sex game?'

'Yeah. In the last few years I've noticed more and more punters want girls to smother them. Either by sitting on their faces, putting a bag over their head or choking them with a belt. It makes them come like an express train.'

'But how…?'

'Don't ask me. Maybe it's like the old stories of men who were hung. When their neck weren't broken by the fall, they would hang there for a couple of minutes slowly suffocating. Many of them were supposed to have come as they died, but you'd have to ask Pierrepoint about that.'

'Who?'

'Albert Pierrepoint,' she said slowly, as if talking to an idiot. 'England's chief executioner for the last thirty years.'

'But that doesn't explain the girl...'

'God, what it is to be innocent. It has the same effect on women.'

Collins tried to hide his embarrassment. 'Do you have any clients who like to choke you?'

'I'm sure some would love to choke Madam. But I don't trust anyone enough to give them a chance to kill me – by accident or intent. But I know a couple of the girls who do offer it.'

'Can you give me their numbers?'

'Sure, but I think they'll tell me more than they will you. How about I speak to them and give you a ring when I've seen them?'

'That sounds fine. Thanks.'

'OK.' They were silent for a few moments.

Collins could see that Mary was thinking. Finally, she asked, 'Have you thought that whoever the killer is he might be more interested in young girls than strangulation? There's much more demand for young girls, and boys come to that, than for girls willing to play strangulation games.'

'Go on,' said Collins.

'For lots of men it's all about the age of the boy or girl. Some like really young kids. Others like kids on the turn. I think they like teaching them about sex. Corrupting them. Moulding them into their own little fuck machines. If that's the case, then strangulation may not be this guy's main interest.'

'Does anyone in Birmingham provide kiddies or young girls?'

'Just one.'

'Only one?'

'When you meet Joey Bishop, you'll understand why there's only one supplier. He doesn't like competition. If you go to see him be careful. Don't go alone. He's a right mean fuck.'

Collins jotted down Bishop's address. His tea finished, he was just about to stand up when Mary said, 'OK, out with it.

What do you want to ask me?'

'I don't have—'

'Rubbish. Every man who comes in here has one of two questions that they ask: "How did you get started on the game?" or "Do you ever come when having sex with a customer?"'

'And what do you say?'

'I lie. With the first question, I tell them a story that fits with their fantasies. For the second, I say that only a very small number of customers can make me come and imply that they are one of the chosen few. Those with half a brain know I'm lying, but play along. Does that answer your question?'

'Not really. I was wondering, what's the most painful thing a punter has asked you to do?'

'Well, at least that's original. Looking to add to your repertoire, are we? Let me think. Some punters like me to beat them, walk on them in my high heels, or kick them where it hurts. A few like me to rub embrocation on their cock and balls, and a very small number, maybe one or two, like me to push the embrocation up their bum. Of course, I use a rubber glove when I do that. How's that for you?' Mary asked, smiling.

Collins crossed his legs and winced. 'How the hell could anyone enjoy that?' he asked.

'Because they're messed up,' said Mary, 'but it doesn't mean they're evil. They don't harm anyone except themselves.'

***

When Collins arrived home, he found Agnes and Jamie chatting in the kitchen. The boy looked a 100% better than he had earlier in the day. Both he and his clothes had scrubbed up nicely. Gone was the cold, tired and dejected kid, and in his place was a vibrant, animated youth. From the way he was looking at Agnes, it was clear that she had done much to engineer the change.

Collins put the kettle on and asked, 'How are you feeling, Jamie?'

'Much better, thanks. Mrs Winters says that I can stay a few days until I get things sorted out.'

'That's grand. Do you want us to talk to your dad and see if you can return home?'

'Jamie doesn't think there is any chance of that happening,' Agnes said.

'What about your mammie? Doesn't she want you back?'

'She's dead,' said Jamie. 'Died when I was little. There's just dad and me and he don't ever want me back.'

'A lot of things get said in anger, especially between fathers and sons. I'm sure that when he's cooled down he'll have you back.'

'No, he won't,' Jamie snapped. 'He don't ever want me back and, besides, I don't want to go back.' Jamie's voice started to break as he wiped away a stray tear.

Collins sat down beside Jamie and placed his hand on his shoulder. 'Why don't you tell me what it's all about? I'm sure either Mrs Winter or me can help sort it out.'

Jamie shook his head.

'He doesn't want to say what the problem is, which, given what's happened to him, is understandable,' said Agnes.

Jamie bit his lip. Head still bowed, he started to cry silently.

Collins looked at Agnes and nodded. She was probably right. Jamie would tell them when he was ready. However, he also felt certain that Jamie needed to tell someone, so he decided to try one last time.

'Look, I'm a copper, but as long as you've not hurt anyone or stolen anything of value, I'm not going to run you in. So, you can tell me or tell Agnes in private what the problem is. That way we'll know how best to help. Come on, Jamie, what do you say?'

Collins handed his handkerchief to the boy, who took it and wiped his nose. When he started to speak, his voice was low, punctuated with sobs of pain and self-pity. 'I shouldn't have told the priest.'

'What priest?'

'Father Murray.'

'What did you tell Father Murray?'

Head still bent, it was hard to hear Jamie's reply. 'I told him that I'd been to the Troubadour in Birmingham. It's a pub where queers go.'

'And you went there to have sex with a man?'

Jamie nodded, adding, 'More than once.'

'And he told your father? Why didn't you tell him in confession?'

'I did, but he asked me to speak to him outside confession. I trusted him. He wanted to help. But then he told Mr Wilson, me headmaster. He's a right sanctimonious bastard and it was him that expelled me and told my father. There is no way back. Me Dad hates poofters.'

Collins patted Jamie's shoulder and looked up at Agnes, who gave him a sad little smile. Maybe Father Murray had wanted to help – but then again Collins had met enough priests to realise that some were duplicitous bastards who applied the letter of the law with the same zealous enthusiasm that the Pharisees had used to implement the Law of Moses. They forgot what Christ had said about the importance of love and forgiveness. Fr Murray may well have trapped Jamie into revealing all outside the protection of the confessional. On the other hand, he may genuinely have wanted to help the boy.

With one final shuddering sob, Jamie stopped crying and pulled away from Collins. 'So what happens now? Do you send me to a home?'

Collins started to reply, but was cut off by Agnes, 'Nothing is going to happen for the next few days. I'm going to talk to some people who might be able to help and I'll have a word with your father. We'll sort something out, I promise, but sending you to a home is not an option.'

Jamie's face broke into a tentative smile and he mumbled,

'Thanks.'

'Now, I suggest you go and wash your face and then you can come down and watch *Bonanza* with me in the lounge. I never miss it.'

Jamie's face broke into a wide grin and he hurried off to the bathroom.

'You were very good with him, Michael. How did you know he wanted to tell us?'

'I don't know. I suppose it was instinct.'

'Well, it was a good instinct.'

'What are we going to do now?'

'Exactly what I said. I'm going to talk to a few people I know in the Education Department and visit his father. See if there's any chance at all of a reconciliation – though I doubt it. Fathers can take it very badly when they hear that their son is a homosexual. They think it's some sort of insult to their own manhood.'

'Well, I've not known many queer fellas, but those I have were always OK with me. I've never understood why people hate them so much.'

'Fear and hatred of the different. The same fear that sent six million to the gas chambers.'

Collins stood up to go. He'd reached the door when he turned and asked, 'Do you mind if I watch *Bonanza* with Jamie? It's my favourite programme, too.'

Agnes smiled. 'Of course not, I'll make us all a cup of hot chocolate.'

Stratford-upon-Avon, 19.10hrs.

The Major was the last to arrive. Colin Spencer was already well into Phillip's whiskey and Trevor was picking imaginary lint from his jacket. They all knew why the Major had called them.

'OK, let's keep this brief. Colin called me yesterday. Two

coppers were at The Palms asking about Andrew. Colin gave them nothing, but they want to speak to Jimmy next week. I'm satisfied that they don't have much to go on. They certainly aren't looking for us, just Andy – and they may not find him. If they do, we'll need to act fast. I'm open to suggestions.'

It was Trevor who spoke first. His soft languid tones were at variance with what he was saying. 'Andy is a liability. He has been since we brought him on board. Yes, he's a good pick-up artist, but he gets too excited and then things go wrong. Last time, it was the overdosed girl. This time, it's a dead girl. What will it be next time? Buggery of the entire choir during evensong?'

Phillip nodded in agreement. 'He was next to useless when we dumped the girl. Nerves shot to pieces. If the police get to him, we'll all be in the shit.'

'I agree,' said the Major. 'Therefore, I propose that if the police do identify Andrew, we dispose of him.'

'We can't just kill him. It would too suspicious,' said Colin.

'Don't worry about that. Trevor and I will look after him. There will be no comebacks, I promise you.'

'Good.'

'One thing, Phillip. Get rid of the Austin van and that includes any paperwork you have on it – just in case. OK?'

'Right.'

'OK, gentlemen, I'll see you all on Saturday at the Club.'

Friday 15th February 1963.
Handsworth, 14.15hrs.

For once, the shift brought no surprises or emergencies. Word of Freddie's accident had got around and several members of the public were keen to offer their congratulations or thanks to Collins and Clark.

'News spreads faster here than in an Irish village.'

'Jungle telegraph, Mickey. Jungle telegraph.'

By 2.15 both men were standing on the steps of the station. The day had grown colder as it wore on and they turned their collars up as they set off in the afternoon gloom.

'I feel like seeing some clean snow for a change. How about we go through the park? I'll show yow a shortcut to your place,' said Clark.

'Fine. I'm in no hurry.'

'I said I'd show yow a shortcut, yow Irish numty. It will be quicker than normal, not longer.'

'From my experience, shortcuts have a habit of taking longer. Things happen when you take a shortcut.'

Clark looked at Collins and tried to work out if he was being set up or if Collins was serious. Unsure, he decided to defend himself with the always useful multi-purpose response of 'Bollocks.'

There had been a half-hearted attempt to clear some pathways in the park and the kids had played their part by trampling down the snow on their way to the big hill that ran from the railway bridge down to the boathouse. It was the best sled ride in the park, provided you could get around the sharp bend at the end. Otherwise, you ran into the iron railings that protected the boats from being pinched in the summer.

The weeping willows that Collins had seen when he was looking for digs were still heavy with snow and ice. The lake was frozen and snow-covered, making it difficult for Collins to see where the land ended and the water began. However, there was no uncertainty in his mind as to the beauty of the scene in front of him. It was perfect, with a few flakes of snow gently drifting to the ground adding a Hollywood touch. Unbidden Collins thought of his favourite film *It's a Wonderful Life I* and the snow in Bedford Falls.

As they neared the pond, Collins saw a movement on the lake, about 30 yards from the shore. At first he wasn't sure what it was, then he realised it was a swan flapping its wings. Pointing, he said, 'I bet he wishes he'd gone south.'

Clark nodded and both men continued to watch the giant bird flap its wings. There was something about the bird's movements that seemed unnatural and as they neared, they could hear its distinctive squawks.

'Bloody hell, I think it's stuck in the ice,' said Clark.

'Poor thing,' said Collins, stopping. 'Is there anyone we can call?'

'Yeah, the RSPCA, but wi could spend all day waiting for them buggers to turn up. So I guess it's down to yours truly.'

'Hang on a minute. I'm not going out on that ice.'

'Too right you're not. Yow're far too heavy. No, twinkle toes here will look after it.'

'Clark, no. It's too dangerous.'

'Na, the pond is froze solid. I'll be fine.'

Stepping carefully, Clark moved slowly across the ice. He placed each foot gently on the snow and tested the ice before transferring his weight. He was only six feet from the bird when a loud crack ripped through the air. Clark spun round and shouted, 'Stay there,' just as the ice gave way beneath his feet and he plunged into the icy waters.

The cold was as bad as anything he'd endured in Norway, but the old training kicked in automatically. *Don't splash about. Orientate yourself. Find which way is up and make your way to the surface. Stay in the hole you fell through. Don't slip under the ice.* After what seemed like minutes but was probably only five seconds, Clark reached the surface. Beside him, the swan was gliding on open water. It looked at him with open contempt, flapped its wings and took off. *Well, at least this ended well for one fucker,* he thought.

Looking around, he saw Collins step onto the ice and start running. 'Stop,' he shouted. 'Go back.' It was no use; Collins was past hearing.

As he ran, Collins struggled out of his coat. *Oh fuck,* thought Clark, *he's going to dive in and kill us both.* But Collins was slowing down. Five foot from the edge of the hole, he lay down on the ice and, holding onto the sleeve of his coat, threw it overarm towards Clark.

The coat fell just short of the water and he tried again. This time, the tail of the coat hit the water and Clark swam towards it. Gripping it with both hands, he shouted, 'Pull!'

Collins wriggled backwards in the snow, legs wide open, spreading his weight as best he could. Twice he stopped when he heard the ice crack beneath him, but nothing happened. Breathing hard, his arms cramping with the effort, he prayed to Jesus, Mary and Joseph to help him. Then, suddenly, the tension was gone. Looking up, he saw Clark crawling towards him on the ice grinning like a maniac. Collins' head sank onto the snow.

'Come on, lad, let's get the hell out of here,' said Clark, his voice choking with the cold.

Back on dry land, the two men stared at each other, then started to laugh. 'That was sodding close, my mad Irish fuck. Thanks. I owe yow,' said Clark and held out his hand.

Collins flicked his coat over Clark and then shook hands. 'I told you. Fecking shortcuts always take longer. We need to get you warm.'

'No problem. I know just the place. There's a Parkees' hut just up that lane. The stove will be on.'

Weary and getting colder by the second, both men trudged

the 200 yards to the green hut. Opening the door, they were confronted by two astonished park keepers and a stove in the corner that was blasting out heat – the distinctive smell of burning coke heavy in the air.

'Yow got room for two more?' asked Clark.

Agnes picked up the phone on the third ring. It was Mary.

'Is your innocent copper about?'

'No, he's not come in yet. He said you might call.'

'OK, I need to make this quick. I have a customer in five minutes. Can you tell him that Della has one customer who might fit the bill?'

'Hold on let me get a pen.' There was a pause as Agnes found a pencil. 'Got it. Which Della are you talking about?'

'Daft Della.'

'OK.'

'One of her regulars, a skinny, blond guy in his early twenties, likes to strangle her. He likes to ride her from the back and wraps a strip of velvet around her throat as a pair of reins. She calls him Bronco.'

'What makes her think he might be our man?'

'He gets a bit rough at times. Pulls that bit too hard. Susan says she's passed out a few times.'

'Why does she still see him?'

'The answers in her name - Daft Della. She hasn't got the sense she was born with. Besides he's a good payer. When he does get a bit rough, he always gives her a big tip. Sometimes it's worth more than her fee.'

'Free with his money then.'

'Well, that's it. It's seldom money he gives her. It's bits of old jewellery, which she flogs for scrap value in the Jewellery Quarter. Reckons she got ten quid for a piece one time. She thinks he probably works in the Quarter. Oh, there's the bell. Tell Michael to call me if he needs to talk.'

Agnes hung up. It did sound like their man. Michael had said that Simone had been strangled with a thin piece of fabric. The trouble was that the Jewellery Quarter was a maze of back allies and tiny workshops, and there were thousands of businesses in it. Finding Bronco or Bucky would take an awful lot of luck and patience.

———————

By the time Clark had dried out, it was nearly 5 pm. By mutual consent, both men agreed not to mention their impromptu swim back at the station. However, they feared it was too good a story for the parkees to keep quiet about.

When Collins got home at 5.20 Agnes quickly reported the contents of the conversation she'd had with Mary. The description of Bronco fitted that given by Mr Wilcox. The similarity of the two names Bronco and Bucky were also too similar to be ignored, but it was mention of old jewellery that convinced Collins he needed to call Inspector Hicks immediately.

The conversation was short and to the point. Collins was to pick up the piece of broken jewellery from Mrs Winston and get back to the nick as quickly as possible and bring Agnes with him.

———————

Agnes and Collins arrived at the police station just before 6. Agnes was given a cup of tea and asked to wait. Collins was marched into Hicks' office by Sergeant York. He wasn't offered a cup of tea. York lent against the door. Collins remained at attention.

'What the fuck have you been up to, Collins? Undertaking your own investigation into the Winston girl's murder. Interviewing a known prostitute on her premises. Involving a member of the public in an ongoing murder investigation. I could have you out on your ear for this.'

'I apologise, Sir. I obviously wasn't thinking straight. It's just that Agnes has a few contacts with prostitutes because of her work with beaten women and I thought that one of them might have seen this Bucky character. It's my fault. I asked her for a name and made a nuisance of meself till she agreed.'

'Do you seriously expect me to believe that bullshit? I made enquiries about Mrs Agnes bloody Winter after she solved our little code problem. From what I could learn of her exploits, she's not a woman who would be badgered into doing anything she didn't want to – especially by a wet-behind-the-ears probationary constable who has more enthusiasm than sense. Do you understand me?'

Collins heard York stifle a laugh. *There's always an element of enjoyment in watching someone else get a bollicking* he thought. When he replied, he was suitably contrite. 'Yes, Sir.'

Hicks sat back in his chair. When he spoke again, his anger had dissipated and he spoke in the tone of voice reserved for conversations that usually began with *"What am I going to do with you?"*

'Look, lad, you've done some great work on this case, but you were out of order on this. Don't you realise the risk to your career that you took visiting a known prostitute on her own premises? If you were seen going in, who's going to believe that you were there to interview her and not shag the arse off her? Oh God, don't tell me you wore your uniform when you paid her a visit.'

'No, Sir, I was in civvies.'

'Thank God for small mercies. Where was Clark when you were being bloody Sherlock Homes?'

'He knew nothing about it. I did it on me own time.'

'That I can believe, because he would have cut your balls off before letting you go. However, it's done now. You need to register this Mary woman as an informant. That way, you have a legitimate reason to visit her. Sergeant York, do you think you can get that backdated a few days?'

'No problem, Sir.'

'As for including Mrs Winter in the investigation, it has to stop. Do I make myself clear?'

'Crystal clear, Sir.'

'Good. Now, let's get Mrs Winter in.'

York left and returned moments later with Agnes.

'Thank you for agreeing to come in to see me Mrs Winter.'

'It was an invitation I couldn't refuse, Inspector,' she said, with a smile.

'Now, Mrs Winter, I don't think you understand how—'

Agnes cut the Inspector off. Smiling, she said, 'I heard the gist of your conversation with Constable Collins.'

'In that case, I must apologise about some of the agricultural language used.'

'No need, Inspector. I can assure you I have heard much worse in my time. It was wrong of me to put Constable Collins in touch with Mary. I should have approached you directly with the suggestion.'

'Yes, you should, but it doesn't seem as if too much harm was done. However, I must ask you to refrain from involving yourself in any ongoing police investigation in future.' Hicks paused and looked Agnes straight in the eye. 'Regardless of anything you might have done during the war. Do you understand?'

'Yes, Inspector, I understand. May I go now?'

'Of course. One last point – and this is off the record – thank you for your help with the code and for Mary's information.'

'You're welcome, Inspector. Goodnight Sergeant.'

York waited until the door had shut and he could hear Agnes' footsteps disappearing down the corridor before he said, 'God, she's a cool one.'

'You've got no idea, Sergeant. OK, Collins, let's see this piece of jewellery.'

Collins took the brooch from his pocket, unwrapped the handkerchief it was in and laid it on the table.

'So, let me get this right,' said Hicks, fingering the brooch. 'We've got Bucky giving girls broken jewellery as a sort of tip. And Mary's told us that one Tom reckons he's a regular of hers and she thinks he works in the Jewellery Quarter. Is that about it?'

'Yes, Sir,' said Collins.

'OK. I think we'll need to canvas the Jewellery Quarter and see if we can track this character down. York, can you arrange that?'

'Yes, Sir. When do you want to start, tomorrow?'

'No, the lads have been working hard. Let them have a break. If this Bucky character is there, he'll still be there on Monday.'

'OK.'

Then Hicks smiled. 'Mind you, it might not be a bad thing to make an early start. You were supposed to be off tomorrow, weren't you, Collins?'

'Yes, Sir.'

'Well, not any more. You can start the enquiry tomorrow and take Clark with you. Both of you will be working without pay. Maybe that will teach you to follow regulations and him to keep a better eye on what his probationer is up to.'

After Collins had left, York sat down in the chair that Agnes had recently vacated. 'You didn't give him any instructions about how to conduct the enquiry.'

'I know. It's way too big a job for two men to do, but hopefully he'll learn his lesson trudging around freezing streets on his day off. We'll start properly on Monday.'

'I don't know, Sir. I think he wants nothing more than to wander around the Jewellery Quarter tomorrow.'

'How do you know that?'

'He was trying not to smile when he left.'

'Bastard,' said Hicks and laughed.

A gnes was waiting outside when Collins emerged from the station. He slid in beside her and she tuned the ignition on.

'I'm amazed that you could hear Inspector Hicks telling me

off.'

'I couldn't.'

'But you heard him swearing.'

'No, I didn't, but I knew that there was a very good chance he would be swearing.'

'But why did you pretend you heard?'

'It took the wind out of his sails and put him on the back foot. Men from Inspector Hicks' background don't swear in front of a lady. When they do, it embarrasses them. It gave me a slight advantage in the conversation.'

'You, Mrs Winters, are a devious woman,' Collins said, with admiration.

'I can be. Anyway, what's your next move?'

'I'm going to visit Clark and tell him that we have to go shop to shop in the Jewellery Quarter, without pay, on our day off as punishment for my visit to Mary.'

'Do you want me to drop you off?'

'Please, and if you were to come in that would be even better. I have a feeling I'll need some protection.'

'Coward.'

'True.'

'I'll wait for you outside. No housewife likes a strange woman to arrive unannounced.'

Saturday 16th February 1963.

Hockley, 09.15hrs.

As recompense for her part in the events that led Collins and Clark to the Jewellery Quarter on a freezing, rock-breaking Saturday morning, Agnes drove both men to Great Hampton Street and dropped them off outside Canning's.

Established over 150 years ago, the Quarter still occupied the same warren of small workshops, streets and alleys that it always had. Clark explained that it wasn't the streets of London that were paved with gold, it was the floorboards in these businesses. There was enough gold dust on most workshop floors to ensure that they were burnt and the gold reclaimed whenever a building was demolished.

Spread over a mere 250 acres, this tiny area contained the largest concentration of businesses involved in the jewellery trade in Europe and produced around 40% of all jewellery made in the UK. It was also home to the world's largest Assay Office, which was responsible for hallmarking over 10 million items a year. With something approaching pride, Clarke explained that at its height, in the early 1900s, the Quarter employed around 30,000 people. Now, the figure was nearer 20,000.

'Right, Sherlock, where the hell do wi start?' asked Clark.

Collins consulted his A-Z of Birmingham and, looking up, said, 'I think we start here on Hall Street. We'll do all the streets that are roughly at right angles to Great Hampton Street first. If we find nothing, we can do those that are parallel. OK?'

'Fair enough, yow do know we're never going to cover the lot by lunchtime.'

'Lunchtime?'

'Yeah, lunchtime. A lot of these characters close up at 1 on Saturdays. Them's manufacturers, not shops.'

'Well, we better get going then.'

By 11.30am, they had visited 21 businesses that offered to buy old gold and jewellery. No one knew of a jeweller in the Quarter who was tall, slim, blond, with a Beatles' haircut and in his twenties. At 11.45am, they called a temporary halt to their fruitless trek and went for a cuppa in Ted's café.

'Morning, gentlemen,' said Ted, 'You pair look froze, if you don't mind me saying. What can I get you?'

Both men surveyed the blackboard menu and simultaneously ordered a bacon butty and a mug of tea. The food arrived minutes later. The tea was steaming and the bacon was contained within two doorstop-size pieces of bread. 'Get that down you, gents. It will stick to your guts, I promise.'

'Looks grand,' said Collins.

'I thought I knew all the local coppers around here. New, are you?'

'Na, we're from Handsworth. Just trying to trace a jeweller around here that deals in broken jewellery. You know, antique brooches and things. He ain't done anything wrong, but we think he could help us,' said Clark.

'If it's antique jewellery, you want to try Carver's on Branston Street. They specialise in repairing and reselling the older stuff. Pete, who runs it, reckons it's coming back into fashion.'

Collins jotted the name and address down in his notebook and got stuck into the sandwich in front of him.

Pushing his plate away, Clark drained his mug of tea before announcing loudly, 'That's the best bacon butty I've had all year.'

Collins agreed it was very good, but suggested that it was no match for the bacon sandwiches that Kevin McDonald sold, just off O'Connell Street in Dublin.

Carver's Fine Jewellery Ltd. was getting ready to close when Collins and Clark arrived. A young, spotty lad was sweeping the floor and an older man was cashing up.

'Could we speak to Mr Peter Carver, please?' asked Collins.

'That's me,' said the older man. 'What can I do for you?'

'Wi'm trying to trace a dealer who specialises in broken jewellery. He's in his twenties, blond, over 6 foot and skinny. Hair cut like the Beatles. Do yow know anyone like that in the Quarter?' asked Clarke.

Carver didn't reply immediately. Shaking his head, he eventually said, 'Sorry, I don't think I do. What about you, Davey?'

'No. No one like that, Mr Carver.'

'Davey is my collection and delivery lad. He knows everyone who works in the Quarter by sight. Don't you, Davey?'

'I suppose I do,' replied Davey, embarrassed by the praise.

'What do you need this guy for anyway?'

'Oh, nothing. We just want to talk to him about this piece of jewellery,' said Collins, holding the broken brooch up. 'Have you ever been offered anything like this?'

Collins couldn't be sure, but he thought he saw Carver hesitate before he took the piece and examined it closely. 'No, I've not seen anything like that before.'

Davey started to say something when Carver cut in, 'Now, if you'll excuse me, I need to close up.'

'Of course, sir. Thanks very much for your time,' said Collins.

Collins waited until they were outside, then asked, 'Did you see that hesitation or was I imagining it?'

'Na, there's nowt wrong with yowr faculties. The sight of the brooch gave him a start. I reckon the kid recognised it as well.'

'I think we should wait for Davey to come out, don't you?'

'I've got nowt better to do.'

Standing in a doorway, they watched Peter Carver and Davey leave the premises. Carver crossed the road and got into a dark blue Jaguar Mk 2. Davey started walking towards Great Hampton Street. Collins and Clark waited for Carver to drive away before they followed the boy.

Ten yards from him, Clark called out, 'Davey, wait up a bit, son. Wi'd like to talk to yow.'

Davey turned, a look of surprise on his face. 'Oh, hi. I thought you'd finished with me. Anything wrong?'

'No. No. Nothing at all,' said Collins. 'It's just that when we showed Mr Carver the brooch we got the feeling that you recognised it.'

'Well, yeah, but it's got nothing to do with the bloke you're looking for.'

'What has it got to do with?'

'You sure this won't get me in no trouble?'

'No chance, lad. Yow've got me word as a lifelong Baggies supporter,' said Clark and fixed the lad with a stare.

Davey looked at the small policeman and wondered if he was drunk or, worse, dangerous, and decided to co-operate. 'Well, about a month ago, this really great looking girl came in the shop. She were half-caste, but really lovely. Nice smile and friendly like. She had about four pieces for sale, all a bit like that 'un. She said that her boyfriend had told her to see Mr Carver, as he'd give her a good price for the items if she wanted to sell them.'

'And did he give her a good price?' asked Collins.

'Na, course not. He's a mean bastard. Anyway, he ended up buying three pieces for twelve quid. But she wouldn't sell him this piece 'cos he only offered her two quid for it.'

'Did she or Mr Carver say anything more about her boyfriend?'

'Na. But Carver can't resist anything in a skirt – no matter how young or old they are. He tried chatting her up. As if she'd fancy an old git like him.'

'Go on.'

'Well. He said to her, *"If you ever want a boyfriend nearer to home than Stratford, give me a call,"* and he gave her his card.'

'Did she say anything?' asked Collins, trying to keep the excitement out of his voice.

'Yeah, she said *"Andy wouldn't like it"* or something like that.'

'You sure she said Andy? asked Clark.

'Yeah. 100%. But even that dain't put the old goat off. He followed her outside the shop and stood chatting to her for a couple of minutes.'

'Could you hear what they were talking about?' asked Collins.

'Na, the door were closed. Hey, you sure this ain't going to get me in trouble?'

'No lad. Yow been bostin. But we'll need your full name and address, just in case wi need to speak to yow again. If I were yow, I wouldn't mention this to Mr Carver.'

When Davey had gone, Clark looked at Collins and said, 'Fuck …'

Collins completed the phrase, 'Me.'

'Wi just found the needle in the proverbial haystack, Mickey lad.'

'Yes, we bloody well have.'

Both men smiled as if they'd won the pools.

Solihull, 13.35hrs.

When Carver got home, he left the car on the drive and rushed into the house. His wife was out and he poured himself a large gin, then picked up the phone and rang a Stratford-upon–Avon number.

'Andrew Young's Antique and Bric-a-Brac Emporium. Can I help you?'

'What the fuck have you been up to, Andy? I had two coppers in the shop asking about you today and some broken jewellery.'

There was silence on the line as Andy tried to compose himself. Finally, he asked, 'What did they want exactly?'

'They wanted to know if I knew a 6-foot, skinny, blond bastard in his twenties who deals in broken antique jewellery.'

'What did you say?'

'What do you think? Fuck all. Is this about that half-caste slag they found last week?'

'I'm not sure what it's about,' lied Andy. 'Look, don't talk about this. I'll ring the Major and tell him. He'll sort it out.'

'OK.'

'Look, I owe you. Are you going to the Club tonight?'

'Yes.'

'Well, I'll bring along a present for you. She's fifteen but looks about twelve, and she's a really tight fit. You'll love her.'

Andy cut the connection and immediately phoned the Major. He was surprised how unfazed the Major was. He assured Andy that he was working on something and if Andy would just hang on for another 24 hours, the police would cease to be a problem. To be on the safe side, he suggested that Andy should give the Club a miss that night.

Young hung up, disappointed. He'd been looking forward to the Club and trying someone new, but he knew better than to argue with the Major. *Still,* he thought, *there's no reason why the night should be a total wash out.* Susan, the girl he'd mentioned to Carver, was sure to be available. Carver would just have to wait. Andy picked up the phone and dialled a Birmingham number.

Handsworth 13.45hrs.

Back at the station, Clark located a business phonebook for Stratford and the two men went to the canteen. Clark started working his way through jewellers, goldsmiths and silversmiths, while Collins got the teas in. After twenty minutes, they had nothing. Nothing. No business starting with A, Andy or Andrew. Disappointed, they sat trying to think what other businesses might deal with jewellery.

'What are you two doing here?' asked Sergeant York. 'I thought that after your stroll around the Quarter this morning, you'd be off home warming your arses against the fire.'

Clark quickly filled York in on what they had found. It was obvious to both men that York's reaction was the same as theirs had been. Excitement, a surge of adrenalin and the belief that they were closing in on the killer.

York sat down, forgetting the reason he'd come to the canteen. After a few moments thought, a smile spread across his face. 'Have you tried antique dealers?' Both men lunged for the directory, but Collins got there first. Within seconds, he'd found *"Andrew Young's Antique and Bric-a-Brac Emporium"*.

'That's it! I can feel it in me water,' said Clark.

'Now, calm down. Without a picture or a description of this Andrew Young character, we can't be sure we've got the right man.'

'Maybe someone at the local station knows him,' said Collins.

'It's worth a try,' said York. 'Come on, we'll phone them from the office.'

The Desk Sergeant at Stratford answered on the third ring. York explained what he was after and the Sergeant promised to call him back as soon as possible.

Fifteen minutes later, the phone rang. York grabbed it.

'Is that Sergeant York?'

'Yes, that's me.'

'Sergeant York, Stratford Police here. We've got no criminal record for this guy, Young, although a teenager did complain that he'd tried it on with her about two years ago. She dropped her complaint, though. His full name is Andrew Young and we did photograph him at the time. I'll send it to you.'

'Great, but could you just describe him for me?'

'OK. Let's see. Slim, with long blond hair. He looks about eighteen, but we've got his age as twenty-seven, so twenty-nine now.'

'Do you have his height on record?'

York could hear the pages of the file being turned. 'Yes, it says six feet two. Is that any use?'

'Oh yes, that's very helpful. Can you hang onto the file and picture? My gaffer will be in touch.'

York hung up. A broad smile spread across his face 'We've got him, lads. We've got him. Time to call the gaffer – this is one interruption to his Saturday afternoon he won't mind.'

Collins slumped back in his chair exhilarated and beaming, while Clark sat and nodded his head.

Thirty minutes later, Hicks was standing in the centre of the office shaking snow off his coat and hat. 'Don't tell me you pair of jokers have found him?'

'I'm afraid they have, Sir,' said York.

'Bloody hell.'

'Does that mean we get paid for today?' asked Clark.

Hicks eyed Clark with sly amusement and said, 'We'll see, you cheeky beggar. Tell me what you have.'

As briefly as possible, Collins and Clark reported what they had found and York outlined his conversation with the Desk Sergeant at Stratford. Hicks listened in silence. He then asked just one question, 'You're sure that Carver was lying?'

'No doubt,' said Collins.

'So he's involved in this, too. Whatever *this* is.'

'Yep,' said Clark. 'He's in it up to his eyes.'

'OK, you two reprobates can push off to the canteen while York and I speak to Stratford. We'll find you when we know what's what.'

Two cups of tea and a bun later, the reprobates were joined by Hicks and York. Collins sighed with relief. Clark had taken the opportunity to educate him in all things Albion while they had been waiting. He'd just started to explain the fourth possible reason for why the Albion's nick-name was the Baggies when he was interrupted.

York nodded at Collins and said, 'Get the Inspector a cuppa.'

Hicks waited until Collins returned with his tea before be-ginning, 'I spoke to Inspector Knowles and he had a word with his Super. They want to do a bit of work before picking him up at work on Monday morning. Seems he has friends on the council and knows the local MP, so they want to get their ducks in line before they act. They'll pick him up at his shop mid-morning. We're invited to attend.' He paused, before continuing, 'I'm sorry, lads, but there's only room for me and York.'

'That's fine,' said Collins, though it was hard to mask his disappointment.

The Club, 21.10hrs.

The party was just starting when the Major arrived at the Club. A local TV reporter was kissing a small girl in the hall, his hand up her skirt. In a corner booth, a teenager was on his knees, his head buried in the lap of a well-known MP who had made his reputation denouncing the collapse of family and moral values in modern Britain. He seemed to be enjoying his own lapse in morality and was encouraging the boy to 'Take it all the way in, you gorgeous boy.' One or two other tables and booths were also occupied, but other than a bit of groping their occupants appeared happy to wait until one of the bedrooms become available.

The Major became aware of someone standing behind him and a familiar voice said, 'Good evening, Major. Just arrived?'

'Yes, your Lordship, and how are you?'

'Damn glad to get away from the South of France. It's a beautiful country, but shame about the people who live in it. Did you bring anything for me?'

'Of course, a very nice redhead. Twelve years old and still in need of breaking in. Trevor is bringing her later.'

'Wonderful. I'll give you a full report afterwards.'

'I look forward to it.' At sixty-eight and nearly 20 stone, the Major doubted that Lord Rattenburg would get up to much. His preference was for the girls to sit on his face while he played with himself. Still, he made a mental note to seek out his Lordship later and ask his *expert* opinion of the girl. A little flattery was a small price to pay for the numerous houses, flats and offices he made available for the Club's use, not to mention his contacts and influence.

Looking up, he saw Trevor enter with the girl. She was still blindfolded from her journey and Trevor was holding her firmly by the arm. If the army had taught the Major anything, it had been the need for security. That's why he insisted on blindfolding all the "young guests". That way, none of them knew the exact location of a party – just in case they were ever inclined to talk – and that's the way he wanted to keep it.

'Your guest has arrived, your Lordship,' he said, nodding in the direction of the door.

Lord Rattenburg looked around and smiled. 'As always, Major, you have excellent taste. Won't you introduce me?'

The Major led the way and made the introductions. When the girl realised that her "date" for the night was a 20-stone tub of lard who smelt like the perfume counter in Rackham's, she turned to Trevor with a silent plea in her eyes. He dug his fingernails into her arm and pushed her towards his Lordship. She smiled grimly and was led away.

Watching her go, Trevor said, 'You can't really blame her. Who the fuck would enjoy having that lard arse as a bedfellow?'

'You mean you don't believe in the possibility of true love, and beauty being more than skin deep?' asked the Major, straight-faced.

'No, I believe in the ability of money, power and position to make even the Hunchback of Notre Dame appear attractive

– in the right light, of course. Will you be playing tonight?'

'That's what I wanted to talk to you about. We need to take care of Andrew. It can't wait. The police were at Carver's today. They have a description of Andy and a piece of jewellery that he gave the girl.'

'Shit.'

'Exactly. So stay sober and we'll slip away around 2.30. OK?'

'Fine. It has to be done.'

Sunday 17th February 1963.
Handsworth, 12.30hrs.

Collins was feeling content. He'd been to an early mass and was now enjoying a late breakfast and reading Agnes' copy of *The Sunday Times* in his room when he heard the phone ring. Moments later, Agnes was knocking on his door.

'Michael, it's the station. It sounds important.'

Collins jumped up, almost dropping his last piece of toast. *What the feck do they want?* he thought, as he hurried down the stairs.

'Constable Collins here.'

'Collins, this is York. Get your arse in gear and get down here fast. Your Mr Andrew Young has been found dead in his home. Seems like he killed another girl, then topped himself. Inspector Hicks and I are leaving in thirty minutes. If you're here, you can come along for the ride.'

'I'll be there.' Collins hung up and ran up the stairs two at a time, shouting to Agnes as he went, 'Agnes, can you give me a lift to the station, please? I'll explain on the way.'

Seven minutes later, Collins was in uniform and sitting beside Agnes in the Rover 100. It was the third time he'd been in the car and it confirmed his previous opinion. The ride was incredibly soft and reminded him of bobbing about on a boat in rough weather. It made him feel queasy. It was not a car he'd ever buy. Fortunately, the journey was short. Shouting 'Thanks' over his shoulder, he ran up the station steps. He found Hicks, York and Clark in the Inspector's office.

'I thought that you and Clark deserved to be in at the kill, but there will be no great satisfaction with this one. It looks like Young was our man. He killed another young girl and, for whatever reason – maybe he panicked – he topped himself. Come on, let's get going.'

Hicks led the way to the rear yard where his car was waiting. 'York, you drive.' He said and climbed into the front passenger seat. Collins and Clark slid into the back.

The journey led Collins through parts of Birmingham that he'd never seen before. Many still showed the scars of the intense bombing that Birmingham had suffered during the war. The Birmingham Blitz had gone largely unreported, for fear the Germans would learn of the damage that it was doing to vital aircraft and munitions factories. Those attacks that were reported on the BBC News had simply said that "A town in the Midlands had been bombed last night but casualties were light." However, the reality was that the bombers had left an indelible mark on large swathes of the city that still lay derelict and unused. Many of the damaged shops and factories had been demolished to ground level and most of the bricks carted away for hardcore. However, that still left the unfilled cellars, underground storerooms and basements for kids to explore and get lost in.

Once past Shirley, the suburbs gave way to a winter landscape that took Collin's breath away. Fields, hedgerows and trees were uniformly dressed in a cloak of thick snow that was four feet deep in many places and virgin white. There wasn't a breeze to disturb the frozen branches and this enhanced the silence that the snow had brought to the entire countryside. Unfortunately, the effect was ruined when Inspector Hicks lit one of his stinking French cigarettes. It was York who broke first and opened a window.

Young had lived in a small hamlet of six houses, 5 miles north of Stratford-upon-Avon. Turning off the main road, Collins found himself in a tunnel of snow. Without the constant flow of traffic, the side road had been reduced to a single lane with eight-foot banks of snow overhanging the track. Signs, covered in thick ice, had icicles hanging from their edges, making them all but unreadable. Collins wasn't surprised when York missed the final turning. With no room to turn around, he drove on for nearly a mile before they came to a junction and he was able to turn back.

***

Collins was impressed by his first sight of Young's house. Approached by a long S-shaped drive, it sat in four acres of land. He guessed that the original house had been built sometime in the 18th century. There was a clear demarcation between the pale soft sandstone that had been used for the original building and the red brick extension that had been added during the Victorian age. Nearby stood a barn, which Collins correctly identified as the garage.

There were two police vans and a police car in the drive. York parked up and, with Inspector Hicks in front, the four men headed for the house. If possible it felt even colder here than in Birmingham and Collins pulled his collar up. As they neared the house Collins caught Clark's eye and nodded in the direction of the front door. Above the door was a small plaque that read *Pan House*.

Hicks showed his warrant card to the officer on the door and asked where he could find Inspector Knowles.

'Inspector Knowles isn't here, Sir. Superintendent Burgess is in charge. I think he's still in the bedroom. Just turn right and up the stairs.'

Hicks' eyes briefly reflected his puzzlement at the mention of a Superintendent leading the inquiry. It was not normal practice, even if Chief Superintendent Lockhart did personally investigate every case in *No Hiding Place* on the telly. He recovered quickly and, nodding his thanks, led the small party into the house. The staircase gave way to a gallery that overlooked the front hall.

Superintendent Burgess was standing outside the main bedroom. He was a big man, well over six foot and weighing close to 18 stone. Despite the layer of fat, Collins had no doubt that there was a frame of muscle and bone beneath.

He'd seen farmers built like Burgess in Ireland. Men who could throw 112 lb sacks of potatoes around all day long as if they were juggling a small ball. However, while he looked like a big honest bear of a man, there was something about his eyes that bothered Collins. They were small, dark, hawk-like and hinted at sly ruthlessness.

Holding out a great ham of a hand, he said, 'Inspector Hicks. Good to meet you at last. I've heard a lot of good things about you from Alfie Thomas over the years.'

'Well, he never had anything good to say about me to my face,' Hicks said and forced a smile.

'That sounds like Alfie,' said Burgess. 'Anyway, it looks like Inspector Knowles was wrong to think that picking Mr Young up could wait until Monday. From what I understand about the first murder, I'm certain he's your man. We don't know who the girl is yet, but she can't be any more than fifteen. Like your girl, she was strangled by a long thin strip of material – in this case, a piece of velvet.'

'Why do you think he topped himself?' Hicks asked.

'My guess is that this was either another accident and he felt remorse, or he thought he'd never get away with two killings. Who knows what goes on in the minds of such scum?'

'Any note?'

'No.'

'Who discovered the body?'

'The cleaning lady. She left her purse here on Saturday and called in for it on the way to church today. Otherwise we wouldn't have known about it until Monday. She called us straightaway.'

'What time was that?'

'Call came in about half seven.'

Hicks looked at his watch. It was 3.20. The call to Thornhill Road from Warwickshire police had been logged at 12.10, nearly five hours after the bodies had been found. 'Mind if we have a look?'

'No, go ahead. The doc's been in and the photographer has

finished taking his pictures. He's just dusting for prints now.'

The girl lay on the bed dressed in the top half of a baby doll nightie. There was no sign of her panties. A large bruise spread down the left side of her face. The velvet strip was still in place. Unless she had been unconscious from the blow, Collins realised that she'd must have died looking her killer in the eyes as he snuffed out her young life. The bed was soiled – her small body diminished further by death.

Young hung from the partially open en-suite door. He was naked. His neck had stretched during the time he had hung on the door. His tongue, deep purple and hideous, lolled obscenely from the left of his mouth. His eyes were bulging, open and sightless. Collins looked at the scrawny body, the floppy blond hair and could hardly believe that this pathetic individual had been responsible for killing two young girls.

Clark walked over and, ignoring the body, inspected the door, running his hand down the panels and looking at the carpet beneath. Only then did he look at the body, checking each hand in turn.

'Mind if I have a butchers at the bathroom? I've not seen one of these en-suite dos before.'

'Be my guest,' said Superintendent Burgess.

Collins followed him in and, with his back to the door, silently mouthed, 'What the feck?'

Clark shook his head imperceptibly and turned to the wash-hand basin where he picked up a pair of nail scissors and inspected them, before returning them to the glass shelf next to a large bottle of Old Spice. Next, he turned his attention to the rope tied to the door handle and examined the knot. Satisfied, he straightened up.

Returning to the bedroom, they found York bent over the young girl. His hands were gently examining her neck. Standing up, he turned to Inspector Hicks and nodded.

'Well, many thanks for your co-operation, Sir,' said Hicks. 'We'll get out of your hair and let you wrap this up. You'll be in touch?'

'Of course.'

A morgue van entered the drive just as the four men walked back to the car in silence. Slipping into the front passenger seat, Hicks slammed the door shut and said, 'Get me the fuck out of here. Then find me a café where I can have a cuppa to help me swallow all the bullshit I've just heard.'

Twenty minutes later, the men were sitting in a truck driver's café watching the few vehicles that were trundling along the A34 on that bleak Sunday afternoon.

'We're off the clock now, lads,' said Hicks, producing a hip flask from his inside pocket. 'Who wants a tot of the hard stuff?'

York and Clark pushed their mugs across the table. Collins placed his hands over his and said, 'No thanks, Sir. I'm teetotal.'

'Strewth,' said Clark, 'now I've heard everything. A teetotal Irishman.'

Ignoring Clark's outburst, Hicks asked, 'What did you make of that?'

Collins kept quiet. It had been his second murder scene and certainly much worse than finding Simone's frozen body. He'd spent much of the time trying not to puke at the smell of recent death and Young's elongated neck. But he'd definitely sensed that something was wrong, but what it was he had no idea. All the time he'd been in the house, he'd had the feeling that an elaborate charade was being played out between Hicks and Burgess. And what the feck had Clark been doing in the bathroom?

'We've always thought that the Winston girl was killed by accident,' said York, 'but this one was hit, possibly knocked unconscious, before she was strangled, so no accident this time. It makes me doubt that he did it, unless of course the first murder gave him a taste for it. But if that were the case, why did he top himself?'

'Fair points. What do you think Clark?'

When Clark spoke, his voice was low and edged with anger. 'If he committed suicide, then me Auntie has a pair of brass balls.'

Collins' head snapped up.

'Go on,' said Hicks.

'He'd been boarded. I seen it a couple of times during the war. When the resistance or special ops wanted to kill an informer but avoid Nazi reprisals, they'd help him or her commit suicide.'

'How?' asked Collins.

Clark took a slurp of his tea, 'First, yow get a piece of wood about the size of a door and a noose. Yow wait until the guy is asleep or, better still, pissed. Then you slip the noose around his neck and before he can wake up, you slide him onto the board. Once on the board, yow just have to stand it upright and pull on the rope. Works a treat.'

'Then, when he's dead, you transfer him to an actual door?' said Hicks.

'That's right, Sir.'

'Why are you so sure that's what happened?' asked Hicks.

'As yow know, Sir, when someone is hanged they usually shit and piss themselves, but there were hardly any mess on the door or the floor beneath him. But there were a big wet patch near the bed. My guess is someone had washed the carpet.'

'You're not wrong Constable,' said Hicks. 'The patch smelt of soap. Someone had cleaned up after the killings.'

'On top of that, even if yow want to kill yourself, you struggle when the noose tightens. However, there were no scuff marks on the door where Young would have kicked, hit the door and smeared his own mess.'

'Anything else?'

'He was a leftie.'

'How do you know he was left-handed?' asked Collins. Then, before Clark could reply, he continued, 'Of course. The scissors was a left-handed pair. I should have seen it.'

'Also, his stuff was lined up on the shelf ready for a left-hander and the knot was tied by a right-hander,' said Clark.

'Why the hell aren't you a detective, Clark?' York asked.

'I tried it once, Serge, it dain't take.'

'Well, if he was a leftie, he definitely didn't kill the girl,' said York. 'There was a big bruise on the left side of her face. Whoever hit her was right-handed and a lot more powerful than that sack of skin and bone.'

'Yow can add to that the fact that his knuckles weren't skinned,' said Clark.

'So, we're agreed that either Burgees is the most incompetent Super we've ever met or he did a spring clean before we arrived. Why else delay calling us?' asked Hicks.

'But why is he covering up a murder?' asked Collins.

'Burgess mentioned my old boss Alfie Thomas as soon as we arrived. He moved to Special Branch in 1959 and Burgess as good as told me that he'd spoken to him that morning.'

'But why is Special Branch interested in the murder of a young girl?'

'They're not, Mickey. Them interested in who done it. Ain't that right, Sir?'

'Yes. My guess is that Young was involved with some important people. Maybe he was the one who got the girls for them. When they found out we had a line on him, they killed him to protect themselves.'

'But the only way they could know we were onto him was if the Stratford Police or Carver told them.'

'My money's on Carver,' said Clark.

'I think you're probably right,' said York. 'Burgess was just doing a bit of damage control – maybe because he was told to do it or maybe because he's in on it.'

'So where do wi go from here, Sir?' asked Clark.

'I think you know that, Clark. The case is closed. My guess is that it will be official by Tuesday.'

'But Sir, what about the evidence?' asked Collins.

'I know, lad, but there's nothing I or any of us can do about it. You and Collins did a great job, but I'm afraid it's over. We've been warned off. Best to heed the warning.'

'Feck. Is that how justice works in England?' asked Collins.

'Na. It's how it works everywhere when the rich or the security services get involved,' said Clark, clearing his throat.

York drove back to the station. The men had their killer but the mood was one of disappointment. Hicks said that he and York would visit Mrs Winston and tell her the news. For her sake, they agreed that all she needed to know was that her daughter's killer had murdered a second girl and then committed suicide.

Collins and Clark walked in silence down Thornhill Road. Both felt cheated of their prize, but what was there to do?

Turning onto Holly Road, Clark said, 'Me Missus wants you to come around for lunch tomorrow. Seems she's got this stupid idea in her head that you saved me life and wants to thank you.'

'That would be grand. Its ages since I had a home-cooked meal.'

'Well, don't get too excited. It'll only be soup or something. She did want you for Sunday dinner next week, but she couldn't wait till then to meet me saviour. The way she's going on, you'd think I were incapable of getting out of a bloody hole by meself.'

'Well, aren't you?'

'Listen, I've been digging meself out of holes of me own creation since I were a nipper,' Clark stopped. 'That din't come out right, did it?'

'No.'

'Fair enough. Just be there for 1.'

Part Two: Nights
Monday 18th February 1963.
Handsworth, 11.00hrs.

Collins had been advised by Clark to sleep until about 9 am and then go back to bed for a couple more hours' sleep in the afternoon, as preparation for his first night shift. But he knew that he would never be able to sleep in the afternoon, so he stayed in bed until mid-morning.

When he finally walked into the kitchen, it was gone 11 and a middle-aged, red-haired woman was emptying a tin of mushroom soup into a small pan. The pocket of her blouse had been torn and she'd been crying, but other than that she seemed to be fine. She gave Collins a timid smile and replied to his greeting with a whispered 'Morning', before returning her attention to stirring the soup.

Collins went to the pantry and took out his loaf of thick sliced bread. With lunch at Clark's, toast would do for breakfast. At that moment, Gloria announced her arrival with a loud crash as she slipped on the last step of the stairs and shouted, 'Fuck it!'

The effect on the woman was instant. Her whole body stiffened, her shoulders hunched up and she pulled on the pan's handle, causing some of the soup to spill. Collins watched as she tried to relax.

Turning slowly, she said, 'I'm a bit nervous. New place, you know.' Her voice sounded middle-class, but her eyes had none of the easy confidence that Collins always associated with such people.

He just had the time to say 'I know the feeling well,' before the whirlwind that was Gloria blew into the kitchen.

'Hello. What you pair up to? You need to watch this guy,

Mary, he'll have your knickers off before you know it. Mind you, I wouldn't mind if he ripped mine off.'

The bruising around Gloria's eye and face had faded. Another couple of days and it would be gone. She was wearing an old dressing gown that trailed the ground behind her and was probably the cause of her slip.

'Stop embarrassing the poor woman,' said Agnes from the doorway. 'Not everyone enjoys your agricultural approach to sex.'

'What yous mean agricultural? I've never been with a farmer in me life.' Agnes smiled and Gloria went over to Mary and put her arm around her. 'Don't mind me, love. I'm as common as muck, but I don't mean no harm. Here, I'll finish warming that soup. Yous sit yourself down.'

'Mary, this is Constable Collins. He lives here. He's here to help if needed. So don't worry. Nothing bad is going to happen to you here.'

Mary responded with a whispered, 'Thank you.'

Collins thought she was about to cry and, by instinct, laid his hand on her shoulder. She jumped at his touch. Removing his hand, he said, 'Agnes is right; you're safe here.' Conscious that Mary didn't like being the centre of attention, Collins turned to Agnes and said, 'What are you up to today, Agnes?'

'I thought I might pay a visit to Mrs Winston. Poor woman must be distraught. Do you mind if I mention your name when I call? It won't get you in more trouble?'

'No, not at all. After all, the case is all but officially closed.' He stressed the word *officially* in such a way that both Agnes and Gloria looked at him quizzically.

Collins arrived at five to one for lunch and was introduced to Ruth, the pretty dark-haired woman he'd seen on his first day on the job and mistook for Clark's fancy woman. Up close, she was even prettier than he had thought. She was maybe 5 foot 4, with jet-black hair, dark eyes that flashed with humour and life, and a smile that burned brightly long after she had turned it off.

Her hand was soft and warm in his and she pressed hard as she said, 'Thank you for saving my stupid husband's life.' Her voice was as soft as a baby's skin, and although her English was perfect her accent was foreign. One of those Eastern European countries, like Hungary or Czechoslovakia.

'How many times do I have to tell yow he dain't save my life. I was in perfect control of the situation. All I had to do was reach me knife and I could've clawed meself out.'

'Yes, of course you could, dear,' she said, winking at Collins.

Collins gave Ruth a box of Cadbury's Milk Tray and followed Clark into the lounge. Ruth went to check on the food.

'This is a grand house. How did you get it?'

'It's one of the new police houses. We were in digs near the park and I got wind that they were building these before them were even announced, and got in first.'

'Well, you did all right for yourself. With the house and Ruth. You're a lucky man.'

'I know it. During the war, I never let meself think of what it would be like after it were all over.' It was the first time Collins had heard him mention the war. 'I'd seen too many of me mates cop it for that nonsense. But if I had, then this is what I would have dreamed about,' he said.

Collins envied his friend's life. He was doing a job he obviously loved, had a happy marriage and didn't want anything else from life.

Clark had described it as lunch. However, when Collins sat down at the table, he was confronted with a steaming bowl of stew, potatoes and a choice of three vegetables. He ladled a large helping of stew onto his plate, and added potatoes and all three vegetables. He saw Ruth smiling and said by way of explanation, 'This is the first home-cooked meal I've had since I left Ireland and it smells wonderful. What is it?

'Beef stroganoff. It's like your Irish stew, but has garlic and a few spices in it.'

'Tuck in,' said Clark.

———

Collins pushed his plate away and sighed contentedly. 'Ruth, that was grand. Can I come again?'

'As often as you like,' she replied, laughing. 'Would you like your dessert now?'

'I couldn't eat another morsel,' said Collins and crossed his hands. 'Can we leave it a bit?'

'Of course.'

They were just about to move away from the table when the phone rang. Ruth answered, listened for a few seconds and then shouted, 'Clive, it's Mom. They've got a burst pipe. Can you go around and give Dad a hand?'

Clive looked to the heavens, but his reply was immediate and without any trace of annoyance. 'Tell her I'm on me way.'

Collins offered to tag along, but Clark told him to stay warm and finish his lunch. Less than ten minutes later, Clark was heading out into the grey afternoon with light snow falling and the temperature heading down yet again. 'Save me pud till I get back, love.'

Ruth made tea for Collins and a coffee for herself, and they sat in the lounge looking at the falling snow. It was barely 2 pm on a mid-February day, yet it was almost dark. Looking to make conversation, Collins asked, 'So where did you and Clive meet?'

Ruth didn't reply immediately. She seemed to be thinking about what to say, which surprised Collins. After all, it was a routine question that she must have been asked many times before.

Finally, she seemed to make her mind up and said, 'We met in Bergen-Belsen.'

Her reply left Michael speechless.

Ruth could see his embarrassment and carried on quickly, 'I was sent there with my parents and sister in 1945. She was fourteen. I was twelve, nearly thirteen. Ester was very ill. I

– 103 –

was sure she was going to die, but then the British came and an English doctor gave her a new drug called penicillin and she started to get better. I still wonder why he gave her one of the very few doses he had.' She stopped and stared at the fire. The memory of what happened was playing like a film in her head.

'About a week after the camp was liberated, we decided to go back to our hut and dig up the only thing we had left from home – our parents' wedding rings. My father had known or guessed what would happen to him and Mama when we arrived at the camp and he gave us the rings. I won't tell you where we hid them. Just as Papa feared, the Nazis separated us at the camp gates. Anyone who didn't follow orders was beaten or set upon by the dogs. Our parents went to the right, to die. We went left, to work and die later.'

Collins sat still, not even sipping his tea, afraid that if he did Ruth would stop talking.

'After the liberation of the camp, there were so many dead and sick people that the British used captured Germans as orderlies and grave diggers. When we reached our hut, two Germans came around the corner. They were drunk. The older one, a big stupid Nazi, was waving a Luger around and laughing. His friend was young and spotty. Hardly old enough to be a soldier. When he saw us, he waved us over with the gun. We were afraid he would shoot. We should have run, but my sister was too weak. Like so many times before, we did as we were told.

'He said to us, "What are you Jewish bitches doing here?" Only, he didn't say bitches. Then the spotty one put his arm around my sister. She pushed him away. He punched her in the face and she fell down. He began to kick her, calling her a Jewish whore and other names. Then he dived on her and started to rip her clothes off, all the time slapping and punching her. I started to scream and the man with the Luger hit me across the mouth. The sight on the gun barrel left this scar.' She pointed to a small v-shaped scar on her left cheek.

'Finally, the spotty one got on top of my sister and started to rape her. She just lay there. He screamed at her to move, but she spat in his face. That's when he smashed her head on the ground and kept doing it until she lay quiet. I can still see the blood.

'I was terrified. I knew what was going to happen to me and I wet myself. Then, this small English soldier came running around the corner. He had a machine gun and I thought I was saved, but he started laughing. Then he said, in German, "Having a bit of fun, lads, before you get shipped back to Germany, are you? Mind if I join in?" The big one laughed and relaxed, dropping the gun to his side. That was when Clive shot him in the head with a single burst of fire.'

Ruth stopped speaking. When she spoke again, her voice was hard and full of conviction, 'He died too quickly. The other one tried to run and Clive shot him in the legs. He fell on his face screaming. Clive came over and helped me up. He then looked at my sister and said, "I'm sorry, love, she's dead." The spotty one was lying on the floor rolling about and screaming. Clive went over to him and placed his foot on the man's chest and raised his gun – but then he stopped and asked, "Do you want to do it?" I think that's when I fell in love with him. I took the gun and shot him in the groin. He screamed even louder and called me names. I let him scream. Then, I shot him in the stomach. He took two or three minutes to die. It was too quick,' said Ruth, a trace of pride in her voice. 'And if I had the chance to kill more of those who ran the camps, I would.'

'What happened afterwards?' Collins asked.

'Clive visited me every day for two weeks. On the last day, he said that he'd arranged for me to be taken to my new home in England. It was only when I reached Birmingham that I realised he'd sent me to stay with his parents – my new Momma and Papa. After the war, I asked him how he'd arranged it.'

'What did he say?'

'Just that he had friends in high places.'

'What did he mean by that?'

'He never told me.' Ruth got up and moved to the sideboard and opened the left-hand drawer. 'It was after we got married that I found this. I think this was his friends in high places.' She handed Michael a small black jewellery box with the royal crest on the lid.

Michael opened it. 'Bloody hell! Sorry. Is this what I think it is?'

'Yes. The Victoria Cross.'

'What did he win it for?'

'He's never told me. When I try to tell him that he's a hero, he always says the same thing: "All the real heroes are dead, love".' Ruth picked up the box and closed the lid gently.

'He doesn't talk about his war service at work. I don't even know which branch of the military he was in.'

'He was in the Commandos. His work took him all over Europe and Scandinavia, but he's never told me any of the details.'

Collins was amazed, yet not surprised. The Commandos and the VC explained a lot of things: how a man who was clearly under regulation height had made it into the force; why he could call the Superintendent Boss instead of Sir and use any language he liked in front of senior officers; why he was given new officers to look after when there were officers twice his size who would appear to be better minders for wet-behind-the-ears probationers. Many of the men at the station had served honourably in the war, many had shown courage, but it was clear from the tiny brass cross, made from the Russian cannons at the Siege of Sevastopol, that Clark was something special.

They sat in silence for a few moments. Rising, Ruth took the medal and returned it to the sideboard drawer. Turning, she said, 'Why don't you help me wash up before I make us both another drink and you can have your pudding. Clive tells me you don't drink. Is that true?'

'Yes.'

'Isn't that unusual for an...' She stopped in mid-sentence, embarrassed.

'For an Irishman, you mean?' Ruth nodded. 'I come from a long line of drunks and I don't want to join them.'

'And you thought you might?'

'Very easily.'

Ruth didn't pursue the subject. Instead, she asked Collins, 'What's your new landlady and digs like?'

Collins was still talking about Agnes twenty minutes later when Clark returned.

Later, as he walked back to his digs, Collins thought about what he had just seen and heard. He'd grown used to Clark's cocky, confident and aggressive nature, but at home he was different. He was softer in how he spoke – less strident, more caring and certainly gentle in how he acted around Ruth. Collins decided that Clark was a very lucky man.

As he opened the house gates, an unbidden thought came to mind. If Clark was able to switch between personalities, like changing his overcoat, which was the real Clark? And were there any more characters lurking inside him?

Handsworth, 15.00hrs.

Agnes rang the bell to Mrs Winston's flat and waited. A few minutes later, she heard footsteps in the hall and the door opened a few inches. 'If you from the press, I don't want to talk. Go away. Please.'

'I'm not from the press, Mrs Winston. My name's Agnes Winter. I'm a friend of Constable Collins. He saw you last week. I know that Inspector Hicks visited you yesterday and explained what has happened. I just wanted to say how sorry I am for the death of your beautiful daughter and to ask you if I could help in any way.'

'Thank you. It's kind of you to come.'

'May I come in?' Mrs Winston looked uncertain. 'I won't stay long, I promise.'

Mrs Winston opened the door and stepped back. Having a white woman come to her home was not something she was used to, especially a lady like Agnes.

Seated in Mrs Winston's flat, Agnes could feel the pain and anguish that engulfed the woman. It flowed from her in dark waves and while it would ease in the years ahead, it would never leave her. It was clear from her hollow, haunted eyes that a part of her had died with her daughter and she would spend the rest of her life longing for the day they would be reunited.

Agnes recognised the symptoms all too well. It was exactly how she had felt when they told her that Simon had been shot down and presumed killed over the Channel in 1940. She'd known him most of her life. They had been childhood sweethearts and had decided to marry the day war was declared in September 1939. Less than a year later she was a widow and looking for a way, anyway, that she could gain some measure of revenge on the Germans.

'Why don't I make us both a cup of tea and you can tell me all about Simone, Mrs Winston?'

Surprised that a white woman wanted to make her a cup of tea, Mrs Winston nodded in agreement.

Two hours later, the women embraced on the doorstep and Agnes pushed her card in Mrs Winston's hand. 'Remember,' she said, 'call me if there's anything I can do to help. And please do let me have details of the funeral.'

Walking back to the car, Agnes hoped that the woman would call.

Handsworth, 21.55hrs.

Collins was looking forward to his first night shift. He was a night person. When others were starting to fall asleep at 11 he was just getting his second wind. He'd always loved the night. The time when darkness obliterated the dirt of the streets and bright lights bathed them in cheap glamour. It was even better when snow covered the ground. He liked to think that within the shadows, there lurked dark secrets and the promise of adventure and romance. He put his romanticising of the night down to seeing too many Jimmy Cagney and Humphrey Bogart films in the local flea pit when he was a kid.

Parade finished, Sergeant Ridley called Collins and Clark over. 'The Superintendent wants to see you pair tomorrow at 4 pm.'

'Do you know what it's about, Sarge?' Clark asked.

'No, but you've been the ones playing detective, so work it out yourselves. If it's any help, York and Hicks will be there too.'

Outside, the weather was as cold as ever, and was made worse by a biting north-westerly wind that cut through gloves and coats and froze the face. 'I wonder what the Super wants?' said Collins.

'From my extensive experience, a summons from the top brass can only mean one of two things. A pat on the back or a kick in the bollocks. As Hicks and York are going to be there, my guess is that this will be a pat on the back – but bring your box just in case.'

Collins wondered what a box was but stayed quiet. Changing the subject, he said, 'Ruth tells me you speak German.'

'She told yow about how we met then?'

'Yeah.'

'Yow should be honoured. She's only ever told four people about that and two of them were me parents. She must trust yow.'

'What about speaking German?'

'I picked a bit up in the war. It's hard to interrogate someone if you don't speak their lingo.'

'Any other languages you can speak?'

'French, Dutch and a bit of Polish and Norwegian. I worked a lot with foreign groups in the war. There were some great lads among them. The Poles were me favourite. There was no messing with them guys. They really hated Jerry. They could hardly wait to cut the bastards' throats. Then, after the war, we betrayed them and handed them over to Stalin.'

'So how is it that you were never able to master English?'

'I walked into that one, dain't I?'

'Yep, but you know what they say about pride before a fall.'

Clark gave Collins a two-fingered salute and the pair walked on in companionable silence, the fresh snow crunching beneath their feet.

Whether it was the cold or something good on the telly, there was nobody on the streets when Collins and Clark started their beat at 10 pm sharp. Two hours later, the most interesting thing they'd seen was a fight between an overweight ginger tomcat and a fox. The fox was younger and quicker but the tom had the experience, and one swipe of his claws had scratched his attacker's nose and left eye and sent him yelping home. Content with his victory, the cat looked at them with unconcealed hatred, hissed viciously and disappeared down the side entry to a row of houses.

By 1.30 they were heading back to the station for a warm-up and some snap. They were near Rookery Road when they first heard the dog. Alternately barking then howling, the sound carried on the wind and set Collins' teeth on edge. 'Some ejit has left the dog out or else it's a stray and it's got stuck somewhere.'

'Yeah, probably,' said Clark.

As they neared Foster Brothers, the sound got louder. It seemed to be coming from somewhere to the right of them. At the wooden front doors of Handsworth Market, Clark stopped and listened intently. Walking on a bit, he turned into the alley that ran along the length of the market and opened out into a stall holder's car park at the rear. 'It's coming from behind the market. It might be Benny's dog.'

'Who's Benny?'

'Old soldier, old tramp, old drunk – take yow pick. Lives in a shed at the back of the market. The stall holders slip him a few bob and he pretends to act as night watchman, but he's about as useful as a chocolate teapot. Seeing as he's always pissed. Come on,' said Clark, and strode up the alley

Turning into the car park Collins' torch immediately picked out the dog. She was sitting outside a small lopsided shed, howling. He had never seen such an ugly dog before. It was entirely black except for a white ring around her left eye, short stubby legs, a barrel-like body covered in muscle that moved as she bounded forward and a set of jaws that belonged to a wolfhound.

He started to draw his baton when Clark said, 'Here, Sheba. Come on, girl.' The dog ran straight past Collins and leapt at Clark, who caught her in his arms. Tail wagging, she started to lick his face.

'What the hell type of dog is that?'

'This, kidda, is pound for pound the best dog in the world. It's a Staffie.'

Collins looked blank.

'A Staffordshire Bull Terrier. If she's out, sommut's up with Benny.' Clark strode forward still carrying the dog, who seemed overjoyed to see him.

Collins followed at a safe distance. He and dogs had never really got on.

Placing Sheba on the floor, Clark knocked on the door. No answer. He knocked again and shouted, 'Benny, are yow there?' He pulled the door open and shone his torch around. Benny was lying on the bed next to the small brazier that he used to keep warm and cook on. The fire was out and Benny was dead. What had killed him Clark had no idea. Maybe his heart or liver had given out. Maybe he'd fallen into a drunken stupor and died chocking on his own vomit. The pathologist would tell them.

Clark withdrew and said, 'He's dead. Yow stay here and play with your new friend, while I phone the station from the call box. See if yow can find some food for her.'

Collins didn't like the sound of that and tried to object, but Clark was already striding away. He looked down at the black monstrosity that was now standing quietly by his right foot. Turning her head sideways, she looked up at him with black pleading eyes. Despite his earlier misgivings, he smiled. 'Looks like it's you and me, girl. Let's see if we can find you something to eat.'

By the time Clark returned, Collins had found a tin of corned beef and Sheba had decided that he was the best human she'd met in a long time. While they waited for the morgue van to arrive, they took the small brazier from the shed, added wood and coke from Benny's small store and warmed themselves. Sheba curled up a foot from the fire and was asleep within seconds. Her job done.

Their shift was nearly over when Collins and Clark returned to the station with Sheba in tow. They took her into the canteen and ordered three bacon sandwiches – one for each of them. The lads waiting to go into Parade came over and patted Sheba. She responded by lying on her back and inviting all present to tickle her tummy. Collins laughed at her antics. 'She may lack looks but she's got plenty of personality.'

'I'm glad yow said that 'cos if we send her to the dogs' home, they'll put her down after a wiek.'

Collins saw immediately what was coming. 'Hang on, I'm in digs. I can't have a dog.'

'I'd take her, but Ruth works Tuesday to Saturday.'

'I don't want a dog and certainly not one as ugly as Sheba.'

'Hush. If yow hurt her feelings, she might turn nasty.'

Collins looked down. Sheba was lying across his feet fast asleep – again. 'Yeah, she looks like a right killer.'

'Yow'd be surprised. As I said, pound for pound Staffies am the best dogs in the world. Look, I'll take her today and yow speak to Mrs Winters. If she says no, we'll take her to the dogs' home tomorrow. Fair enough?'

'OK' said Collins doubtfully.

Tuesday 19th February 1963.
Handsworth, 14.00hrs.

Collins emerged from his room at 2pm then had a leisurely shave and shower, before donning his uniform in anticipation of his meeting with the Super at 4.

The kitchen was empty and he was able to cook and eat his lunch of scrambled egg, bacon, sausage and toast in peace. He was just washing up when Agnes entered.

'You're up and dressed a bit early for someone who's not on duty until 10 tonight.'

'True enough, but Clark and me have to report to the Superintendent at 4.'

'Nothing to do with me and my meddling, I hope.'

'No. I'm pretty sure it's to do with closing the case down. Anyway, how's Jamie doing? I haven't seen him for a few days.'

'He's doing fine. I have him working on odd jobs around the house and garden. He spends most of his free time raiding my library. He must have read four books since he arrived. Gloria thinks he's wonderful.'

'And with her record of boyfriends and pimps, she's a good judge of character, is she?'

'I think she knows people.'

'That's probably true,' Collins conceded. 'Anyway, what are we going to do with him?'

'I've been thinking about that. He says there is no chance whatsoever that his father will take him back. I'm going to visit Mr O'Conner to see if that really is his position.'

'And if it is?'

'I don't want Jamie to go into a home. He has something. A sort of raw intelligence that, if nurtured, might even take him all the way to university.'

'Well, you would know more about that than me.'

'His handwriting is terrible and his spelling is worse, but he can write and he has a wonderful vocabulary.'

'So if he's not going home and he's not going into a kids' home, are you suggesting that he stay here?'

'That's what I'm thinking, yes. A friend of mine runs a day school in Harborne. He's already said that he will take Jamie if I support him with extra tuition at home.'

'And you're willing to do that?'

'Oh yes. I think I would enjoy it.'

'Well, I can't think of a better place for Jamie to live.'

'Neither can he.'

'You mean he's started to drop hints and suggestions already?'

'He's been doing that since the day he arrived.'

'When are you going to see Mr O'Conner?'

'Tonight, after he returns from work.'

Collins could think of no easy way to introduce a 28-pound bundle of muscle, teeth, evil black looks and a vivid personality into the conversation, so he jumped in with both feet. 'Talking of waifs and strays, Clark and me had an interesting time last night.' He was only three-quarters of the way through the tale when Agnes said, 'You want to know if you can bring the dog here.'

'That's about it,' said Collins sheepishly. Not beyond trying to play on Agnes' sympathies, he continued, 'Clark says that if she goes to the dogs' home, they'll put her down after a week.'

'I'm not so sure. I have the women to think of.'

Collins saw the hesitation in her eyes and quickly said, 'Just think of her as another female in need of help.'

Agnes looked at him and burst out laughing. 'Is that your Irish charm and blarney at work, Mr Collins?'

'Sure, I have no evidence to indicate that I possess any charm whatsoever, Mrs Winters, especially when it comes to the ladies. Mind you, I did find me way into Sheba's heart with a tin of corned beef.'

Still smiling, Agnes said, 'All right. We'll give it a try... for six weeks. After that, we will revisit the decision. All right?'

'Fine by me, Agnes.'

'And so that we are absolutely clear about this: she's your dog. You feed, train, exercise and clean up after her. Agreed?'

'Agreed.'

———

At 4.02 pm precisely, Inspector Hicks, Sergeant York and Constables Clark and Collins filed into Superintendent Hollis' office. He had company. Assistant Chief Constable Morris was sitting beside him. Both looked pleased with themselves. All four men came to attention and saluted the ACC.

'Come in, men. I'm sure you all know ACC Morris.' Collins didn't have a clue who he was, but nodded in agreement with the Superintendent's statement. 'The ACC will explain what this is all about.'

'Thank you, Superintendent. Like you men, I usually have to deal with trouble of one kind or another, so it's particularly pleasing that for once I've been asked to do something that is entirely pleasurable. The Chief Constable wants you to know that he's very impressed with the speed and professionalism with which you solved the murder of the little half-caste girl. He particularly wishes to extend his congratulations to Constable Clark and Probationary Constable Collins, who Inspector Hicks tells us showed great initiative and commitment by working on their day off to uncover the vital evidence required to close the case. I'm delighted to say that you will all receive a formal commendation in due course.'

'I, too, would like to congratulate you on a job well done. You're a credit to the force and this station,' said Hollis.

'Thank you, Sirs,' said Hicks, 'but as I indicated in my report, there are one or two lines of inquiry that I'd like to follow up before signing off on this case.'

'Good man, Inspector Hicks. Always the perfectionist. I'd expect nothing less from a man with your record,' said the ACC. 'However, I've had a word with Superintendent Burgess and he feels that his team are best placed to tie up the loose ends. I have to say I agree with him. So onwards and upwards to the next case and again well done to you all.'

Inspector Hicks laid four drinks on the table. A pint of mild for York, bitter for Clark, orange for Collins and a half for himself. The Endwood Pub had just opened and the men were happily ensconced in the small snug behind the main bar, away from prying eyes and ears. The gas fire was on full and if anyone asked, they were just four friends enjoying a quiet drink.

But the atmosphere was flat. They all knew their investigation had been cut short. They waited for Hicks to speak. Pulling his chair away from the fire, he lit up another of his noxious French cigarettes.

'Lads, although they're blowing smoke up our collective arses, I want you to know that you deserve the commendations coming your way. Tracking down Young within a week was good police work. Well done.' He raised his glass and there was a chorus of "Cheers" around the table.

'It's just a shame we dain't get to finish it, boss.'

Hicks looked at Clark, well aware of what he was thinking. 'If you're wise, you'll let it go and get on with your jobs.'

'Boss, I'm from the Black Country. Wem well known for strong arms and weak heads.'

'It's the same with the Irish, Sir. We're famous for always getting into the wrong fights.'

'Well, that's very commendable, lads, but I've been here before.'

'How so?' asked York.

Hicks considered just how much he should say. When

ready, he replied, 'You've all heard the rumours about me – how I screwed up my last case at the Met. Well, essentially, I was set up.' Hicks paused and took a sip of his half. None of the men rushed him. They knew he had to tell his story in his own time. 'There was a right little shit on my patch by the name of Howe. He was a nasty vicious little bastard, responsible for a string of robberies that had left a lot of people in hospital. I was getting real close to him when word came down to lay off. Why, I had no idea. Anyway, I ignored the message and a few weeks later a crucial piece of evidence went missing in another case of mine. My name was in the evidence log as the last person to book it out.'

'Did you ever find out why you'd been told to lay off, Sir?' Collins asked.

'Only a rumour. Howe ran a couple of gyms and apparently he supplied specially selected young boxers for swish city gents and others of similar ilk, who fancied a bit of rough.'

'Bloody hell,' said York. 'Why did you stay in the force?'

'I sometimes wonder myself. Anyway, I'm telling you this because Young smells just like Howe. Important people are involved, I'm sure of it. If you start stamping all over their little beehive with your size twelves, you're going to get stung. I can't afford to get another black mark against my name. The wife's ill and my son is off to university in September, if the lazy bugger passes his exams. So if any of you decide to do your own private investigation, you need to realise what you're up against. And while I'll try to cover your back, I can't promise you full protection.'

'Fair enough, Sir,' said Clark.

Twenty minutes later, Hicks and York left. No one had proposed doing anything after what Hicks had said. If anyone wanted to take independent action, the fewer people who knew about it the better.

'So, Clarkee, what are we going to do?'

After the slightest pause, Clark said, 'We go after the bastards.'

'Good man yourself. I'm with you.'

'Good. Any ideas where wi start?'

'A few. We need to find Simone's diary. It has to be in one of three places: her home, the school or at a friend's house. We need to check all three again and talk to her school friends. We'll also need to identify these influential friends that Young was supposed to have. We should also go back to The Palms and have a chat with that guy Ravenal, see what he knows about Young. While we're at it, we should go and sweat the manager. As we're off book, maybe we could have a firm chat with him after work one night. Do you think that could be arranged, Constable Clark?'

'No problem at all.'

'Have I missed anything?'

'Carver? I can feel it in me water that he's the one who set Young up.'

'I agree. Maybe we could catch him at work.'

'And have a firm chat with him as well, Constable Collins?'

'You read my mind, Constable Clark.'

Plan of action settled, the two men ordered a second drink and Clark regaled Collins with the early history of West Bromwich Albion. He explained how they had been formed by a group of factory workers from the George Salter Spring Works in 1879. Initially called West Bromwich Strollers, they changed their name to West Bromwich Albion within two years. And as any half-educated bog dweller would know, Albion was the old English name for England. Collins tried hard to keep his eyes open.

Villa Cross, 18.15hrs.

At about the same time as Collins was trying not to chew off his right hand from boredom, Agnes was standing outside the house that Jamie had called home. It was a run-down terraced house off Villa Road. She tried the bell, and when she heard nothing, knocked loudly on the flaking paint with her gloved knuckles. She heard footsteps and a few moments later, the door opened.

'If you're a Jehovah's Witness, you can piss off. We're Catholic here.'

The smell of beer was on his breath, shirt, jumper and trousers, but there was no mistaking Jamie's Dad. They had the same compact body shape and the same sharp, well-defined facial features. However, whereas Jamie's eyes were green, his father's were brown. If he'd been sober, cleaned up and wearing a suit, O'Conner would have been considered by most as handsome.

'I'm not a Jehovah's Witness,' said Agnes. 'I'm here to talk about your son, Jamie.'

'He ain't here.'

'I know. He's staying at my house. May I come in so that we might talk in comfort?' Agnes didn't wait for a reply and stepped past O'Conner.

'You better come down to the dining room. It's the only place with a fire.' O'Conner led Agnes down a long hall and into a small room that was no more than 10 feet by 12, which contained a table and four chairs, a sideboard and one red velvet armchair, under which newspapers from the last month were stuffed. A 17-inch TV sat in the corner, courtesy of Rediffussion Rentals. A second door led into the kitchen. The room smelt of boiled bacon, cabbage and cigarette smoke.

'So where is the little ponce? In a home?'

'No, he's at my house. I'm looking after him.'

'You fostering him?'

'Unofficially, you might say. Jamie says that you won't allow him to return home under any circumstances. Is that correct?'

'That's right. I'll not have a queer as a son.'

'I see. Well, in that case, I was hoping that you'd be willing to sign this,' said Agnes, taking a large brown envelope from her bag and removing two sheets of typed paper.

'What is it?'

'A child can leave home legally at the age of sixteen. Jamie is fifteen. If he is to stay at my house, I need you to confirm that you have given permission for him to do so until he reaches the age of sixteen. I've had these documents drawn up and I can assure you that they are entirely legal.'

'And why are you so interested in the little queer?'

'Please stop calling him that. He's just a child and he is still your son.' O'Conner stiffened at the rebuke and drew his lips back, baring his teeth like a dog. For a moment, Agnes thought that she'd gone too far and that he would strike her. Instead, he snatched the papers out of her hand and started to read them.

Agnes had lied. The papers weren't legally binding. She had written them herself that afternoon. Their purpose was to protect her against any charge of kidnap or hiding Jamie from his father.

After reading them twice, O'Conner said, 'You still haven't told me why you want to help him.'

'He's a child and he needs a home. He's also bright. He writes well, even though his spelling is terrible and I think that with some help he can progress. Maybe even take his O Levels.'

'So you're going to educate him, is that it? What's the matter, got no kids of your own?'

'That's correct. I have no children. My husband was shot down over the Channel in 1940 before we had time to start a family.'

'I'm sorry,' said O'Conner. 'No offence meant.'

'None taken. Are you willing to sign the papers or not? As you can see, they clearly state that you will be able to see Jamie any time you wish.'

'I won't be making any visits, but I'll sign. It's better that he's with you than on the streets or in some home.'

'Well, I think that's something we can both agree on. While I'm here, may I also collect Jamie's belongings? He was particularly keen that I take the books that his mother left him.'

'You can take whatever's in his room. Margaret bought those books one a month for four years when he turned five. Started reading them to him when he was six. When she died, he would spend hours reading and rereading them. I reckon that's what turned him queer. He should have been out playing football and tag with his mates, instead of burying his head in those fucking books.'

Agnes didn't reply immediately. When she did, it was to ask for directions to Jamie's room. It took less than ten minutes to pack the boy's clothes, photo albums and odds and ends in the battered suitcase O'Conner gave her. However, three further trips were required to carry the fifty-odd *Everyman Library Books* to the car.

As she climbed into the Rover, O'Conner came out and leaned against the roof of the car. He seemed to want to say something, so Agnes asked, 'Do you have a message for Jamie?'

'Tell him that for as long as he's a queer, he's no son of mine – but that he should look after himself for the sake of his mother. Tell him that. OK?'

Agnes thought that she detected a catch in O'Conner's voice and said, 'I will and thank you.'

As she drove away, she looked in her rear-view mirror. O'Conner was still standing by the side of the road. He looked lonely and beaten, and Agnes felt sorry for him. He was a broken man, trapped by his own prejudices.

A gnes arrived home a couple of minutes after Collins, whom she found boiling the kettle in the kitchen.

'Cuppa?' asked Collins.

'Please.'

'How was it?'

'Strangely upsetting. He can't cope with the idea that his

son might be a homosexual.'

'I thought we'd confirmed he was?'

'Maybe. Maybe not. A lot of young boys have homosexual experiences in their teens. For some, it's a time of experimentation; for others, they're looking for a father figure. Then, there are those who know what they are and never change. Only time will tell which path Jamie takes. Anyway, how did your meeting with the Superintendent go?'

Collins told her what the Super and ACC had said. She seemed as disappointed as Collins with the decision. 'Isn't there anything you can do to change their minds?'

'No. Something's going on. Strings have been pulled. That's what Clark said and we can't un-pull them. Hicks and York want to go on, but they can't for a variety of reasons.'

'You mean like pay, promotion and pensions?'

'I don't think that's fair. Hicks as good as said he would try and look after us if we did continue the investigation informally.'

'Are you going to do so?'

'Oh yes. Me and Clark have worked out a plan of action.'

'What are you going to do?'

'First and most importantly, find Simone's diary. We're going to see this guy Ravenal tonight and then we plan to speak to Mr Carver and Mr Spencer again.'

'Well, I'll speak to Mrs Winston and ask her to look for the diary. I know the police have been there, but mothers have a habit of knowing where their daughters hide things. Mine certainly did.'

Collins called for Clark at 8.30 and they quickly walked the half mile to The Palms. The dance hall closed at 10.30 so they calculated that Ravenal would take a break at around 9. They weren't wrong. As they entered the dance hall, he was just stepping off stage. Pushing through the crowd of teenagers and twenty-somethings, they followed him. There were two dressing rooms. Only one had a cardboard sign hanging on the door, which read "Jimmy Ravenal". Collins knocked.

'Sod off, I'm busy.'

Clark hammered the door twice with his fist and walked in. Ravenal was sitting on a chair, with a girl of about sixteen on his knee. Her jumper was rolled up, showing the bottom of her white bra, she quickly pulled it down.

'Sorry about that, kidda. I could have sworn I heard you say come in.'

Collins saw a flash of anger shoot across Ravenal's face, but it was quickly gone as he registered the uniforms. 'No harm done. I thought you were another autograph hunter.'

'Like this young lady?' asked Collins.

'Yeah,' replied Ravenal, 'but she's just leaving, aren't you, love?' The girl stood up and brushed between the two policemen.

Turning, she asked, 'Will I catch you after the show?'

'Yeah, do that.'

She went out and closed the door. Ravenal grinned broadly. His smile reminded Collins of a leering hyena he'd once seen in a cartoon – all teeth and sneering cold eyes. 'If you're in this business, you have to beat them off with a cricket bat. What can a man do as long as they're legal, eh lads?'

'And what if they ain't legal?' asked Clark.

'I never touch 'em. Anyway, how can I help you? Did I park the van in the wrong place or something?'

'No, we just wanted to ask you a few questions about Andrew Young. You might know him as Andy.'

'Sorry, friend. I don't know any Andy.'

'Tall, skinny, blond-haired guy. He was at the kids' dance just after Christmas,' said Clark.

'No wonder I don't remember him. You have any ideas how many jobs I've done in the last six weeks?'

'We have a witness who says he was chatting to you.'

'Lots of guys and gals talk to me. Doesn't mean I know

them.'

'She says you were real friendly with him and the half-caste girl he were with,' said Clark.

'Don't remember him or her. Look, what's this all about. Missing girl or something?'

'Yeah, yow could say that. She's missing all right – missing about fifty years of her life,' said Clark.

Collins watched as Clark held Ravenal's stare, waiting for a reply.

Ravenal was the first to look away. He picked up a towel from the dressing table and wiped his face. 'I'm sorry to hear that, but I know nowt. Now, if you don't mind, I have to get back on stage.'

As he moved to the door, Collins stepped in front of him. 'Just one more thing before you go, Mr Ravenal. Could you give us your home address and telephone number, please? Just in case we need to speak to you.'

Again, a flash of anger, of barely concealed rage, clouded Ravenal's features. He felt in his back pocket and pulled out a card. 'I travel a lot, but you can always get a message to me if you ring that number.'

Collins took the card and stepped aside. 'Thank you very much, Mr Ravenal.'

'We'll be in touch, Mr Ravenal,' Clark said and winked.

Neither man spoke as they walked down the stairs. In the lobby, they buttoned up their coats before stepping into the night. Slow, lazy snowflakes were floating gently to the ground. For a few seconds Collins watched a single flake as it spiralled silently to the ground, illuminated by the light from a lamppost.

'What did you make of him, Mickey?'

'Odd bloke. He seemed ready to blow his top at any time.'

'Yeah, I noticed that. He wants to be top dog in every situation. Can't bear it if someone is sticking it to him – but were he lying?'

Without hesitation, Collins said, 'As sure as the Pope is a

Catholic.'

'Well, wi agree on that.'

'What about Spencer? Have we time to see him?'

'Na. We'll catch him tomorrow when things are quiet. Best if no one sees us going in to talk to him. Now, come on, Ridley will have a fit if wi late for parade.'

As they began to walk, Collins asked, 'Did you mean it when you told Ravenal we'd be speaking to him again?'

'For sure. That sod's up to sommut and I'm going to find out what.'

Wednesday 20th January 1963.

Handsworth, 15.00hrs.

Collins was still half asleep when he called for Clark. He'd managed to get about six hours sleep, but it had been disturbed by noises in the house and the failure of the curtains to blot out the weak winter sunshine. *I'll need blackout curtains if I'm to get a decent sleep*, he thought, and rang the bell.

Collins wasn't sure what Clark was going to do. Was he going to give Spencer the full "Welcome Wagon" treatment or just put a scare into him? When he asked, all Clark would say was, 'Follow my lead, yows can't plan these things until you see how the guy reacts.'

Collins looked at the empty, locked-up Palms and wondered why so many picture houses, dance halls and theatres looked depressed and dead in the daylight. It wasn't just that the night hid the damaged drainpipes, peeling paint and dirty windows. It was the lack of life. The lack of movement. Looking up, he saw that there was a light burning in what he guessed was Spencer's office.

Casually, Clark walked down the alley to the stage door. He leaned against the door and was surprised to find it open. 'At least wi won't have to break in,' he said, and walked through.

Collins followed Clark up the backstairs to the second floor and along the landing to Spencer's office. Clark didn't bother to knock. He flung the door open.

Spencer was at his desk and shot up as the door slammed against the wall. 'What the fuck…'

'Afternoon, Mr Spencer. Mind if wi come in?'

'What the hell is going on?'

'Wi just came to have another chat with yow about your teen dance, a long-haired streak of piss called Andrew Young and a pretty little half-caste girl called Simone Winston.'

'And when we've finished with them, we'd like to hear what you have to say about Mr Ravenal,' said Collins.

Regaining some composure, Spencer straightened up and, trying to appear indignant, said, 'I told you before I know nothing about any half-caste girl or this Andrew Young character you keep on about. As for Jimmy, he's just a DJ we use. Now, will you please leave?'

'Na, wi can't do that. Yow see wi both think you're a lying sack of shit.'

'How dare you? If you don't leave immediately, you'll find yourself in a whole lot of trouble.'

Collins watched as Clark sauntered over to Spencer. 'Now, I wish you hadn't said that. Yow see, I hate threats. They make me nervy and when I'm nervy, I do things like this.' Clarks hand shot out and grabbed Spencer by the balls, squeezed and twisted.

Agony registered on the manager's face. He stumbled forward, mouth open, gasping like a fish out of water, unable to speak and paralysed with pain. Without letting go, Clark pushed him back into his chair. Still squeezing his balls, Clark whispered in his ear, 'Now, unless yow want a whole world of pain, yow going to tell me and my mate here what yow know about Andrew Young.'

'I told you I never saw him.'

'Wrong answer,' said Clark. He released his hold momentarily and punched Spencer in the balls. Spencer doubled up. A new type of pain contorted his face. After another fifteen seconds, he said, 'I told you I don't know him.'

'Wrong answer again,' said Clark and pressed his thumb into the bottom of Spencer's neck just above the collarbone. Spencer screamed with pain and continued squirming until Clark released his hold.

'Now, what do yow know about Andrew Young?'

'All right. Give me a minute,' pleaded Spencer.

Clark stepped back.

Collins could almost see the wheels in Spencer's brain turning. The little so-and-so was trying to work up a story that he and Clark would swallow.

Thinking done, Spencer raised his head and said, 'OK. I never knew the guy's name, but he was a regular here. He liked the girls and used to slip me a fiver if I put him onto a good thing.'

'So you pimped underage girls for him, is that it?' asked Collins.

'No, I never put him onto a kiddie.'

'What about his friendship with Ravenal?' asked Collins.

'What friendship? They didn't know each other.'

'We have a witness that says he was real friendly. Constantly talking to him throughout the dance,' lied Collins.

'He didn't know Jimmy. It was just part of his pick-up routine to pretend he was friends with the DJ. He did it all the time. You know what these girls are like. A bit of glamour and you're halfway there.'

'OK,' said Clark, 'we'll check out what you've said and if you've lied, we'll be back – and yow will be sorry, I promise yow.'

'I'm not lying.'

Back in the alleyway, Clark turned to Collins and asked, 'What yow think?'

'He was lying through his back teeth. He said he *used* to know Young, so how does he know he's dead? It's not been in the *Birmingham Mail* yet. I looked.'

'Well spotted, Mickey lad. It may have just been a slip of the tongue, but everything he said was bollocks.'

'So why did you stop?'

'Strewth, yowm am a vicious little sod, aren't you?' Clark said, with some approaching admiration. 'Yow got a future in this police force. Wi were never going to get him to spill his guts with just one visit. Besides, me main aim was to stir the wasps' nest a bit. Now, we just sit back and see what develops. All sorts of nasties may creep out of the woodwork looking to scare off a couple of cocky coppers working off the books.'

'And if nothing develops?'

'Wi visit him again.'

Thursday 21st February 1963.
Handsworth, 14.00hrs.

Agnes answered the phone on the fourth ring.
'Hello, Agnes Winter speaking.' She waited as the caller pressed Button A, the four pennies dropped into the phone box and the line was cleared.

'Hello. Is that Mrs Winter?' a voice asked nervously.

'It is.'

'Hello, this is Mrs Winston. I really didn't want to bother you, but you were so kind when you called round. I was wondering if you could help me.'

'If I can, I will.'

'I've had a letter from the Ice Rink in Hockley. They heard of Simone's death and they've written to me asking if I want to empty her locker. I didn't know she had a locker or I would have told the police. Not that it matters anymore. Anyhow, I can't go into town today. I have to go to the funeral home. Could you collect her things for me?'

At the mention of a locker, Agnes' heart missed a beat. *Could that be where Simone's diary was?* 'Of course I can. That will be no problem. I'll pick them up right away and bring them over to you.'

'Thank you. You're very kind.'

Agnes hung up and went to wake Michael. She knocked once, but there was no response. She hit the door hard and shouted, 'Michael, I need to talk to you. It's urgent.'

From beyond the door, she heard movement and a sleepy voice. 'OK. I'll be down in a few minutes.' Collins rubbed the sleep from his eyes and reached for his trousers. *I have to get a fecking dressing gown,* he thought, as he rummaged in the chest of drawers for a shirt.

Once downstairs, Collins gratefully accepted the cup of

coffee that Agnes pushed across the kitchen table. 'I think we've had what you call a break in the case,' said Agnes.

'Really?' he said and suppressed a yawn.

'Yes. Simone had a locker at the Hockley Ice Rink.'

Collins head snapped up. Suddenly he was very much awake. 'Who told you?'

'Her mother rang. She said that the Ice Rink had written to her asking if she wanted to collect Simone's belongings from her locker. She asked if I would pick them up.'

'Did she say what was in the locker? Is Simone's diary in the locker?'

'She doesn't know, but I thought that you and I should find out.'

'I think you might just be right,' said Collins, smiling, and on impulse hugged Agnes, and kissed her on the cheek. Realising that he may have crossed a line, he quickly broke away and muttered, 'Sorry.'

Agnes, a surprised look on her face, said quietly, 'No, that's fine.'

While Collins shaved and dressed, Agnes called the ice rink and arranged a meeting with the manager Mark Carney.

———

Collins surveyed the ice rink. Mid-week, during term time, it was nearly deserted. There were two ice hockey players practicing turns and blocking in one corner. In another, the rink's professional was giving a lesson to an old married couple. They had the look of people who might have been pretty good on the ice thirty years before, but they'd taken time off to marry, fight a war and raise a family. Maybe it had been a New Year's resolution to recapture their skating prowess or just a desire to get out of the house – either way, they were enjoying themselves.

A man, who was repairing one of the seats that ringed the ice, directed them to the manager's office on the first floor. The office was small and neat with pictures of ice dancers adorning every spare inch of wall space. Like his office, Mark Carney was also small and neat and, except for the thinning brown hair, he looked exactly like the young man who was smiling out from nearly every picture. Although he was probably in his forties, Carney looked ten years younger. There wasn't an ounce of fat on him. He moved with the natural grace of a dancer. A trait that takes years and thousands of hours' practice to achieve.

Collins was surprised by the strength of Carney's handshake and the calculated manner in which he appraised him. 'Terrible business, this thing with Simone.'

'You knew her?' asked Collins.

'No, I didn't, but I'd seen her. We don't get many coloured people skating. You might say she stood out from the crowd.'

'Did she have any particular friends here?'

'I wouldn't know, but I saw Peter, one of our stewards, skating with her more than once.'

'Is he at work today?'

'No, you misunderstand me. Our stewards aren't employees. They're more like prefects in a school. We let them in for free and they sort of police the rink. Nip any trouble in the bud.'

'When will he be in?'

'He'll be here tomorrow and Saturday night.'

'What about Simone's belongings?' asked Agnes. 'Are they still in her locker?'

'No, I emptied it. I have them here.' Bending down, Carney lifted a small cardboard box onto his desk. 'Not much really, but given the circumstances I'm sure her mother must want everything that belonged to her daughter.'

Agnes and Collins moved forward and opened the box. It had been carefully packed by the manager and he'd laid a single pink rose along with a card to Mrs Winston on top. There were pictures of Simone and her friends taken at the rink and one of her mother standing outside Buckingham Palace. They rested on a white cashmere sweater that had a London label, and beneath that were a pair of skate guards, a small bottle of cheap perfume, lipstick, a tin of talcum powder and an open packet of sanitary towels. Lining the bottom of the box was a clear plastic Mac, beneath which Collins saw the back cover of a foolscap book.

Looking at Agnes, he gave a nod and watched as the tension left her face and shoulders. All he wanted to do now was get out of the rink and examine the diary.

'We won't keep you any longer, Mr Carney,' said Agnes. 'You really have been very kind. I know that Mrs Winston will really appreciate your letter.'

Shaking hands with Collins, Carney replied, 'I'm only too pleased to help. It's been a pleasure to meet you, Constable Collins. If you do call in to see Peter, please drop by and say hello.'

Collins again had the feeling that he was being closely examined by the older man, who seemed reluctant to let go his hand.

Outside, Agnes said, 'Well, you certainly made a conquest there.'

'What do you mean?'

'Good Lord. You really didn't notice, did you?'

'Notice what?'

'Carney. He was practically drooling over you. He couldn't take his eyes off you.'

'That's nonsense.'

'Believe me. That man was undressing you with his eyes from the moment you walked in the room.'

Collins blushed, remembering how Carney had held his gaze and hand. 'But why would he think I'm like that?'

'Like what?'

'You know, *queer*.'

'Some homosexuals are strongly attracted to heterosexual men. They see it as a challenge.'

'Well, I'm one challenge he's not going to win,' Collins said firmly.

'Or, of course, he may just have picked up that you harboured some latent homosexual tendencies of your own.' Agnes let her statement hang in the air and watched as Collins wriggled on her hook. Unable to keep the pretence up any longer, she burst out laughing. 'I'm only teasing you. I don't think you display any homosexual tendencies!'

'Thank God for that,' said Collins, but he remained concerned.

———

Desperate as they were, Agnes and Collins waited until they got home before unpacking the box. Other than two condoms, which they decided not to return to Mrs Winston, they found nothing new. The diary started in August 1962. Most of the entries were mundane and dealt with school and friends. There was even a list of Christmas gifts she had hoped to get. Topping the list had been a Dansette record player. Only a few of the entries were in code and even those were a mixture of plain English and the odd encoded word or phrase.

While Agnes worked on deciphering the coded entries, Collins busied himself making tea and toast. It was a close call, but Agnes finished just before Collins buttered the last piece of toast. *She's quick,* he thought, before asking, 'So, what have we got?'

'There are eight entries of interest. Here, have a look.' Agnes pushed her notepad across the table to Collins. He started reading while Agnes spread jam on her toast and sipped her tea.

- *27/12/62. Thursday. Met Andy at Palms dance. Carol was sick. She'll be mad that she didn't meet him. He's lovely. He gave me a drink and tried to touch me up. I might let him next time.*
- *29/12/62. Saturday. Andy picked me up in town. We*

went to Stratford. He's got a great house. I had my first
champagne and he gave me some pills that really made
me feel great. Not sure what happened after that, but everything felt lovely. He thought I was a virgin! He gave
me some money afterwards. Said it was to buy some nice
things. Don't know what I'm going to buy with it.

- 4/1/63. Friday. Andy took me to his house again. He
gave me a lovely dress and a cashmere sweater. After we'd
fucked (that's what Andy calls it – he says only kids call
it making love) we went to the Green Man, a really posh
restaurant near Warwick. Andy's friend Phillip was there.
He has a Jaguar E-Type and gave me a ride! I knew he
fancied me from the start. Gave me his number Stratford
2357. I might call him.

- 15/1/63. Tuesday. Andy picked me up from school. Went
to the Green Man again. Afterwards Andy took me to
a hotel and gave me some underwear and another lovely
dress. He wanted me to get dressed up and show him my
knickers before we went to bed. I had to lift my skirt up and
tease him. Then he took pictures of me sitting on a chair
with me legs open. He said I looked beautiful. Afterwards
I only had to touch him and he came. He wanted to tie me
up but I said no.

- 18/1/63. Friday. Met up with Phillip at hotel. He was
with his girlfriend Marie. We all went back to Andy's.
Andy had some more of those pills I like – much better than booze. Andy started to snog Marie so I sat on
Phillip's lap. Not sure what happened but ended up in
bed with Phillip. Then Andy and Marie came in. It was
like a dream. They all wanted to touch me. And kiss it. I
touched Marie's. She was so soft.

- 25/1/63. Friday. Mom was doing an extra night so I
rang Andy. I couldn't do anything because I was on, so
Andy said we should meet up with Phillip at his house.
Phillip had a new girl with him. She was younger than

me and a bit nervous. Phillip asked me to chat to her and get her to take some pills. It looked like we were going to have fun. But Phillip got a call from some man called Major and had to leave for an hour. When he came back he found Andy fucking his girlfriend and me watching, but he just laughed and asked me to wank him off. His cock's bigger than Andy's. It was a real laugh. On the way home, Andy said there was going to be a party on the 16th of February in Birmingham and that we should go, as there would be lots of people there who could help me with my writing if I made a good impression. I'll have to see if Carol can cover for me.

- *6/2/63. Wednesday. Phoned Andy and said I could make it on Friday. He's going to pick me up by the cathedral. He said he had a new game he wanted to try. He's daft, he is. Said he'd get some new, even better, pills. Great.*

'OK, so what new information does this give us?' asked Agnes, pen poised to start writing.

Collins looked at the transcript again and dictated:

1) *Andy has a friend by the name of Phillip. He owns an E-type Jag and a Stratford telephone number 2357. Don't know if this is a business or private number.*

2) *At least two other girls were involved with Andy and Phillip.*

3) *Marie sounds as if she is older, maybe in her twenties. She may have been used to encourage Simone to play around with Phillip and to try out pills. The other girl was probably younger than Simone, and this time Simone was used to encourage her to take some pills.*

4) *Do Andy and his friends use pills to knock the girls out/ lower their inhibitions?*

5) *There's someone called Major. He must be important because Phillip was willing to disrupt his evening to meet with him. Might be worth checking if any of Andy's important friends are called Major.*

6) *There was a party planned for the 16th February in Birmingham at which important people were due to attend.*

7) *On the 6th February, Simone says Andy wanted to try out a new game. Was that game strangling?*

'What do you make of it?' asked Collins.

'It's obviously important. You have three new names to try and track down – Phillip, Marie and the Major – although I don't think Marie is that important.'

'I agree.'

'It does seem to confirm that there is a group of men involved in this. It wasn't just Andy and a friend. There's enough of them to arrange parties for *lots of people*,' said Agnes.

'Yep, that's what I was thinking. It might also explain how they operate. One of the men chats a girl up and gives her pills and gifts. Then he accidently meets a friend, who just happens to be with an older woman. Between them, they create an atmosphere in which it seems natural for Simone to be handed around. They pretend that this is the way sophisticated adults behave and if she wants to be part of their clique, she has to go along with it.'

'What are you going to do?' asked Agnes.

'Talk to Clark. The easiest guy to trace is probably Phillip. There can't be that many red E-Types in and around Stratford.'

'Michael.'

'Yes.'

Agnes hesitated, trying to find the right words to express the feeling of disquiet that was building within her. 'Michael, if you are dealing with the type of people I think you are, you need to take care. These people aren't common criminals. They're respected, powerful members of the community and they have influence. If you become a threat to them, they won't hesitate to squash you like a bug. I know, I've seen it happen.'

For the first time, Collins could see concern in Agnes'

eyes – not for herself, but for him. For some reason, it made him feel joyful. 'Don't worry about me. I'm very fond of me skin and intend to stay attached to it for as long as possible. Besides, I have Clark to protect me,' he said, and laughed.

Friday 22nd February 1963.
Handsworth, 01.00hrs.

With the moon waning, the night was dark and cold. It was nearly 1 am, and Collins reckoned that he and Clark were the only people out and about on Soho Road that night. Stopping every now and then to check that shops had been locked up, both men felt that the whole night was a waste of time. As Clark had remarked earlier: 'No self-respecting burglar would risk his goolies on a night like this.'

The quietude gave Collins plenty of time to bring Clark up to speed about the contents of Simone's diary. Clark agreed that Phillip would be the easiest to trace and said he had friend in the Birmingham car registration office. He'd be able to get the info from Stratford with no bother and no one would be any the wiser.

Collins felt content. It might be freezing cold, but they were making progress. Instinctively he knew they were on the right track, and given time and a bit of luck they'd catch the bastards who were behind Simone's death. He was certain of it.

They occasionally heard a noise at the back of a premises and would have a quick look to confirm that it was nothing more than a fox, stray cat or large rat that had knocked a bin lid over in its scavenging.

'Another hour and we can get a bit of snap back at the station. And I can count me knackers to make sure none have dropped off,' said Clark.

'You know, I think in another life you could have been a poet.'

'Yow think so? I've always thought I had a way with words.'

'I do. Of course, it could just be that me brain is so fecking cold I'm hallucinating.'

'Yeah, that's probably what it is. It's only to be expected,' replied Clark.

'Why?'

'Because yow got such a small brain in that big skull of yows that there's extra water in there, to stop it rattling around, and in this cold it's probably frozen solid.'

Collins was still thinking of a suitable response when they heard the sound of a window breaking at the back of Burton's. Both men stopped and listened. There it was again. The unmistakable tinkle of shards of glass being broken to make room for someone to climb through.

'Hear that?' whispered Clark.

Collins nodded. Drawing their truncheons, they moved quietly towards the alley. The alley was eight feet wide and ran the full length of the shop, before turning sharp left at the end. As they edged toward the corner, they could hear the sound of someone breathing hard and muttering softly to himself.

Clark put his mouth next to Collins' ear and whispered, 'Noisy bastard, ain't he?' Collins had to fight down the urge to laugh. Clark clearly wasn't at all concerned about what they might find.

At the turning, with his back flat against the wall, Clark risked a quick look. He held up one finger and whispered, 'Ready?' Collins nodded.

Stepping beyond the edge of the wall, baton in one hand and torch in the other, Clark said, 'Evening. You'll never earn a living as a burglar if you can't keep the noise down. I could hear you at the lights.'

The man stepped away from the window and it was then that Collins saw he was carrying a crowbar, and didn't seem in the least worried about being caught.

A voice from behind Collins made him spin around. 'Who says we're burglars, short arse?'

Clark turned and looked at the man who had spoken. He was maybe 6 foot 2 and looked lean, strong and wiry. He was holding a knife. His eyes were shining with excitement. He grinned, showing a full set of smoke-stained teeth in the torchlight. Beside him was a smaller stockier man with a doubled-up length of motorcycle chain. He swung it casually in circles by his side and looked faintly disinterested in the events unfolding. He even had time to run his free hand through his crew-cut hair. They'd been standing by the bins hidden in the shadows. Clark cursed himself for being so careless.

'We've got a message for you from some friends of ours. Stop messing in things that don't concern you.'

'OK,' said Clark, 'we've got the message. Thanks. We'll be on our way.'

'Lads, the short arse has a sense of humour. It don't work like that. We have to deliver the message in full, so there won't be any misunderstanding.'

'Did yow hear someone say that on TV or did you dream it up yourself?'

'You really are a smart arse, aren't you? I'm going to enjoy taking you apart.'

'That's a pity, 'cos it means this is going to get right painful for yow.' Turning to Collins, Clark asked, 'Can yow remember what I said on the first day?'

'Yep.'

'Good lad.' Turning back to the leader, Clark said, 'Come on then, let's get on with it.'

This was not the reaction that the big man had expected. Annoyed, he said, 'Fuck you,' and charged.

He came in, slashing wildly with his knife. When he was within reach, Clark waited for the swinging backhand to miss him by an inch. He then pivoted 45 degrees on his left heel and kicked out sideways, stamping down hard on the man's exposed kneecap. The knee buckled, bent backwards and snapped. As the man fell to the ground, the screaming began and didn't cease.

Unperturbed, Motorcycle Chain advanced quickly. Clark

waited for him to get within range and swing. As the chain whistled towards his head, Clark brushed it aside with his baton. The chain wrapped around the truncheon as Clark knew it would. Then, using the man's forward momentum, he pulled hard, bringing the man closer. Simultaneously, his left arm shot out and upward, the heel of his hand hitting Chain on his upper lip, just below the nose. However, he wasn't aiming for Chain's lip or tip of the nose. His target was two inches inside the man's mouth. Teeth, gristle and bone gave way as he found the bulls-eye. Chain staggered backwards and fell to the ground unconscious.

Clark grabbed Collins, who had been holding off Crowbar with his baton, and flung him to one side. Crowbar hesitated. He'd seen what Clark could do, but freedom was beyond the little man – and fear of going back to prison outweighed everything. Screaming loudly, he charged.

Clark waited for him to come. Then, raising his right knee, he snapped out a straight kick, which caught the man flush in the groin. Crowbar stopped. Like a scene from a cartoon he stood there, frozen in motion. His raised arm poised in mid-air. Unable to breathe, unable to cry out, he began to fall forward onto his knees. As he did so, Clark kicked him in the face. Crowbar's head snapped back and he went sprawling on the floor unconscious. His jaw was broken, and his red-tipped teeth spread across the snow.

Looking at Collins, a smile spread across Clark's face, 'You OK, Mickey?'

Collins nodded his head, amazed at what he'd just witnessed. In the space of five or six seconds, Clark had laid out three armed men, all bigger than himself, and he wasn't even breathing hard. Instinctively Collins knew that if the little man's pulse was taken at that precise moment, it would be normal – unlike his, which was pounding in his ears, twenty to the dozen.

Walking over to the leader, Clark hunkered down and said, 'Thanks for the work out, kidda. If yow ever want a rematch,

I'll be happy to oblige. Now, I've just got one question for yow before I ring an ambulance. Who sent you?'

'Fuck off, cunt. Look what you did to me knee.'

'That's the wrong answer. Shall wi try again?' said Clark and dug his baton into the man's shattered kneecap. The man stifled a scream and swore. Releasing the pressure, Clark continued. 'Your mates are out cold. They'll never know you spilled your guts, so save yourself a whole lot of pain. Who sent you?'

'Bishop,' he whispered.

'I can't hear yow.'

'Bishop sent us.'

'Why did Mr Bishop send yow?'

'He was told to by some guy.'

'Told to? And who were this guy?'

'I don't know. Just some posh bastard who phoned him.'

'How do you know he were posh?'

'It were me who answered the phone.'

'And did this guy have a name?'

'He just said, "It's the Major. Put Bishop on." For fuck sake, call an ambulance.'

'I will, kidda. Just one last question. What's your name?'

'Shepard. Johnny Shepard.'

'OK, Johnny. Make sure you never cross me path again or next time I'll cripple yow for life. And if you or your mates ever go after me mate over there or anyone we care about, I'll fucking kill you and they'll never find the pieces. Understand?'

Shepard nodded.

Collins had watched the interrogation with fascination. There was no doubt in his mind that Clark meant every word of this final exchange. What was more important, so did Shepard.

'Come on, Mickey, let's get these boys an ambulance.'

They found a phone outside the post office and Clark di-alled for an ambulance. In a convincing German accent, he explained that he'd just seen three injured men in the alley next to Burton's on Soho Road and that they needed an am-bulance. When the operator asked for his name, he hung up.

'Aren't we going to arrest the bastards?' asked Collins.

'Na, them's small fry. We got what wi need. Proof that this Major guy exists and that he's got enough pull to tell Eddie Bishop what to do.'

'Hell of a way to find out,' said Collins, still finding it dif-ficult to comprehend what he had witnessed. 'Mary said Bishop ran underage girls.'

'So you told me, but he's into a lot more than that. I'll tell yow about Mr Bishop this afternoon.'

'Why this afternoon?'

'Cos that's when wim going to pay him a visit.'

Collins didn't try to pursue the conversation and instead changed the subject. 'Was it the Commandos who taught you to fight like that?'

'Yeah, I were taught by the best.'

'No wonder you won the war,' said Collins, with feeling.

Clark smiled at the compliment. 'You did all right yourself, lad. You dain't panic. Yow covered me back. That's all I ever ask of a partner.'

Collins had never been so pleased by a compliment in his life. The approval of this little man meant more to him than he could explain or understand. 'Could you teach me how to fight like that?'

'I can teach you the basics.'

'Why just the basics?'

'When I were taught it, I needed it to stay alive and kill people. That meant I was willing and able to spend hours, days and months getting it right. Yow don't have the same kind of motivation. Yow just need enough to deal with scum-bags like them back there. We can do that in a few months, part-time.'

'When can we start?'

'As soon as yow like, but yow need to know that not every-one takes to it.'

'Why not?'

'Even the basics require patience and a lot of hard work. Not to mention the bruises, sprains and the odd broken bone yow can pick up along the way.'

'Sounds grand.'

Clark looked at his young partner and laughed, 'Just re-member that the Commandos motto is: "Train hard, fight easy". Yow can't say I dain't warn yow.'

A little later, as they turned into Thornhill Road, an am-bulance rushed silently past. It didn't need its bell on the deserted roads.

Birmingham, 15.25hrs.

With Clark's mother and father visiting family in Coventry, there was no chance of borrowing their car. Instead, Collins and Clark caught the number 70 bus to Birmingham. The sight of two uniformed police officers on the bus mid-afternoon was unusual enough for the conduc-tor to refuse to take their fare and more than one passenger turned around to gawk at the pair.

Collins wished that they'd stayed downstairs. There were only five other passengers on the top deck, but they were all smoking and no windows were open. To take his mind off the drifting smoke, he asked, 'Have you ever met Bishop?'

'Na, can't say I have. But I know him by reputation. Every copper in Brum does and we'd all love to nail the bastard.'

'So what's his game then?'

Clark outlined what he knew of Bishop. Some of it was fact, some supposition and a bit myth, but even myths have their origin in a truth of some kind. He confirmed what Mary had said, that as well as running several discreet brothels, there were well-founded rumours that he supplied underage girls for overage men.

But Bishop was a lot more than just a pimp. He also ran protection rackets aimed at small shop owners, a string of dirty bookshops, most of the illegal gambling in the city, and Central CID were convinced that he'd financed and organised more than one raid on jewellers, and knocked off the wages from several companies. 'They even reckon that he's gone along on a few of the jobs. Apparently, he likes to keep his hand in. That and the fact he probably gets a hard-on when knocking some poor sod over the head with a pickaxe handle,' said Clark.

Collins asked, 'If there's so much circumstantial evidence against him, why haven't we been able to pin anything on him?'

'I've often wondered that meself. My guess is he has a few well-placed coppers in his pocket that can tip him the wink when plod is getting close. That would account for some of it, but he's also a clever sod. With the exception of the robberies, he seldom gets his hands dirty. Prefers to work through Benny and Brian – a couple of brothers. Right nasty bastards. Built like brick shithouses, the pair of 'em. All three grew up within spitting distance of Villa Park, in the slums of Aston.'

'It sounds rough.'

'Oh, don't get me wrong. I ain't saying that Aston is the end of the world, but yow can see it from there.'

'Your objective opinion of Aston wouldn't have anything to do with the fact that they have a football team that even I've heard of?'

'Na, of course not, but now that yow mention it. Ever since the Villa won a couple of league titles back in the 19th Century, when the Royal Engineers were a big team, them believe they're sommut special. Arrogant sods, the lot of em.'

'And the Albion aren't?'

'Na, we're nice, wi am.'

Collins decided to change the subject. 'I suppose if he's

running pros, he could also have a few councillors, even judges, in his pocket.'

Clark looked at Collins and nodded, 'Yow could be right, but there's also the small matter of at least four people who were thinking about squealing, who slipped on various towpaths around Brum and ended up dead in the canal. That's just a rumour you understand,' said Clark and winked.

They got off at Colmore Row and walked past St Philip's. The graveyard that surrounded the Anglican Cathedral was covered in snow, except for the heavily used pathways that had been cleared and gritted. Today, its pathways and benches were deserted. It was hard to believe that in a couple of months, the flowerbeds would be in bloom, the grass neatly cut, and office workers would be eating their sandwiches under the trees.

As they walked past the Council House, Town Hall and the city's wonderful red-brick library, Clark said, 'Bishop will be a hard nut to crack but I've been thinking. I'll try to get him feeling secure and in control, and then yow hit him hard with sommut. He won't expect a sprog like yow to challenge him. It'll hurt his pride and with a bit of luck, he'll react.'

'Hit him with what?'

'Search me. Yow can't rehearse these things. Just pay attention, follow me lead, and then ask yowr question. If it surprises me, it will sure as hell surprise him. OK?'

'OK,' Collins replied, doubtfully. He wasn't at all sure that he could come up with a suitable question. Besides, he had the distinct feeling that this wasn't going to be an interview – more a confrontation. That thought was enough to trigger a release of adrenalin into his system. He felt his heart beat faster and the familiar dryness in his mouth as he mentally prepared himself. Because it would do no harm, he silently prayed to Jesus, Mary and Joseph that he wouldn't let Clark down.

Bishop's office was behind the old Bingley Hall, just off Broad Street, in a three-storey Victorian townhouse that had been converted into offices around the time that the Great War was just getting started and people still believed it would "all be over by Christmas". As far as Collins was concerned, the house was certainly showing its age, with flaking brickwork, peeling paint and green stains streaking the walls. It didn't look occupied, but a small sign in the doorway read: E. Bishop Ltd. 3rd Floor. There didn't appear to be any other occupants in the building. Both Collins and Clark eyed the ancient lift with suspicion and simultaneously decided to head up the oak stairway.

Reaching the third floor landing, they followed the sign to Reception. There was little sound and a complete lack of movement, but they could hear two women talking quietly. Collins opened the door and walked in. Sitting at separate desks were a set of identical twins, except that one was dressed entirely in black and the other in white. Neither was doing any work and they seemed surprised that a visitor had had the temerity to disrupt their conversation.

Standing up, the woman in white said, 'Good afternoon, gentlemen. Can I help you?'

'We'd like to see Mr Bishop.'

'I'm very sorry but he's out and won't be back today. If you'd like to leave a message, I'll get him to call you. Or I could make an appointment for you.' As she said this, the woman in black casually stood up and walked over to the filing cabinet. Opening it, she took out a file and slammed the drawer shut. Not content that it had fully closed, she repeated the process.

'Oh, we don't mind hanging about, love. Tell you what, we'll make ourselves at home in Eddie's office while we're waiting.'

'You can't go in there,' said the woman in white and tried to step in front of Clark. But she was too slow and he brushed past her.

'Well, would yow look at this, Constable Collins. Mr Bishop and his associates are in here. Either them snuck in the back way or those young ladies were telling us porkies. Which is it, Mr Bishop, lies or incompetence?'

Collins entered the room just in time to see Bishop stand up and say, 'Neither. I pay Miss Train to keep the riff-raff out.' He was not what Collins had expected. Standing 6 foot 3, with brushed-back grey hair, a strong Roman nose and a well-proportioned mouth that showed off a set of brilliantly white teeth every time he opened his mouth, he was an imposing figure. The Savile Row, single-breasted, charcoal grey pinstripe suit and immaculate white shirt from Jerymn Street with a muted red tie added to the image of a highly successful businessman. Unfortunately, that image was shattered the moment he spoke. His voice was high pitched and screeching and had the same effect on Collins as someone running their fingernails across an enamel basin. The man's accent was a strangulated combination of Received Pronunciation mixed with Aston slum.

There were two other men in the room. One was young and slim, with blonde hair spilling over his collar and soft feminine features. He was almost too pretty to be called handsome. Beautiful was a better description. Dressed in a dark blue, made-to-measure suit, white shirt, striped tie and black shoes, he looked as if he had just stepped out of a shop window. Collins wondered if the smell of expensive perfume came from him or the White Twin standing behind him.

The other guy was built like a beer barrel, with a massive chest and a football-sized head that seemed to grow straight out of his chest without any evidence of a neck. He'd stood up when Bishop had risen and was waiting quietly to see what his boss wanted him to do with these two hick coppers. Collins moved towards him and stood blocking any run he might take at Clark. Fortunately, Bishop's next words calmed the situation. 'I'm always happy to help the police, but I do prefer to be given advance notice of any visits. Now that you're here, though, why don't you sit down. You can go, Susan.'

Susan closed the door, but not without giving Clark a stare that she had probably used to shrivel many a man's amorous intentions. It didn't even register with Clark.

'Na, we'll stand, Mr Bishop, if it's all the same. Wi ain't going to be long.'

'Suit yourself,' said Bishop and resumed his seat. 'So, what are you here for? A donation to the Police Benevolent Fund or tickets to the police ball?'

Clark ignored Bishop's attempt at humour. 'Yow heard about the half-caste girl who got killed and dumped on Hill Top?'

'I saw something in the paper.'

'Well, wi was wondering if you knew her?'

'Now, why would I know her?'

'Because yow run a string of underage girls from all accounts.'

'I'm sorry to disappoint you. Those old stories about me are just that – stories. Put about by jealous competitors.'

'I didn't think yow had any competitors. The way I heard it, they usually end up dead in the canal.'

'What can I say? More rumours put about by people who want to do me and my legitimate business interests harm.'

'So yow've never heard of Simone Winston?'

'Never heard of her. Never met her.'

Collins was wondering why Clark was talking about Simone. They knew that she wasn't one of Bishop's girls, although that didn't mean he had never met her.

'What about Andrew Young, the guy who killed her. Ever hear of him or meet him?'

'Sorry, doesn't ring a bell.'

'You sure? A long, blond, skinny streak of piss?'

'I'm sure.'

'Well, thanks for your time, Mr Bishop. We'll be going now. If you think of anything, please give me a ring at the station.' Clark crossed to the desk, picked up a gold Waterman fountain pen and scribbled the station's number on the pristine blotter.

'Sorry I couldn't be of more help.'

Clark turned without reply and headed for the door.

The bull in the corner stood up and spoke for the first time. 'Don't let the door hit you in the arse as you leave.'

Collins could see that Clark was desperate for him to ask his question, but instead he turned and headed for the door. Even with his back turned, he could feel the waves of disappointment coming from his friend. Only when he grasped the door handle did he half turn and ask, 'When was the last time you spoke to the Major, Mr Bishop?'

Bishop's head snapped up and, for just an instant, Collins saw the rage that lay behind his normally cold, lifeless eyes. Here was the true Bishop. The animal Bishop who enjoyed wielding a pickaxe handle and exercising his power over those that couldn't fight back. As quickly as it had appeared, the anger retreated into its cage.

When he spoke his voice was higher pitched than before, but he chose his words carefully, 'I'm sorry I don't know any Mr Major.'

'Not Mr Major. *The Major*. An army man, probably. He lives near Stratford.'

'You're losing me again. I don't know any army major and I've never been to Stratford. I'm not a big Shakespeare fan. I prefer Tennessee Williams and that Osborne guy. There's always a chance of a bit of sex in their plays.'

'So you've never provided the Major with girls for his parties then? Underage girls.'

'I've told you already. I have nothing to do with any underage girls'

'Not even the little one found dead next to Andrew Young last Sunday?'

'No. None,' said Bishop, the pitch of his voice rising. 'Now, if you don't mind, I've got work to do.'

'I'm sure you do. Number one on your list will probably involve calling the Major. Give him our regards and tell him we're looking forward to meeting him.' Collins didn't wait for a response but quickly left, with Clark just behind.

Clark waited until they were out of the office and halfway down the stairs before he said, 'I know I said surprise the bastard, but that were a right shock to his system. Did yow see the look he gave you when you mentioned the Major?'

'You think I overdid it?'

'No, lad, yow got a rise out of him, which confirmed he's in this up to his neck with whoever is running things from Stratford. Trouble is, there will be repercussions from what you said. Let's hope wi can deal with 'em. Yow'll need to put your steel helmet and box on again.'

Collins wanted to ask what the hell this box was that Clark kept on about, when he stopped on the second-floor landing and looked at the two doors each side of the stairs. 'What do you reckon is behind them?'

Clark smiled, 'I'll check the two on the left.'

The first door Collins tried revealed a storeroom full of old files and broken furniture. The second was locked. Looking up, he saw that Clark was picking the lock on his first door. Collins joined him just as the latch sprang back. The room was neat, tidy and painted light pink. There was a queen-size bed in the corner, heavy curtains on the window, an empty drinks table, wash basin and mirrors on three walls. Clark flipped open the small trunk that sat on the floor at the bottom of the bed. It contained an assortment of ropes, handcuffs, whips and hoods.

'I doubt that much sleeping goes on in here,' said Clark, with a grin.

The next door was also locked, but Clark was now up to speed and quickly picked the lock. This room was almost identical to the first except that it was painted blue and had a picture of a naked young man fondling himself.

'Pink for girls and blue for boys?' suggested Collins.

'Could be. Let's see what's behind the last door.'

'Maybe it's for those who can't make up their minds.'

Clark gave Collins a pitying glance and shook his head.

The last room was a surprise. It was huge for a start. Maybe

20 by 30 feet, it looked like a small dance hall with a parquet floor, a fair-sized bar in one corner, a row of leather booths down the left side, and small round drinks tables and leather chairs down the right. Every window was covered with new wooden shutters and the lighting was subdued and intimate.

Collins felt his excitement build.

Clark quickly relocked the ballroom while Collins checked the other doors, before they slipped quietly out of the building. Once on the pavement, they looked at each other and both broke into a huge grin.

When Clark returned home, Ruth handed him a message she'd received from his friend in Vehicle Registration. *"There are four E-Types registered to addresses in Stratford, but only one features the name Phillip and that's Phillip Morrison Motors of Stratford Road. Hope that answers your question. You owe me a pint. Don."*

Clark gave a little whoop of delight and kissed Ruth on the lips. Slipping her arms around him, Ruth responded to his kiss. That's when he decided he had better things to do at that precise moment than ring Collins with the news.

Saturday 23rd February 1963.
Handsworth, 12.00hrs.

With his parents back from Coventry, Clark was able to borrow his father's car and, as arranged, pick Collins up at 12. Collins had only slept for three hours. Half the trouble was that bloody dog, Sheba – or, more precisely, the noisy fuss that Jamie, Gloria, Mary and even Agnes were making of her and the banging of doors as they pursued her around the house. This, combined with his first full week on nights, had wrecked him. He felt like a half-resurrected corpse. His mind felt disassociated from his body as he curled up in the corner of his seat. He was asleep before they had reached the A34.

Morrison's Motors was easy to find. It occupied a large site at the side of the main A34 road, about two miles from Stratford. There was a selection of new Fords in the showroom and outside was a variety of second-hand cars including Fords, Austins, Vauxhalls, a few old Humbers and even a pristine Morris Traveller, nearly all of which had been taken in part exchange.

Collins began to casually meander among the cars looking for an A35 van, while Clark checked out the parking space at the rear of the showroom. It quickly became obvious that there was no A35 on the lot.

Shaking off the snow from their boots, they entered the showroom. A young man in his early twenties approached and asked, 'Can I help you, officers?'

'We'd like to speak to Mr Morrison, please,' said Clark.

The young man disappeared into the back of the showroom and moments later reappeared with Phillip Morrison. 'You wish to speak to me, officers?'

Morrison was pretty much what Collins had expected.

Well-dressed, in a smart Italian suit, pale blue shirt and matching knitted tie, he had light brown hair, hazel eyes and the looks of an older James Dean. This was coupled with innate self-confidence, born of privilege, and it was obvious why Simone had been attracted to him. Collins disliked him on sight.

'Yes, sir. We'd like to talk to yow about your friend Andrew Young,' Clark said.

'You mean my acquaintance, Andrew Young. We were never close friends. We'd be better off talking in my office, if you'll follow me.' They followed him down a short corridor to a small office overlooking the parking area. Once settled, he asked, 'Can I get you gentlemen a hot drink?'

'That's very kind of yow sir, but this won't take long. Just a few details wi need to clear up for our report,' said Collins.

'That's right, sir. Little things, but important,' said Collins.

'And what report would that be?'

'The report into the unlawful killing of Simone Winston by Andrew Young,' replied Collins.

'I thought the local police were dealing with that, not Birmingham's finest.' His words were laced with sarcasm.

'They are, sir. But, yow know how it is, every force has its own records to keep and our boss likes to tie up any loose ends,' said Clark.

'I see, and that's what you're doing here. Tying to tie up loose ends?'

'Correct, sir. Now, yow say Andrew Young wasn't a friend of yowrs, more an acquaintance. Is that right?'

'I'd known him for many years to say hello to. We were at school together, but not in the same year. We were never what you would call friends. However, in a small town like this, it was entirely natural that we should move in the same circles. Besides which he used to buy his cars from me. If I'm honest though, I always thought he was a bit off – if you know what I mean.'

'No, I don't think I do, sir. Can yow explain?' asked Clark.

'Not one of the lads. Not very sporty. To tell you the truth, I thought he was queer.'

'Why's that, sir?'

'Well, even in prep school he seemed to prefer playing with little girls. Doctors and nurses, that sort of thing, rather than rugger or cricket.'

'But yow dain't play with the little girls, is that it, sir?' asked Clark.

'That's right. I preferred playing with the bigger boys and girls.'

Collins knew that Morrison was baiting them and decided to give him something to think about. 'If that's the case, sir, how is that you had intercourse with Simone Winston, aged fourteen, on the 18th January 1963 and had her wank you off on the 25th January 1963?'

The details contained in the accusation hit Morrison like a blow to the stomach, but he quickly recovered his composure. 'I assume that you have proof to back up these ridiculous claims?'

'Oh yes, sir. We have her diary. She provides detailed descriptions of the nights she met with you, Andrew Young, a woman called Marie and an unknown girl, probably about her own age.'

'That's absolute tosh. I've never been invited to an orgy, let alone partaken in one.'

'I didn't say anything about an orgy, sir,' said Collins.

'Don't be pedantic, officer. You know what I mean.'

'That's the thing about the law, Mr Morrison. It's very pedantic in matters like this,' said Clark. 'So if these events never happened, how do yow account for Simone having yowr telephone number and describing the car you drive as a red E-Type? Yow do drive a red Jaguar E-Type?'

'I don't like your tone, officer.'

'Yeah, I get a lot of complaints about it. It keeps me awake at night, worrying about what people think. But yow see, I'm from the Black Country and there ain't many cows there, so

I can smell bullshit whenever I'm within a mile of it and I don't like it. Now, how did she get your name and a description of your car if she never met yow?'

'That's very easy to explain. I used to lend the car to Andrew on occasions.'

'That's very generous of you, Mr Morrison. Lending your posh new car to just an acquaintance,' said Collins.

'Well, perhaps I should have said rented. I had an arrangement with Andrew that he could borrow the car for special occasions, provided he filled it up before returning it to me.'

'And that was financially worthwhile?' asked Collins.

'Do you know how much it costs to fill an E-Type? A full tank costs more than you earn a month in overtime.'

Collins felt elated, but hid it well. Morrison was rattled. Clark could take the next swing.

'What about yowr name and phone number? How did she get that?

'Isn't it obviously? Young must have mentioned where he got the car from and she probably found one of my old business cards stuffed in the glove compartment or some such thing. The rest she made up to impress her friends. You know what schoolgirls are like.'

'What about the A35 van you have for sale? Where's that? asked Collins, hoping that the change of direction would unsettle Morrison further.

It didn't. His reply was instant. 'I don't have an Austin A35 on the books. I haven't had one since about September last year.'

'Yow sure of that, sir?' asked Clark.

'Positive.'

'Well, in that case, wi won't take up any more of yowr time.'

'No need to show us out, sir. We'll find our own way,' said Collins. As they walked through the showroom, Collins spotted a copy of the local newspaper, *The Stratford Bugle*, lying on a table. Folded in two, it had a picture of Morrison shaking hands with an older man on the forecourt. On impulse, he picked it up.

As they made their way back to the car, Collins studied the picture and read the caption beneath it. It showed Morrison shaking hands with a big man in a Crombie overcoat and scarf. The heading read *"Local MP praises businessman's support for orphanage."*

As he closed the car door, Clark's irritation finally broke free. 'Lying bastard,' he spat. 'Did yow see the way he was playing with us? Cocky sod. I'll have 'im. I swear I'll have 'im. If it's the last thing I do.'

'Calm down. It's not as bad as it seems. We've already got him.'

'What do you mean? I can't see how the hell wi can get past his story. Wi know he's lying thought his teeth, but it's his word against the scribblings of a dead girl.'

'Oh, I wouldn't say that. Have a look at this,' said Collins, handing his partner the paper.

Clark slowly scanned the front page. Finally, he spotted the small photo near the bottom of the page. 'Sorry, kidda, I don't see the significance.'

'Look at what's in the background.'

Clark brought the paper closer to his face and squinted. It was barely more than an out-of-focus blur, but it was enough. 'Sod me. That's an Austin A35 or I'm a Chinaman. When was the picture taken?'

'Well, the paper is 15th February so the photo had to be taken some time before that. It means the car might have been on the lot on the 8th February.'

'The day old Wilcox saw it. Wi better get over to the paper. Do yow think it'll be open?'

'It's worth a try.'

⬥

Less than ten minutes later, they were outside the offices of *The Stratford Bugle*. But one look was enough to tell Collins that the place was closed for the weekend. He should

have known. Just what you'd expect from a small local week-
ly newspaper. Once they'd covered the Saturday morning
weddings, staff would be off for the weekend.

Clark was in the act of reversing when an elderly man
emerged from the front door and started to lock up.

Collins didn't wait for the car to stop. He jumped out and
slammed the door shut. 'Excuse me, sir, my colleague and I
were wondering if it would be possible to have a look through
your archives?'

'Can't it wait until Monday? I've just locked up.' The man
was hunched over, his arthritis-ravaged hands struggling to
turn the key. His skin an unhealthy yellow, with patches of
green shading under his eyes. Collins had seen this before.
Liver disease. The poor sod would be dead before Christmas.

Clark joined them just as Collins considered his options.
On nothing more than a hunch and a little knowledge about
old reporters, he decided to be frank with the man. 'I'm afraid
we can't come back on Monday. You see, sir, my partner and
I have been specifically told not to investigate this matter.'

The old man tried to straighten up, a sudden gleam illumi-
nating his eyes. 'You'd better come in then. We'll go in my
office. It's the only place that's heated on a Saturday.' He led
them to the back of the building to an office with the name
"Victor Begley, Editor and Proprietor" in gold lettering on
the door. He unlocked the heavy oak door and the three men
stepped into a stifling hot room. The office wasn't that large,
but had oak-panelled walls, a mahogany conference table
with eight chairs and a bookcase holding bound copies of every issue published by *The Bugle* since 1815. It was impressive
and spotless. There wasn't a scrap of paper in the wrong place
and the whole room smelt of fresh furniture polish.

'Take your coats off, gentlemen; no one in good health can
stand the heat in this room for long. Take a seat and I'll make
us all a cup of tea. Or would you prefer something a little
stronger, seeing as this is an unofficial visit?'

'Tea would be grand, sir.'

After Begley had left, Clark lent across the table and asked, 'Did I hear yow right when yow told him this was unofficial? Why?'

'I worked on a paper just like this for two years before I came over. Mr Begley is a paper man down to the soles of his feet. Good reporters are mavericks. They break the rules. I gambled he wouldn't be able to resist the chance of a good story about two coppers working a case on their own time.'

'Well, let's hope he don't go blabbing about it to his rich friends. It might be them wem after.'

'You don't know reporters. They never blab in case someone pinches their story, and the good ones would hang their granny for a great story.'

'Nice people then.'

When Begley returned minutes later, he was pushing a small tea trolley. On it were three cups and saucers, a large pot of tea, the bottom half of a cottage loaf, butter, cheese, arrowroot biscuits and a near-full bottle of Johnny Walker Whisky. 'I thought you might be hungry and a drop of whisky in your tea doesn't count as a drink in my book. Shall I be mother?'

For ten minutes, the men drank their tea, enjoyed doorstep-sized slices of bread and cheese, and spoke about the weather and the effect it was having on the sporting calendar. Clark complained about the lack of football and Begley was bereft at the suspension of horse racing. He'd not had a bet in weeks. Only when they had finished eating and piled everything back on the trolley did Begley lean forward and place his clasped hands on the conference table. 'Right then, gentlemen. How can I help you?'

'We're interested in this picture,' said Collins, sliding his copy of *The Bugle* across the table.

'Phillip Morrison and our esteemed local MP, Sir Marcus Tobin. What is it that interests you about the photo?'

'We'd like to know when it was taken,' said Clark.

'And why are you interested in that?'

'There's a van behind the two men. Wi need to know if it were on Morrison's lot before the 8th of February.'

'The 8th of February, you say.' Collins watched as the old man pulled together various disparate ideas that were forming in his mind. 'Nothing happened in Stratford around that date. Even if it did, the local police would be looking into it – not two Birmingham coppers. So the question is, what happened in Birmingham around that time important enough to bring you here on your off day and in miserable weather? I should imagine it's something serious. A robbery, maybe, or a murder?'

Begley stopped and looked at both men. 'Am I getting warm?' he asked.

'About as warm as this room,' said Collins.

'There was no major crime reported in the *Birmingham Mail* on the 8th or 9th of February. However, on the 11th, they reported the death of a half-caste girl. Am I warm?'

'Roasting, sir,' said Collins.

'In that case, I'd better go and check the photo records in the archive and cool down,' said Begley, with a smile.

'He may be old and sick, but he's still got all his marbles that 'un,' said Clark, after Begley had left the office.

'I was thinking…'

'Careful now, that could be dangerous, seeing as yow do so little of it.'

Collins ignored the comment and continued, 'He probably knows everyone who's anyone in Stratford. We should do a deal with him. Tell him the entire story, as far as we know it, in return for every bit of title-tattle and gossip he has about the important people of Stratford.'

'He'll want the lot.'

'So we give it to him on condition he keeps us out of the story.'

'I ain't sure. Yow can never trust a reporter. Tell yow what, let's see what he brings back.'

'OK.'

When he returned, Begley was carrying a photo and two old copies of *The Bugle*. Sitting down, he spread the three items out on the desk. 'The photo was taken on 5th February,' he said, and turned the photo over to reveal the date it had been taken. 'You can also see part of the van's registration number clearly in the original.' Both Collins and Clark smiled. 'Better than that, though, I can prove the van had been on the lot for at least three weeks prior to the 17th of February.'

'How?' asked Clark.

Begley slid a copy of *The Bugle* that was dated 17th January across the table. It had been opened and folded in two. The bottom of the page contained a quarter-page advert for Phillip Morrison Motors of Stratford, listing a selection of the cars and vans for sale and fourth entry down was an A35 with the same registration number as in the original photo.

'Mr Begley, sir,' said Clark, 'you've just proved that a certain gentleman lied to us. Thank you.'

'My pleasure.'

'What's the last paper?'

'Oh, I almost forgot. It's this week's issue. We led with the deaths of Andrew Young and the unknown girl. Now, what I want to know from you, gentlemen, is: what is the connection between Phillip Morrison, Andrew Young and the death of two teenage girls?'

Clark and Collins looked at each other, still undecided about revealing everything to a reporter.

In an attempt to break the impasse, Begley said, 'Gentlemen, I'm seventy-two years old and, with the exception of two wars, I've worked as a reporter or editor my whole life and I've loved every minute of it. My one regret is that I've never broken a really big story. I'd like to do it just once before I die. The doctors say I have maybe four or five months to live. Liver cancer. So this is probably my last chance to beat those bastards in Fleet Street and land a whopper. I'll do anything you want and agree to any conditions you set, as long as you give me the full story when you can.'

'What if we aren't able to prove it all?' asked Collins.

'Then I'll print what you can prove, and that way you can at least string the guilty up in the court of public opinion.'

'If wem right, yow could make yourself really unpopular among some important people round here. They might go after yow or your family.'

'That's really not a problem. As I said, I'll be gone soon enough. My wife died in 1957. We had no children and I think my only living relative lives somewhere in Canada. When I go, the nearest thing I have to a family, this paper, will close. After 148 years, it too deserves the chance to go out with a bang.'

'What if the government slap a D Notice on yow?' asked Clark.

'I've never liked being told what to do, so I don't care if they slap a D Notice on me. The story runs. Anyway, they can only slap a Notice on me if they know about the story in advance and they won't. The first they'll know about it will be when the paper hits the street. Then let them try and stop it. After that, who gives a flying stuff? I'll be dead before they can put me in jail.'

Clark was satisfied. Looking at Collins, he said, 'OK, but on two conditions: One, yow leave our names out of it and two, yow wait until we give you the go-ahead to print it. Deal?'

'Deal.'

'OK then. Tell him, Mickey. Tell him all of it.'

It took Collins nearly twenty minutes to relate the entire story. The old man only interrupted twice to ask questions of clarification. Collins finished by telling him about their visit to Bishop the day before.

'Eddie Bishop, you say. Long time since I heard that name. Nasty piece of work. Whatever he might have told you, he knows Stratford. He tried to rob a jewellery shop in the high street back in the early fifties. Left the manager with a fractured skull, but someone saw him take off his balaclava before he jumped in the getaway car. They picked him out in an identity parade. The police were certain he was going down for six or more years. Anyway, the case went to the Assizes Court, but fell apart when the witness failed to recognise Bishop. Of course, it may have been amnesia from the nasty crack on the head that the witness suffered when he slipped and banged his head.'

'That sounds like the Bishop I know and despise,' said Clark.

'All right, what can I tell you that may be of use? I've definitely seen Phillips and Young together. There is a third character that hangs around with them, Trevor Kent, but there's nothing unusual about that. Stratford isn't a big place and they are of a similar age and move in the same social circles – the tennis club in summer, the hunt in winter and the Young Conservatives throughout the year. They also have links to the same business organisations, such as the local Chamber of Commerce. What's more interesting, and relevant, is that Kent left the army under a cloud. Seems the young lieutenant smuggled a woman into the barracks.'

'Nowt odd about that. Just about every officer I ever knew under thirty did it. Almost part of the initiation ceremony,' said Clark.

'Yes, but this one ran half naked onto the parade ground and screamed the house down. She claimed that he'd tried to rape her. Of course, the army hushed it up and his short commission became even shorter than he expected.'

'Do any of them hang around with someone called the Major?' asked Collins.

'There are a lot of retired majors and the like living in and around Stratford – many from the First World War – but I've never seen either Young or Phillips with any major I knew. I'll look into it and check out some of the ex-majors we have in the town.'

'What do yow know about Superintendent Burgess?'

'Ambitious. Doesn't want to rock the boat, just in case it scuppers his chances of promotion. It's very likely that if he was told to close the Simone case down, he'd do so and ask no questions.'

'And Sir Marcus Tobin?' asked Collins.

'Lower middle-class, maybe even working-class background. He had a good war. He started out in the ranks but won a battlefield commission. When he came home, his accent had changed along with his name. He dropped Mark and started calling himself Marcus. Anyhow, he managed to charm Miss Mary Singleton out of her knickers and in so doing married money and began his political career. He's a Tory Whip at the moment but the rumour is he'll be in the Cabinet if Macmillan wins the next election.'

Collins looked at his watch. 'I'm sorry, Mr Begley, we need to be on our way.'

'That's quite all right. I'll give you my number and you better give me a private number I can reach you on. We don't want to set any tongues wagging in the station, do we? I'll come in tomorrow and go through the files and see if anything jumps out at me. I'll call you no later than Monday night.'

'Thank you, Mr Begley, for all your assistance.'

'No, thank you, gentlemen, for making the last few months of an old man's life interesting.'

Victor Begley was still smiling as Clark and Collins drove away. The biggest story of his life had just landed in his lap.

Part Three: Afternoons
Sunday 24th February 1963.
Handsworth, 12.55hrs.

Ruth and Clark arrived at 12.55 for Sunday lunch. Ruth brought a box of Black Magic chocolates for Agnes and Clark gave Sheba a large beef bone, which she immediately grabbed and took to her temporary bed in the kitchen.

They were joined by Jamie for a dinner of roast beef and all the trimmings. By the time the pudding of apple pie and custard was served, everyone was feeling full and relaxed.

'Michael tells me that you can speak several languages, Clive. I did some translating during the war. Which languages do you speak?' asked Agnes.

'I'm not up to the level of a translator but I can get by in French, German and Dutch, and I know a bit of Polish and Norwegian.'

'That's very impressive,' said Agnes in German.

Clark replied in German and for a few minutes he and Agnes showed off their linguistic skills as they switched between various languages. Eventually, Ruth joined in, leaving Collins and Jamie to lament their lack of any foreign language training. At a break in the conversation, Collins winked at Jamie and launched into a recitation of the last verse of the W.B. Yeats poem *Easter 1916* in Gaelic. When he'd finished, he said, 'I just thought you polyglots would like to hear what a real foreign language sounds like.'

'I think he's telling us to talk in English,' said Ruth.

'Where did you do your translating during the war?' asked Clark, who seemed to have moderated his Black Country accent.

'Oh, here and there. I was based in London at first and then a backwater where nothing ever happened called Bletchley. After the war, I was in Berlin and Nuremburg.'

'At the trials?' asked Collins.

'Yes.'

'My unit did a bit of work around Bletchley. As a training exercise, we used to try and break into various places. The idea was it kept them on their toes and gave us a bit of practice. There was one place near Bletchley, sort of a country house that we did twice. First time we tried, it was easy-peasy – like walking into an open house. Second time, one of me mates got a bayonet in his side for his troubles. He was OK, though. I think it was called Station X.'

'How exciting. But I can't say I've ever heard of Station X. As I said we were the quietest of quiet backwaters,' said Agnes, standing up. 'Would anyone like some more tea or coffee?'

Ruth curled up on the settee, enjoying the heat from the open fire. Agnes sat in her favourite rocking chair, drinking tea. They could hear Clark shouting in the garden and Jamie laughing as Collins set about building a snowman.

Agnes felt relaxed and contented. It had been a very pleasant few hours. Clark had surprised her. She suspected that he was a lot more intelligent than he let on. His German was certainly very good. She was also certain that he had seen past her denial that she'd never heard of Station X. He may not know what had gone on at Bletchley, but he knew that it had been important. Strangely, she felt as though a weight had been lifted from her shoulders. For eighteen years, she had kept secret the nature of her work. Now someone had an inkling of what she had done and that shared secret – never fully explained and only hinted at – had a liberating effect on her.

'Michael tells me that you came to England as a refugee and found yourself billeted with Clive's parents. Was it love at first sight when he came home?'

For a moment Ruth was uncertain just how much Collins had told Agnes, but her words were not tinged with sympathy. Collins had kept her secret. 'Well, I was only fourteen when he came home from the war and he was twenty-two. Mom and Dad were kind. They'd always wanted a girl, but Clive's sister had died at birth. I became their daughter and Clive's little sister, but I always knew I loved him and that I wanted to marry him. But I said nothing.'

'What happened?'

'Well, I think eventually Mom guessed how I felt about him. I mean, I'd never had a boyfriend. Not even a date. On my 21st birthday, she and Dad went to stay the night at Auntie Diane's. I think Mom arranged it. Clive took me to a Chinese restaurant. Have you ever had Chinese food?'

'Yes. It can be very good if you get the right restaurant.'

'We should all go one night. You can choose the restaurant. Anyway, when we got home, there was a feeling in the air that something might happen. I know that Clive felt it because he was very quiet. Then, he kissed me on the forehead and rushed off to bed. Well, I'd had enough. I'd been waiting for him to do something for seven years. So I took off all my clothes, went up the stairs and got into bed with him. And that was that. We were married three months later.'

'Did you ever find out why he hadn't said anything to you?'

'Oh yes. First, I was too young. Then he thought he'd be taking advantage of me because I was living with Mom and Dad. Then, when I was older, he was afraid to tell me how he felt in case I left home. Amazingly, he had no idea that I'd loved him from the moment we met.'

Agnes smiled. 'Men can be pretty stupid when it comes to anything that involves feelings. Take Michael. He's mentioned Clive to me once or twice and I've only seen them together for a few hours, but it's obvious that he'd do anything for him.'

'I've noticed the same with Clive. I think the fact that

Michael risked his life on the ice to pull him clear meant a lot to him – even though Clive insists he could have got out of the water using his knife.'

'What ice?'

'Didn't Michael tell you?'

'No.'

Ruth retold the story that Clark had told her to explain why his normally immaculate uniform was crumpled, stank of stagnant water and generally looked as if he'd slept rough in it for a week.

'Well, it seems Clive is not the only man around here who doesn't like to talk about what he does.' Looking up, Agnes could see that the boys' snowman was reaching completion. 'That snowman needs a hat and I have just the right one. Come on, grab your coat.'

Minutes later, Agnes and Ruth appeared in the garden wearing green wellies and Agnes carrying a battered top hat.

'Agnes thought that the snowman needed a hat in this weather.'

'That's a grand idea. Come on, Agnes, give his lordship his topper.'

Agnes responded to Michael's urgings by walking very solemnly towards the snowman with her arms outstretched, carrying the hat as if it were a crown. As she prepared to crown the snowman, the men removed their own hats and she placed the topper on the snowman's head. 'Let it be known,' she intoned in her best Shakespearian voice, 'that this snowman will henceforth be called Clive Michael Jamie the First, ruler and protector of the back garden for as long as the frost doth last.'

A ragged cheer went up from the assembled throng.

Turning, Agnes bowed deeply and was hit on the side of the head by a snowball thrown by Collins. 'You swine, sir. You'd hit a lady when she was unprepared?

'Yes,' said Collins, and threw another that missed.

Jamie immediately sided with Agnes and Ruth, and they

attacked Collins and Clark. Ruth, in particular, was amazingly accurate and managed to hit both men several times. However, what Clark and Collins lacked in accuracy, they made up for in speed. Their constant barrage was slowly pushing Jamie and the women back. Defeat seemed inevitable, but then the backdoor burst open and led by Sheba, Gloria, Mary and the latest arrival Susan stormed to the rescue. While Sheba ran around Collins and Clark, yapping and jumping, the Agnes force regained the initiative and within minutes were rolling both men in the snow.

Knowing he was defeated, Collins shouted, 'Stop. Stop. We surrender.'

'What do yow mean wi surrender? I've never surrendered in me life.'

'Well, this is a good time to start,' said Collins. Standing up, he raised his hands.

———

Ruth and Clark were just leaving when the phone rang. Agnes picked it up, listened briefly and then held it out for Collins. 'A Mr Begley wants to talk to you.'

At the mention of Begley's name, Clark closed the front door and waited.

Collins took the receiver. Even before he had finished introducing himself, Begley cut him short. For the following three minutes of the conversation he just listened. The call ended when Collins said, 'We'll be there, 10 tomorrow morning.'

By this time, Clark's impatience was obvious. 'Where are we going to be tomorrow at 10?'

'He wants to see us. He suggested we meet at his house.'

'OK, but what's he found?'

'From the sound of it, quite a bit,' said Collins, dragging the moment out.

'For goodness sake, Michael, stop teasing Clive and tell him what Mr Begley has found – before he starts chewing my carpet.'

'Sorry, I couldn't resist it. He's found a link between Tobin, Bishop and Burgess.'

Clark's face broke into a wide grin.

'It seems that Detective Sergeant Burgess was the arresting officer when Bishop tried to rob the jewellers and Tobin was the magistrate that granted Bishop bail pending his appearance at the Assizes. He's also found some interesting notes on Morrison, Young, Carver and a couple of other characters.'

'I love that man,' said Clark, with feeling.

'Agnes, can we borrow the car again tomorrow?'

'No,' said Agnes, sternly. She paused just long enough for disappointment to register on Collins' face before continuing, 'I'll drive you. Why should you have all the fun?'

Ruth suppressed a giggle and Clark glared at her and said 'Well, wi know whose side yow're on.'

Monday 25th February 1963.
Stratford-upon-Avon, 09.55hrs.

Agnes, Collins and Clark pulled onto Begley's drive just before 10am. Begley was standing in the bays window waiting for them and had the door open before they reached the step.

'Come in, come in. You had no trouble finding the place then?'

'None at all,' said Collins, 'but then Agnes was driving. Mr Begley, this is Mrs Agnes Winters – a friend of ours.'

'I'm very pleased to meet you, Mr. Begley.'

'And I you, my dear. You've just turned a very good story into a great one.'

'How so?' asked Clark.

'Why, gentlemen, every great story needs a beautiful woman, and here she is.'

'I can see we're going to have trouble with yow,' said Clark.

Begley led them into the dining room before excusing himself. He returned minutes later with a tea trolley containing a pile of freshly buttered bread, a bowl of crisp bacon and two racks of toast, along with a selection of jams and honey.

'You'll have to forgive me, Mrs Winters, I wasn't expecting a lady. I was only expecting two policemen, who, from my experience, have never been known to refuse a bacon sandwich. I hope I can interest you in some toast and honey, though. The honey is made locally.'

'Well, actually, I think I may succumb to a sandwich myself. The bacon smells gorgeous, and please call me Agnes.'

'I've always found that the smell of bacon and coffee promise far more than the taste can deliver, but it's never stopped me from enjoying both. Please help yourselves.'

As on the previous Saturday, no mention of the case was

made until after all four had finished eating. Collins wondered if not talking business while eating was a habit that Begley always followed. If so, it was a very civilised way to behave and one that Collins thought he might adopt.

'So you enjoyed yourself in the archives yesterday?' said Collins.

'Oh yes. One of the very best days I've ever had as a reporter. Come,' he said, 'the results of my search are on the table.'

Begley had arranged his findings in four neat rows of paper. In its symmetry, it reminded Collins of someone playing a careful game of patience. Each folder and slip of paper was aligned exactly with the page above and below it, and each row was as straight as a newly made ruler.

Pointing at the first row of material, Begley said, 'These documents are the various stories we ran on the jewellery robbery, including our coverage of the trial and Bishop's acquittal. As you can imagine, it was a big story back in the early 50s, and Bishop's acquittal was something of a scandal. The last document, you might find particularly interesting. It's a letter from Colonel Reginald Quinn. It was never published, because in it he suggests that Tobin had known Bishop during the war when Bishop was briefly seconded to his office as a supplies clerk. He surmises that it may have been Tobin who supplied Bishop with the witness's details. Of course, such information could have been obtained in any number of ways.'

'But why make such an allegation? British colonels are not renowned for making unsubstantiated claims,' said Agnes.

'My thoughts exactly, Agnes. That's why I called the Colonel after I spoke to you last night.'

'What did he say?' asked Collins.

'He wanted to know why I was investigating something that had happened over ten years ago. I told him I was doing a profile on Sir Marcus and had been intrigued by his claims against a respected member of local society.'

'What did he say about Tobin and Bishop?'

'Tobin joined his regiment as a Lieutenant at the end of the war and was assigned a logistical role while awaiting return to England. Bishop was his Sergeant. Under their control there was a very significant increase in stock losses, but despite ordering a snap audit he couldn't prove anything – though that wasn't what worried him the most.'

'What did?' Clark asked.

'There were stories that if you wanted a woman, Bishop and Tobin could supply one.'

'Nowt strange in that,' said Clark. 'Most regiments have a supplier of Toms.'

'The Colonel said the same. His concern was that a couple of twelve-year-old girls were discovered in one hut. They wouldn't say who'd brought them onto the camp or who they'd been with, but it was obvious that they'd been "used", as the Colonel put it, by more than one man.'

'Desperate people do desperate things,' said Agnes. 'I saw a lot of child prostitution while I was in Berlin. Sometimes, mothers even hawked their own children around the bars and streets.'

'Yeah, I saw that too – but what wi got here is another bit of information that links Tobin to Bishop and underage girls,' said Clark.

'There is more to come,' said Begley, picking up the second row of paper. 'I found this spiked story from 1959. A young girl complained to the police that her boyfriend and another man had raped her at a party. Morrison and Young were questioned under caution at the police station following the alleged assault. One of our trainee reporters was hanging around the station when they were brought in. They were never charged, which is why it was spiked.'

'How come they weren't charged?' asked Clark.

'It seems that one of the officers on duty recognised the girl. He'd arrested her for soliciting four months earlier while she was on the run from an approved school.

'The Custody Sergeant told our lad that she was probably

trying it on with Young and Phillips. Looking to scare a few pounds out of them.'

'If circumstantial evidence were allowed in court, we'd already have them by the short and curlies,' said Clark. Then, realising what he'd said, he started to apologise.

Agnes cut him off, 'Don't worry about it.'

'If that's circumstantial, the last piece of information is pure speculation,' said Begley, holding up a 6 x 8 picture. It showed a group of men about to board a coach. The caption underneath read "Local Chamber of Commerce Members look forward to a day at Wolverhampton Races". 'Recognise anyone?'

Clark took the photo and, with Collins looking over his shoulder, said, 'That's Morrison, Young and Spencer. And that looks like Tobin in the back row. The guy at the end looks like Carver, but may not be.'

'Correct on all counts, and the man standing next to Tobin is Trevor Kent.'

'So, other than confirming that Carver knows Young, Morrison, Spencer Tobin and Kent, what does it prove?' asked Collins.

'Maybe nothing. Maybe just a bit more circumstantial evidence.'

Collins could sense that Begley was holding something back. Like the good reporter he was, he was building suspense and saving the best until last.

'It was the date that caught my attention, the 1st August 1960. I've always been good with linking dates to stories. Give me a date and I can usually tell you what was making the news around then.'

'So what story broke on the 1st August?' asked Clark.

'None, but by Friday 5th August, we were leading with the story of an eight-year-old girl from Wolverhampton who'd gone missing the previous Monday. She was never found.' Begley dropped the newspaper on the table.

No one spoke. Everyone was thinking the same thing.

Much of the drive back to Birmingham was made in silence. Agnes in particular seemed quiet and withdrawn. When asked a question her responses were monosyllabic. Finally, as they reached the outskirts of Birmingham she said, 'I have a friend from the war. He's just a clerk, but he may be able to provide us with some additional information about Tobin and his friends. I'll call him when I get home.'

Collins was about ask who the friend was, but an imperceptible shake of the head by Clark cut him short.

Handsworth, 12.30hrs.

After dropping Clark off, Agnes drove home and parked in her usual spot. Michael climbed out of the car and immediately spotted a trail of blood leading from the porch to where a car must have been parked near the garage. Agnes quickly unlocked the front door and was confronted with more spots of blood on the hall's parquet floor.

Fearing that Gloria's pimp had come calling in her absence, Agnes rushed to the kitchen where a cacophony of excited voices could be heard. Collins followed closely behind. Gloria was on her knees wiping blood from the linoleum. Mary was cradling Sheba in her lap and the new girl, Susan, was waiting for the kettle to boil. All three were speaking, but no one was listening. The window over the sink was smashed, and broken cups littered the floor.

'What's happened?' demanded Agnes.

'Yous missed it, Agnes. It were great.'

'It was amazing,' said Susan.

'Wonderful,' said Mary in agreement and tickled Sheba's tummy.

'What did I miss?' All three woman started to speak at once. 'One at a time, please.'

'Mary, it were your husband. Yous tell her.'

'About twenty minutes ago, there was a knock on the door.

Susan was in the kitchen, so she answered it.'

'I'm so sorry,' said Susan. 'I didn't know who he was, but he looked so respectable that I let him in.'

'He said he just wanted to talk to me,' continued Mary, 'so I came down. Gloria and Susan were here so I felt safe, but as soon as I came in the kitchen he started shouting at me. Calling me a whore and a bitch for walking out on him. He said my leaving was just a pathetic attempt to embarrass him and gain attention, but that now he'd come to take me home.'

'So I told him to fuck off,' said Gloria. 'Yous ain't taking Mary anywhere, I said, unless she wants to go. That's what I said.'

'That really annoyed him and he called Gloria all sorts of names,' said Susan.

'Water off a duck's back, love.'

'Poor Sheba was so terrified by all the shouting that she hid under the table,' said Mary.

Collins looked reproachfully at the dog. So much for Clark's assertion that pound for pound Staffies were the toughest dog in the world.

'I said I wasn't going and there was nothing he could do to make me. That made him really angry and he started to smash the cups and saucers, and hurled one of the chairs at the window.'

'That's when he made a grab for Mary,' said Susan.

'I managed to get in the middle of 'em, but he punched me in the face and grabbed Mary by the hair,' said Gloria.

'I was shouting and trying to slap his hand away,' said Mary.

'But then he started screaming in agony. Like he had his balls in a wringer or sommut.'

'That's when I saw Sheba. She'd got hold of his leg and sunk her teeth into his calf,' said Mary.

'Yeah, he were screaming like a stuffed pig. Hopping about on one leg trying to get Sheba to let go.'

'He hit poor Sheba with the kettle, but she wouldn't let go. He even smashed her against the cabinet but she still hung on,' said Mary.

'Sheba was wonderful. He tried to get out of the kitchen, but she wouldn't release him. She just shook her head and the more she did, the more blood was sprayed around the kitchen,' said Susan.

'He dain't like the sight of his own blood, I can tell you. Scared him shitless, it did,' said Gloria.

'I think it was Sheba that scared the living daylights out of him,' said Mary, and laughed. It was the first time Collins had seen her laugh and he found himself laughing with her. 'Finally, he sort of half ran, half hopped to the front door with Sheba still attached to his leg. It was like a scene out of the Keystone Cops. I've never seen anything so funny. She only let go when he opened the door.'

'Then she trotted back in here like cock of the walk. I tell yous, that dog is a bloody marvel.'

Collins looked down at Sheba again and conceded that Clark's judgement about Staffies had been correct. She was asleep again, her left ear twitching as she dreamed of sinking her teeth into another leg.

'Well, it seems that the ladies of the house now have two protectors,' said Agnes. 'We need to get this place cleaned up, check Gloria's eye and see if Sheba has any injuries. So let's get on with it.'

Mary gently lifted Sheba off her lap and placed her in the cardboard box by the radiator that had become her home.

As Agnes led Gloria away to look at her latest black eye, she turned to Clark and whispered, 'I think you can assume that Sheba has passed her probation.'

Collins smiled and joined Mary and Susan in cleaning the kitchen and hall.

———————

Collins met Clark by the Park Gate Stores and the two men walked the remaining 300 yards to the station. Collins relayed the news of Sheba's heroics and Clark was only too pleased to say, 'I told yow, Staffies were the best dogs in the world and them great with kids.'

'I'm not so sure about that. If Sheba got hold of a kid in those jaws, she'd kill it.'

'No chance. Them known as the Granny Dogs in West Brom. Yow see, for years, if an owner saw any hint of aggression from a Staffie towards kiddies, he'd kill it. No messing. Shoot it. Drown it. That way, any aggression towards babbies was bred out of them. In fact, yow got to be careful about hitting a kid around a Staffie. He's likely as not going to go for yow if yow do.'

Sergeant Ridley entered the Parade Room four minutes late. No one could ever remember such an occurrence. Standing at the desk, he cast his eyes around the assembly. Spotting Clark and Collins at the back, he stopped and slowly shook his head. 'I need to see you pair after Parade.'

'I don't like the sound of that. What you been up to, Mickey lad?' Clark whispered.

Collins didn't have the time to reply before Ridley launched into his briefing.

As the afternoon shift filed out, Collins and Clark hung back. When the room was empty, Ridley closed the door. 'Super wants to see you and he's right pissed off. He's had Chief Superintendent Wise from Central CID with him for the last hour and you pair were the topic of conversation for most of it. What the fuck have you been up to?'

'Honest, Sarge. I ain't got a clue. Nowt we've done is connected with anything Central would be interested in.'

'So you admit you have been doing something?'

'Us, Sarge? Never. It was just a figure of speech, like.'

'Well, for your sake, I hope so. Get in there and get it sorted, and then I want you to deliver a death message to Mr Fred Hopkins. His wife, Edith, passed away at 12.45 pm today in Dudley Road Hospital. Here's the details.'

Clark took the message slip and, folding it twice, he placed it carefully in his breast pocket. As they walked out, he said, 'This is the worst part of the job, Mickey, delivering a notice of death. It never gets any easier. I've done dozens of them. The worst is when it's a kiddie or a young mother. There's nowt yow can say then.'

Collins nodded and remained quiet. He'd never had to tell anyone that someone they loved had died, but he remembered how he had felt when his father had woken him at two in the morning to tell him his mother had died. It was the feeling of total devastation, of a loss so great that it didn't seem to have a beginning or an end. It was anger at an unseen God. The wish that it was his father lying on some cold mortuary stone and not his mother. He pushed the memory of that night from his mind and pulled his tunic down as Clark knocked on the Superintendent's door.

Clark and Collins marched into the Super's office and came to attention. Sitting beside Hollis was Superintendent Wise. Tall and lean, he looked like a hungry vulture with a beaked nose and a huge Adam's apple that moved up and down like a yoyo. Sitting behind them, near the door, was a third man that neither Collins nor Clark had noticed as they entered.

Superintendent Hollis lost no time on introductions. 'I told you pair to stop working on the Winston Case and leave it to Burgess, didn't I?'

'Yes, Sir,' said Clark.

'Then why the hell were you at Eddie Bishop's gaff last Friday?'

'Wi were just trying to tie up a few loose strings from our side, Sir.'

'A few strings my arse. You deliberately disobeyed my orders and those of the ACC. Tell me why I shouldn't put you both on a disciplinary?'

'It were my fault, Sir. The lad was just following me lead. If anyone should be disciplined, it should be me.'

'That's not true, Sir. It was me that suggested we go and see Bishop. Constable Clark was against the idea.'

'Yow see what I have to put up with, Superintendent?'

For the first time, Superintendent Wise spoke, 'Hell knows, every copper in Birmingham wants to bring Bishop down and from what I've heard you did a good job of rattling him.'

Collins and Clark exchanged glances. How the hell did he know that they'd rattled the great Eddie Bishop? Come to that, how did he know they'd even visited him?

'But, you see, you fucked up a four-month investigation we had going. Gentlemen, may I introduce you to Detective Sergeant James Richards, our man on the inside of Bishop's operation.'

Turning to look at the man behind them for the first time, it took a few seconds to recognise the face without the pancake make-up, the touch of rouge and the elaborately styled hair.

'Nice to see you again. I have to say you made quite an impression on Eddie. He really would like to cut your balls off and stick them down your throat. Me, I'd settle for giving you pair a right good kicking. But judging from what you did to Shepard and his pals, Constable Clark would probably put me in hospital before I laid a glove on either of you.'

'Yes, we know all about your little escapade on Thursday night. An incident that you also failed to report,' said Superintendent Hollis.

'Sorry, Sir. Just trying to save on paperwork.'

'Careful, Constable Clark, you're walking a tightrope.'

'Excuse me, Sir,' said Collins, 'could I ask how our actions have interfered with Central's robbery investigation?'

'You tell them Sergeant,' said Wise.

'We heard that Bishop was eyeing up a fashion company in Digbeth, but he wanted a man on the inside before he'd do it – so I took a job there. I've spent the last four months trying to get Bishop to trust my alter ego, Queen Reggie, enough to finally do the job. It was all set up for next Friday. He was even going to go along for the ride. We'd have caught him and his entire gang red-handed. But your visit threw a scare into him and he's decided to batten down the hatches and play safe until this Simone thing blows over.'

Collins and Clark let the new information sink in. If only they had waited a week, Bishop would have been in custody and who knows what he might have been willing to say about the Major and his friends for a reduced sentence. The truth was that they had screwed up, but, even so, Collins wasn't sorry for what they had done. He was surprised when he found himself saying, 'We'd like to apologise, Sir, to Superintendent Wise and Sergeant Richards for messing up their operation, but the truth is that Bishop is into worse things than armed robbery – and no one is doing anything about it.'

'And you thought it was your job to do something?'

'Yes, Sir.'

Superintendent Hollis shook his head in exasperation and said, 'You may be right, Constable Collins, but in this force you follow orders. I've told you once, and now I'm telling you for the second and last time. The Simone Winston case is no longer your concern. Lay off it or you'll both be for the high jump. Clear?'

'Yes, Sir,' said Collins and Clark in unison.

'Good. Now, get out and don't let me see you in this office again.'

<hr>

Collins and Clark walked slowly up Soho Road. Neither was looking forward to delivering their message and both were still thinking about how they had comprehensively ruined the police's best chance in years to arrest Eddie Bishop and his mates.

'Yow know, Mickey lad, wi got off lightly today. The Super

could have thrown the book at us. I've come to the conclusion that it can only be me innate charm that's keeping us safe from the sack.'

'We're not going to stop, are we?'

'Not a chance Mickey. Not a snowball's chance in hell.'

Collins smiled and lowered his head into the wind.

Mr Hopkins' house was a three-up, three-down on Boulton Road, which had been built around 1900. The snow had been cleared away from the pavement outside the house and gritted, as had the short path and steps leading to the front door. Collins rang the bell and waited. Mr Hopkins was in his mid-sixties and of average height, with grey receding hair and a slight build. He was dressed in a white shirt with the starched collar removed, a brown jumper and corduroy trousers to match. The clothes were old but spotless.

He looked at Collins and said, 'She's dead, isn't she? My Edith is dead.'

'I'm very sorry to say that she is, Mr Hopkins. Your wife died peacefully at 12.45 pm in Dudley Road Hospital,' said Clark. 'Mind if wi come in?'

'Aye, come on in. The day's not fit for man nor beast.'

Inside, the house looked like it had been given a full spring clean in the last day or two. Every surface had been wiped down and polished. Each ornament and book had been taken down, dusted and put back in its place. Collins realised that he'd done it for his Edith. He thought she was coming home.

Mr Hopkins led them through the front room and into the living room where a roaring coal fire was burning, above which was a framed picture of the Sacred Heart.

'Sit yourselves down, lads, and I'll make you a cuppa. You must be perished.'

'No, Mr Hopkins. Why don't yow have a sit down and Constable Collins here will make yow a cuppa. He's a dab hand in the kitchen. Aren't yow, Mickey?'

'That I am,' said Collins, already heading for the kitchen. He put the kettle on and then stood in the doorway, watching as Clark engaged the old man in conversation.

'Is that your wedding photo, Mr Hopkins?'

'That it is, May 1919. I'd wanted to marry her sooner, but her father wouldn't allow it until the war ended. He didn't want her to be a widow. There were a lot of young widows hereabouts.'

'You made a bostin couple.'

'I don't know about me, but she were beautiful. There were a lot of lads after her, but she chose me. I'll never know why.'

'Oh, that's easy, she picked the one she thought were the best of the bunch, and if yow stayed together for forty-four years, she must have picked right.'

The old man smiled and, leaning across, patted Clark on the knee, 'You're a kind man, Constable, but I'd expect nothing less from a man with the Victoria Cross,' he said, pointing at the ribbons above Clark's left breast pocket.

Collins was surprised to see Clark blush. Stepping forward, he pointed at a picture of a young man in a naval uniform that sat beside the wedding photo on the sideboard. 'Is this your son?'

'Aye. That's Jimmy. He were on the Arctic convoys when he got killed in 1942. Edith were never the same again. You see, he were her only child. Something went wrong when he were born and she could never have any more kiddies. Not right; not fair.'

Collins wasn't sure if it was his son's death or his wife's condition that he was referring to but didn't ask. The kettle whistled and he went out to make the tea. 'There's some chocolate digestive biscuits here. Do you want a couple, Mr Hopkins?'

'No, lad, but bring 'em in for you and your mate.'

They sat and drank their tea, and Mr Hopkins told them of the first day he'd seen Edith, of how terrified he'd been to ask her out. And the golden days when they'd put little Jimmy in his pram and take a walk around Handsworth Park, and listen to the band or chase him through the raked piles of autumn leaves. These and other small ordinary moments were remembered and recounted.

After an hour, Clark asked, 'Is there anyone you'd like us to call, Mr Hopkins?'

'No, lad, there's no-one. There were always only the two of us and, for a while, we were three.'

On impulse, Collins said, 'I'll drop in tomorrow before me shift. See if there's anything you need.'

'No need, lad, but thanks anyway.'

As they walked away from Boulton Road, neither man spoke until they had reached Soho Road. Collins said, with feeling, 'Poor old sod.'

Clark nodded in agreement.

———————

When Collins and Clark returned to the station for their snap at 6, they were surprised to find Sergeant Richards in the canteen. Stocked up with a mug of tea each and a plate of sausage and mash with onion gravy and peas, they sat down beside him.

'Sorry about messing yowr case up,' said Clark.

'Don't worry about it. The wages job is just delayed, not cancelled – provided I can continue to string him along, we'll get him in the next six months or so.'

'Can I ask you a question?' asked Collins.

'Certainly.'

'How are you able to keep the act up? I mean, what if some man had tried it on?'

'That's easy, darling. I'm what's known as a choosy queen,' replied Richards. He extended his right arm, made his wrist limp and pointed his fingers down as if he was expecting Collins to kiss the back of his hand. 'Unfortunately, very few men ever come up to my requirements,' he lisped. 'Therefore, they are all rejected with varying degrees of rudeness and humiliation. This feeds my reputation as a real bitch and makes most men wary of me. As for all my conquests, they consist of men that no one knows or have ever met. You see, I let it be known that I'm particularly attracted to straight men, which explains why no one meets them.'

The change in Richards' voice and demeanour had been total and instantaneous. He was like an actor who had totally inhabited his role. Throwing off his Queen Bitch character, he returned as quickly to his Sergeant Richards persona. 'But tell me about your murder and this Major guy,' he continued. 'I've never heard Bishop speak of him, but when you mentioned the name, he looked like Hamlet when he first saw his father's ghost.'

Clark looked at Collins and gave an imperceptible shake of the head, before launching into a summary of the case. Collins was content to stay quiet and get on with eating his dinner and drinking his tea, but listened intently to what Clark said and didn't say. It was obvious to him that Clark was providing Richards with a much abridged version of their investigation, one that contained no reference whatsoever to The Palms, Spencer, Ravenal, Carver or Begley. The only link that their case might have to Bishop, he said, was a tip off from an unnamed Tom who said that Bishop supplied underage girls, and they wanted to know if he'd supplied Simone to this Major character.

As Clark finished his story, Richard's pushed his tea cup away and, leaning forward, smiled. 'I know you've only told me half the story and I understand why. I also know that regardless of what your Super says you're going to go on investigating this case and I don't blame you. I'd probably do the same thing myself – *Qui audet adipiscitur* and all that. All I'd ask is that you keep me informed so that we don't get our lines crossed again.'

Taking out a small business card, he wrote a telephone number on it and handed it to Clark. 'Call me any time, day or night, and I'll do anything I can to help.'

Outside, the wind had got up and was blowing in the men's faces as they tramped towards Soho Road.

'There's something wrong about Richards, isn't there? That's why you didn't want me to say anything.'

'Yowr right. The thing is, I think he wanted us to know that he weren't kosher. If yow can survive four months under cover with Bishop, yow don't drop Latin and Shakespeare into the conversation when yowr talking to a couple of fellow coppers unless you are sending them a message.'

'But what's the message?'

'I ain't sure, but I think he were telling us that he ain't a regular copper. That we can trust him. My guess is he works for MI5 or Special Branch, sommut like that.'

'Why them?'

'Because public school oiks – and he is one of 'em, I'm sure – don't join the police. After school, they go to university and then into the forces or security services if they want a bit of excitement.'

'How do you know he went to public school?'

'I can smell 'em. They think they're superior to the rest of us and don't mind letting it show. Besides, his queer act is too good to be entirely untrue.'

Collins considered what Clark had said. He started to nod his head. 'If he is Special Branch or MI5, why is he interested in a gangster like Bishop?'

Clark raised an eyebrow and said nothing. He waited as Collins joined the dots up.

'He's not interested in Bishop. He's interested in the Major or whoever Bishop supplies girls and Toms to. Important people. They're potential security risks.'

'That's one possibility. Or, if the Major is someone important, he may be protecting him by making sure that his links with Bishop don't come out.'

'We need to find out what Richards is really up to.'

'True enough. Yow should ask Agnes to raise it when she speaks to her friend in London.'

'Why would he know anything about Richards? Her friend is just a clerk. He wouldn't know anything about Richards.'

'If yow believe that, you must be in love with her. Agnes ain't going to see some piss ant clerk. She's seeing someone important.'

'How do you know?'

'Call it a hunch, but for half a second she got flustered when I mentioned Station X at lunch on Sunday. Then she covered it like a pro.'

'But she never worked there.'

'Mickey, Station X were special. I doubt that anyone who ever worked there would admit it. I don't know what they did, but the word was that if Jerry ever bombed Station X about fifty percent of the brainiest people in Britain would be wiped out. So, they could only have been working on one of two things. The A-bomb or intelligence gathering. My guess is it were spying. Yow dain't need linguists like Agnes to make a bomb, but them bloody useful if you were eavesdropping on Jerry.'

'And you think Agnes was involved in that?'

'I think she worked at Station X, which means that she mixed with some very important people. Many of 'em are probably still in intelligence. I'll bet me next wage packet that she's gone to see an old friend who can give her the lowdown on Tobin and his friends.'

'But why would she want to hide something she did nearly twenty years ago?'

'A little thing called The Official Secrets Act. Wi all signed it and wi all took it seriously. It were true what they said in the war: loose talk did cost lives. Besides, if wi were to gab on about some things, even now, we'd end up in the clink – which ain't a nice place for ex-policemen.'

'Is that why you don't talk about the war.'

'Na, I just want to forget about the war.'

'Even your VC?'

'Especially me VC.'

Something in Clark's voice registered with Collins. He knew instinctively that now was the time to ask the question he'd wanted to ask since Ruth had shown him the medal. 'Why don't you want to talk about the VC? Why do you want to forget that?'

Clark stopped and looked at Collins. The wind was blowing harder and the people on Soho Road flowed around Clark as if he was a rock in the middle of a river. All they were interested in was getting home, putting their feet up and watching one of the nine million stories from *The Naked City* on telly that night. Slowly, Clark smiled. 'Yow've got the gift for asking the right questions at the right time, yow know that? OK, let's grab a brew at The Boundary Café and I'll tell you about it. After that, yow never raise it again. Deal?'

'Deal.'

'And remember, avoid any puddles yow see in the café, especially the yellow ones.'

As always, Sid was pleased to see Clark, whose frequent visits and reputation was sufficient to ensure that his café never had any problems with the local Teddy Boys. 'What'll it be, gents?' he asked, ushering the two men to a nice warm table near the kitchen and out of any drafts.

'Just tea and toast, Sid,' said Clark.

While they waited, neither man felt the need to talk. Instead, they relaxed and rubbed some circulation back into their hands and face, content to be warm for the first time since leaving Mr Hopkins' house.

Within a couple of minutes, Sid reappeared with their order and left. Only then did Collins lean forward and ask, 'So why do you want to forget something that any man would be proud of?'

'Because it was a fuck-up from start to finish and a lot of good men got killed for nothing.'

The force of Clark's response surprised Collins. It was the first time that Clark had allowed his emotions to show since they had met. There was real anger in his voice and eyes – an anger he'd not seen when they had found Simone's body or when Shepard had stepped out of the shadows with knife in hand. Collins decided to say nothing and waited.

'Wi was dropped behind Jerry lines the night before D-Day with instructions to capture and hold a small bridge. It were chaos, and me and four mates ended up about five miles off target and separated from the rest of the unit. During the night, we hooked up with some American paratroopers. They were even further away from their drop zone then wi was. They were heading towards the coast where they was going to meet up with the troops coming ashore.

'At about 07.00 hrs, we was about 2 miles from the beach-head. By then, you'd have to be deaf, dumb and blind not to know that the invasion had started and every Jerry were on full alert. Anyhow, as wi approached this crossroads, a machine gun opened up. Jerry were dug-in at the top of this hill covering the crossroads. We all dived in the roadside ditch where we were comparatively safe, provided we dain't stick our head out. Unfortunately, the Yank Lieutenant had seen too many war films for our good. He'd missed his main target and he dain't want to report back without at least getting involved in a fight.'

'He wanted to go after the guns?'

'Yow got it. Now, wi had nothing but hand grenades, one Bren, and a couple of Browning automatic rifles. We were no match for three dug-in heavy machine guns. Me and the lads tried to reason with him. This was his first time in action and he dain't know what he was taking on. The clever thing to do were wait for a tank or a platoon with grenade launchers or mortars and we could've take 'em out easy.

'There were no reasoning with the guy. We could have refused. Should have refused, but yow can't back down when a bunch of Yanks are looking at yow. So we joined them. Fortunately, he let us choose our positions and we picked the left flank as there were a few hillocks on that side which we could use for cover.'

Clark stopped talking. Once again he was seeing the road, the steep 60-yard hill that lay beyond it, the neigh-on impregnable heavy machine guns and, worst of all, the bodies of his dead friends. Gathering himself as he must have done on that day, he continued, 'On his shout, we moved out of the ditch. Two or three Yanks got it even before they cleared the road and I was about 20 yards up the hill before I noticed that there were no sign of the Lieutenant. Well, I reckoned the prat had bought it and kept going.

'The Yanks on the right and in the middle got the worst of it. Brave buggers they were. They charged them guns … Anyways, I don't reckon any of them got more than 30 yards up the hill. Once they were down, Jerry turned on us. They dain't have the best angle on us, but even so two of me mates copped it and the other two were wounded.

'Funny things happen to you in battle. I were the only one not wounded or killed and I was angry. I wasn't scared. I were just pissed off. Pissed at the Lieutenant for being a stupid pillock, at the Jerries for what they had done to me mates, and with meself for not doing more to stop the stupid bloody charge.'

'But what could you have done?'

'I could have shot the stupid bastard. That way I'd have saved fourteen lives.'

'And probably lost your own.'

'Maybe. Anyways, I still don't know how I covered the remaining 30 yards to the first nest without getting hit. A couple of bullets went through me trouser legs, but nothing touched me. I kept firing from the hip and suddenly the first machine gun went quiet and I dived into the nest. One of the Jerries was wounded, the rest dead. I finished him off with me knife.

'Then, a couple of potato mashers landed by me feet. If they'd landed a few yards away, I wouldn't have had the time to throw them back. The first exploded in mid-air and I caught some shrapnel in the shoulder, but the other wiped out nest two.

Nest three were now paying me full attention. While they were moving their gun to get a better angle, I made it to nest two. As soon as I got there, I lobbed a couple of grenades at Jerry. When they exploded, I charged. By the time I reached them, they were all dead.'

'My God, Clarkee, how can you not be proud of that?'

'Three reasons. One, there were no need to launch the attack. Two, fourteen men died. Two of 'em were me mates and six others were wounded. Three, the Lieutenant hadn't bought it. He'd not even been wounded. Seems he sprained his ankle getting out of the ditch and fell back into it. That were the official version. My guess is that as soon as he stood up and Jerry opened up, he dived for cover.

'When I got back to me unit, I wrote a full report signed by me and me two mates criticising the actions of the Lieutenant. But he wrote a different report in which his brave decision to protect advancing troops had been magnificently carried out by me under covering fire from his courageous troops and himself. He ended by recommending me for the VC.

'His was a better story and did a hell of a lot more for troop morale and Anglo-American relationships then mine, so his account became the official version. He received a commendation and a bloody Purple Heart – for a sprained ankle. And me, I got a VC for my part in one almighty fuck-up. Now do you understand why I don't talk about it? Fourteen men died needlessly so that I could get a bloody medal.'

Collins remained silent for several seconds. He understood Clark's feelings but still marvelled at the courage of any man who was willing to charge three machine guns alone. Finally, he said, 'There's an old saying among reporters: "When the facts conflict with a good story, print the story". It's not your fault that the wrong story got told. But you did show "conspicuous bravery in the presence of the enemy".'

'Yow been reading up on the subject?'

'A little. The point is that whatever the circumstances, you

showed incredible bravery and you deserve your medal.'
  'Tell that to the fourteen mothers who received a telegram.'

Tuesday 26th February 1963.

Handsworth, 12.00hrs.

Tuesday started quietly for Collins with a late breakfast and a walk across Hill Top with Sheba, before he put on his uniform and headed for Mr Hopkins' house. When he arrived, he found the curtains drawn. It was the traditional sign of a death in the family, but something was wrong. Collins could feel it. He could hear it in the sound of an empty house. A bottle of milk on the step, had frozen solid, expanded, and pushed the foil top off, and the morning paper was sticking out of the letterbox.

Collins rang the bell. No response. He tried again. Still nothing. He tried knocking on the door with his fist, but the house remained stubbornly silent. As he turned away, a neighbour opened her front door. 'I'd keep trying if I were you. He's in there. I've been cleaning the front room all morning and not seen him go out. Is it about his wife?'

'Yes.'

'Gone, has she?'

'Yes.'

'I'm sorry to hear that. A lovely woman, but we all knew it would be quick once the cancer got her.'

Collins returned to his task. Nothing. Now worried, he found the side entry that allowed access to the back of the houses and walked around. The curtains in the back bedroom were also drawn, but the window was open. An open window on a freezing day like this didn't add up.

He found an old pair of step ladders in the garden shed and, using them, was just about able to push the window up enough to pull himself up and slither head-first into the bedroom. Mr Hopkins lay on the bed, dead. His hands were placed across his chest as if he had been posed by an undertaker. There was an empty bottle of pills at his side and an envelope in his hands.

To whom it may concern,

I'm sorry for the fuss and extra work that this will cause you all. But you'll find my will on the sideboard downstairs and all my affairs have been tied up best as I can.

I know it's wrong but I've taken all my pills. It's for the best. It means that at last Edith, Jimmy and me can be together again. I know the Church won't forgive me for what I've done but I'm sure God will.

Signed: John Alfred Hopkins 25th February 1963

PS. Please thank Constables Clark and Collins who called last night. We had a lovely chat.

Collins read the note with a lump in his throat. He knew that he should call the station, but he was thinking about the picture of the Sacred Heart over the fireplace and Hopkins' note. Instead, he picked up the empty bottle of pills and read the name of the chemist who had issued the prescription. Taking the bottle, he found the house keys hanging on a hook in the kitchen and left.

Wright's Chemists gave him the name and number of Mr Hopkin's doctor and Collins called him. Thirty minutes later, they were both standing beside the body. Collins handed him the note and the empty bottle of pills. The doctor read the note and said, 'I'm sure you know that since the Suicide Act of 1961, suicide is no longer a crime, but it is still has to be reported to the coroner.'

'Yes, sir.'

'So why did you call me and not the police surgeon or station?'

'It's the last sentence in the note, sir. He's a Catholic. Most people don't know it, but the Church does bury the majority of suicides in consecrated ground on the basis that those who kill themselves are usually suffering from a mental illness. But it's clear from his note that Mr Hopkins was entirely sane, so the Church won't bury him in consecrated ground. That means he won't be buried with his wife.'

'I see. And what would you like me to do about that?'

'Well, last night, sir, he took the news very badly. Lots of tears. Very upset, he was. He looked really unwell when I left. That's why I came back this morning. I think that delayed shock might have killed him.'

The doctor looked at Collins over his glasses and pursed his lips. 'I think you missed your calling, Constable. That's precisely my diagnosis. Indeed, only last week I told Mr Hopkins that he should avoid any stress and shocks if at all possible.'

With that he handed both the suicide note and pill bottle back to Collins for disposal and took out his pad of death certificates.

<hr>

Clark and Collins left the station at just after 2. Collins explained what he'd found when he'd returned to see Mr Hopkins. Clark was in full agreement with what he'd done and said, 'If there is a God, then I reckon he'd be on yowr side with that one.'

'You don't believe in God?'

'I don't know. I saw some things that don't sit right with the idea that there's a God.'

'In the war?'

'Yeah. But also in the service.'

'Such as?'

'There were a woman whose hubby was killed just before war ended. She had a couple of babies. With him gone, they got in the way of her having a good time so she locked them in the coal shed. Neighbours could hear 'em crying for a day or two but did nowt. Doc reckoned they took about three days to die of thirst. The eldest was four, the other just two. It was me an me mate that found them. Where were God for them?'

'There's always been evil and always will be. Two thousand years ago, some Romans enjoyed watching Christian virgins being raped by donkeys and horses before they were killed. You see, the Romans considered it bad luck to kill a virgin.'

'So, me question remains. Where were God 2,000 years ago and where were he for those babbies?'

'I like to think he was there at the end.'

'He weren't there for Jesus at the end. Why else did he call out: "My God, My God, why have you forsaken me"?'

Not wanting to get involved in a debate about why an all-powerful God allowed evil in the world, Collins decided to shift tack and asked, 'What happened to the mother. Did she hang or get away with pleading insanity?'

'Neither. She was on remand. Kept in solitary for her own protection and not allowed to mix with any other prisoners. She was even kept on suicide watch – although the bitch didn't seem at all sorry. No one knows how they got into the bathroom, where she was, without being seen. They reckon there were at least three of them...'

'They drowned her?'

'No. They filled the bath three quarters with boiling water and threw her in. Held her under with mops. It took her three days to die. Much like her babbies.'

Collins had no reply and the men walked on in silence. At the Palladium Cinema, at the bottom of Hockley Hill, Clark called the station from the police pillar and reported in.

Handsworth, 22.50hrs.

Glad to be home at last, Clark brushed the snow from his coat and boots and opened his front door. There was a large brown paper envelope waiting for him on the mat. Picking it up, he shouted, 'I'm home love. Yow gone to bed?'

Ruth appeared at the top of the stairs with a toothbrush in her hand. 'Almost. What's that you've got?'

'Don't know. It were on the mat.'

'I'll make you a cuppa. There's some soup and fresh bread if you want it.'

'That would be good.' He struggled out of his top coat and slipped his boots off, before padding into the lounge in his socks. Dropping into the settee, he ripped the envelope open. A handful of photos and a typed note landed in his lap. Picking up the photos, he went through them slowly. Four of them featured Ruth. One showed her at the bus stop, one leaving work and two had been taken of her standing in the lounge. The other two showed his parents outside their house. He felt anger start to form in his stomach. The sort of anger he'd not felt since the war. It was the same cold, mind clearing anger that had helped him survive when others had died.

The note was short: *You've had one warning. This is your second. There won't be a third. Back off now or your pretty wife and parents are not going to live long enough to regret your actions.* It wasn't signed.

He slipped the photos in his pocket and neatly folded the note and placed it in his tunic's top pocket. Walking into the kitchen, he said, 'Leave that, love. I need yow to pack a few things. Yow, Mom and Dad need to go away for a few days to Auntie Dianne's.'

Ruth turned and saw that he was serious. He'd had the same look on his face when he shot the German outside her hut. 'What's happened?'

'Nothing, love, and nothing will, but I have a few things to do and it's best that I don't have to worry about yow or Mam. So be a good girl and get cracking while I ring Dad.'

Mr Clark answered the phone on about the twelfth ring. 'Yes?' he barked.

'Sorry to wake you Dad, it's me.'

'What the hell are yow ringing for so late?'

'I need you and Mam to pack a few things. Enough for a week. Then come round here and pick up Ruth.'

'And where are wi going?'

'Somewhere safe. I were thinking Auntie Di's.'

'I take it I won't be going to work for a while?'

'Yow ain't wrong there.'

'All right, son. We'll be around in about forty minutes. Yow can tell me the details when yow've sorted it out.'

Clark was grateful for his father's lack of inquisitiveness. Just as he had never asked Clark about what he had done in the war, he was willing to accept his son's judgement that he and the women needed to get away quickly.

Clark's next call was to Collins. Agnes answered the phone. She listened briefly, then said, 'I'll get him.'

Collins barely had time to say, 'What's up?' before Clark cut him short and explained what had happened.

'What do you want me to do?'

'Ask Agnes if yow can borrow her car. Wem going to pay Mr Bishop a visit.'

His last call was to Sergeant Richards, who was happy to supply Bishop's address and a description of his house without asking any questions.

While waiting for Collins and his parents to arrive, Clark told Ruth what the envelope had contained. She didn't question his reasoning. If he thought it was a serious threat, that was enough for her. She put her arms around him and, holding him close, whispered, 'You do what you think is right, but please be careful.'

Clark kissed her and said, 'Ain't I always?'

'No.'

'Don't worry, love. Mickey and me will sort it out. Yow'll see.'

Half an hour later, the civilians had been packed off to Coventry and Collins and Clark were talking in the kitchen.

'You're sure it was Bishop?'

'Oh yeah. It were him all right. He may have discussed it with the Major, but it were him.'

'So what are we going to do?'

'Pay Mr Bishop a visit.'

'At this time of night. That's really going to piss him off. I can't wait to see his face.'

'Sorry, Mickey. He ain't even going to know that I've been until I've gone.' With a wink, he left Collins standing in the lounge and paid a quick visit to the garage. When he returned, he was carrying a black rucksack and a gray boiler suit. 'I'll get this on, then we're off.'

'Don't I get one?'

'Naw. What I'm doing, I do alone. I just need yow to sit in the car.'

Wednesday 27th February 1963.

Sutton Coldfield, 01.20hrs.

Bishop lived in a private estate opposite Sutton Park. Richards had said that the house, a flat-roofed Art Deco mansion was surrounded by a large wrought iron fence that backed onto Roman Way. Clark didn't think it would be hard to find. Only once, on a whim to see how the other half lived, had he driven round the private estate in his father's old Ford Popular. He'd quickly been stopped by an officious gardener who thought he looked suspicious. Without pause, Clark had produced his warrant card and said that he was investigating a spate of recent burglaries on the estate by bogus gardeners, and asked to see the man's identity.

He vaguely remembered seeing a huge flat-roofed monstrosity and wondered at the time if that was where the singer Dorothy Squires and Roger Moore of *Maverick* fame lived.

As they approached Roman Way, Clark pointed to a row of shops set back from the road. Outside the general store and post office, there was a telephone box. Clark pulled up beside the familiar red box and jumped out. 'I'll only be a tick,' he said. 'Switch seats.' Thirty seconds later, he was back in the car, satisfied that the phone was working.

'OK, Mickey. About 400 yards down the road, there's an island. Drop me off there and then come back here and wait. If I'm not back in 35 minutes, call 999.'

'OK but what if someone asks me what I'm doing parked outside a post office in the middle of the night?'

'Show them yowr warrant card. Yow do have it with yow, don't yow?'

'Yes, I've got it,' said Collins and pulled away with a jerk. 'Sorry,' he said, 'I've not had much practice recently.'

'I'm just impressed yow can drive. I thought that your lot

still drove pony and traps.'

'I'm from Dublin. We have cars, electric lights and indoor plumbing – something a lot of the houses in West Bromwich don't have.'

'Less chat, more driving.'

Clark slipped out of the car at the roundabout. By the time Collins looked in the mirror, he'd disappeared. Only a sliver of the moon showed in the cold night sky. However, with the snow reflecting what little light there was, Clark was able to pick his way through the heavy undergrowth that bordered both sides of Roman Way. He knew it was probably unnecessary, and he could have ambled down the road at this time of night and not be seen, but he couldn't ignore his training and the maxim that had been drummed into him: "Never take unnecessary risks, no matter how small they may appear".

Clark veered slightly to the left. After seven minutes, he found the railings that ran alongside Bishop's house. He hunkered down and surveyed the house and grounds. The snow on the lawn was pristine with no evidence that any dog or guard had walked on it in days. Slipping off his rucksack, he threw it over the fence. He then jumped up and caught hold of the top bar and pulled himself up. Unbidden, the memory of Upright Freddie came to mind as he carefully avoided impaling himself on the 12-inch spikes that topped the fence. Satisfied that he was clear of all snags, he jumped and rolled forward on landing. He lay there for thirty seconds, waiting to see if anyone had seen or heard him. Nothing.

Picking up the rucksack, he ran parallel to the fence until he was at the side of the house. Again he stopped, looked and listened. Again, nothing. No sound. No movement. *Bishop clearly doesn't know how to protect himself*, he thought. Then, he realised that as the number one villain in Brum, Bishop had no reason to fear being done over by a burglar. Everyone was too shit-scared of him to try such a suicidal move.

Clark moved out of the shadows and crossed to the kitchen door. He shook his head in disappointment as he saw that all he had to get through was an old Yale lock. Bishop was making this too easy. In less than twenty seconds he was inside and striding quietly across the tiled floor to the hallway.

There were three reception rooms downstairs. Clark selected the one that looked like Bishop's study. The room had been furnished like a gentleman's club. A captain's chair stood behind a fine mahogany desk. The centre of the room was dominated by two Chesterfield settees and an oak coffee table, and a fine series of glass-fronted bookcases covered three walls.

Clark quickly checked out the books. Most had never been opened, but those housed behind Bishop's desk had clearly been read. They were mainly military memoirs and first editions by various playwrights including Arthur Miller and Tennessee Williams. *So, Bishop did know his Osborne from his O'Neill,* thought Clark. Good – that would make what he was about to do even more personal.

Clark silently started to remove the first editions from behind Bishop's desk and build a small wigwam of books and rolled-up newspaper on the carpet in front of the desk. He left the centre of the pile hollow to allow for a good draft. Opening his rucksack, he removed a two pint bottle of petrol and sprinkled it liberally on the 3-foot mound of books. Taking a small bundle from the rucksack, he unwrapped a cheap Timex watch, a 9-volt battery and a small detonator.

Checking his watch, he set the alarm for eleven minutes and placed his homemade charge in the centre of the wigwam. Even if someone was in the room when the detonator went off, the charge was too small to harm them, but it was more than enough to ignite the books and with it the whole study. Clark hoped that it would prove to Bishop that he was dealing with someone just as willing to kill as he was. After one last check, Clark stood up, sprinkled the last of the petrol over the books, desk and chair and laid the empty bottle next to the improvised bomb. Standing up, he took his rucksack and left.

Once over the fence, he checked his watch. Eighteen minutes since he'd left Collins; barely three since he'd set the timer. Retracing his steps, he reached Collins at the row of shops six minutes later.

Without stopping to talk to Collins, he went straight to the phone box and waited. With less than one minute to go before the incendiary went off, he called Bishop's number. The phone was answered on the third ring.

'Is that Eddie Bishop?'

'Yes. Who the fuck is ringing me at nearly two in the morning?'

'I'm the guy who has just been in your house. You have about 20 seconds before your nice collection of books goes up in flames. I wouldn't go in there before you hear the bang or you might hurt yourself. After that, yow'll be able to put the fire out fairly easily.' Message delivered, he hung up.

As they drove back along the Queslett Road, Clark explained what he had done. 'What about innocent people in the house?' Collins asked.

'You mean wife and kids? He ain't got any.'

'There could be others.'

'There could, but do you really think that anyone staying at Bishop's is innocent? Besides, if he stays outside the room until the fire starts I doubt anyone will get hurt.'

'You doubt!' said Collins.

'Mickey, that's the difference between us. Yowm a copper and one day you'll be a great copper. Me, I'm a soldier. I know from bitter experience that the only way to fight someone who is trying to kill you is to show him that yow are just as ruthless as he is. That way, he may back off.'

'And what if he doesn't back of?'

'Then you kill him before he can kill yow.'

They drove on in silence. For the first time, Collins realised why Clark didn't talk about the war. He'd been part of a war that had required him to slit a man's throat in cold blood or hang a woman on the back of a door and make it look like suicide. He'd been turned into a killer by experts at the age of twenty and he'd remain a killer until the day he died. No one, except maybe Ruth and his fellow Commandos, would ever fully understand that.

At the end of the Queslett Road, Collins pulled over to a phone box and Clark jumped out. Bishop answered his call on the second ring.

'Did yow get there before the fire took?'

'You bastard. I'm going to kill you.'

'Now, now, Mr Bishop. It's your threats that got you in this mess in the first place. Yow say that yow warned me twice. Well, I've given you fair warning. Come after me, me family or friends and I promise you that I'll fucking kill you and everyone and everything you hold dear. Understand?' Clark didn't wait for a reply and hung up.

Collins eventually pulled up outside Clark's house. They sat in silence for a few minutes, before Clark said, 'I'll see yow later, Mickey' and started to open the door.

Collins caught his friend by the arm. 'Clarkee, I know we're different, but I want you to know that I'll always back you up. No matter what.'

Clark pushed the door open and, without looking back, said, 'Thanks Mickey. I knew I can rely on yow.'

London, 11.00hrs.

Agnes sat with her ankles crossed and looked at the portraits on the wood-panelled walls. They were a collection of military leaders, none of whom Agnes could name, but two of which were very fine examples of 19th century portraiture. She'd been waiting twenty minutes but didn't mind. It had to be important. She knew how much Aubrey loathed poor punctuality and he'd be mortified that he'd kept her waiting.

The telephone on the secretary's desk rang. She picked up

the receiver, listened for a few seconds, hung up and then in the most condescending voice that she could muster said, 'Sir Aubrey will see you now.' Rising, she opened the door behind her and ushered Agnes into the holy of holies.

As Agnes entered, Sir Aubrey leapt from his chair and came round the desk. 'Agnes, my dear. I'm so sorry that I kept you waiting.'

'That's perfectly all right, Aubrey. I'm sure it was unavoidable.' At the use of Sir Aubrey's first name, Agnes could feel the secretary stiffen beside her.

'Miss Florin, would you be so kind as to bring us some tea and biscuits? Chocolate biscuits, not the usual rubbish we give visitors.'

The mention of chocolate biscuits was the last straw and Miss Florin's one word reply of 'Yes' was as cold as the ice covering the window sill. She withdrew and the atmosphere in the room immediately became warmer.

'My Lord, it's good to see you, Agnes. How long has it been?'

'A while,' Agnes replied, knowing full well that Sir Aubrey knew exactly when and where their last meeting had taken place. Not even he could blot out the memory of a dead double agent at his feet.

'Anyway, what have you been up to?'

'You mean you don't know? My word, your spies must be very second rate. I thought you kept a close eye on all of us oldies.'

'In your case, just a watching brief. Your discretion and loyalty were and never will be in doubt.'

'Then you'll know that I'm on a number of Quaker Committees and look after beaten women.'

'No regrets that you left the service?'

'None. The work at the Park and then after the war in Europe was enough for me.'

'Pity. Oh, do you know who I ran into just yesterday? Ian. I said I was meeting you today. He sends his love. I think he still sees you as the one that got away.'

Agnes smiled. 'How is he? Still writing?'

'He didn't look too well, but he's still scribbling away.'

There was a knock at the door and Miss Florin entered carrying a tray, which she deposited on the table next to Sir Aubrey's desk. She moved to pour when Sir Aubrey said, 'You can leave that, Miss Florin. I'll do it.'

'Very well, Sir,' she said. But really it wasn't well at all that Sir was pouring tea for some unknown middle-aged woman, who apparently could get an appointment with the Assistant Director of MI5 with one phone call and all without going through her. Outrageous.

Handing Agnes her tea, Sir Aubrey asked, 'So, what's brought you here today. It sounded important on the phone. What have you been up to?'

'Me, nothing, but friends of mine have become involved in something that you may have an interest in.'

'You mean your tame policeman?'

'So you have been watching me.'

Sir Aubrey smiled and raised his shoulders in a shrug.

'He's investigating the death of a fourteen-year-old half caste girl. Her body was dumped in Handsworth, but the trail seems to lead back to Stratford-upon-Avon. The names Sir Marcus Tobin and Superintendent Burgess have cropped up. I was wondering if you had anything on them? There is also mention of someone called The Major, who may or may not be either Tobin or Burgess.'

Sir Aubrey sat back in his chair and made a steeple with his fingers. Looking over the rims of his glasses, he exhaled a long 'Hmmm' before answering. 'Sir Marcus Tobin, Chief Whip of the Tory Party. He definitely knows where all the bodies are buried. Very powerful behind the scenes. No one wants to cross him.'

'Aubrey, I could get that information from *The Times*. What's in his file?'

'Are you asking me to divulge state secrets despite the fact that you always refused to sleep with me?' he said, jokingly.

'From what I recall, you never tried that hard.'

'True. I suppose I loved Claire too much. Still do, in fact. Anyway, Tobin. A nasty piece of work. Was commissioned from the ranks in 1944, I think. At the start of the war, he was assigned to special ops. He had a talent for killing people quietly and took out several important targets for king and country. Came back to England. Married into money and started to forge a career in politics.' Sir Aubrey hesitated.

'What else?' asked Agnes.

Sir Aubrey seemed to be making up his mind. 'There is evidence that he likes the company of young people.'

'You mean children?'

'No, older. Teens seem to be his preference.'

'Why haven't the police done something about him?'

'There's no hard evidence.'

'You mean you won't give it to them.' Agnes was starting to feel angry.

'Agnes, that's a little unfair. We have no hard evidence, just a lot of stories and innuendo. Besides, he has some very powerful connections. Some of whom may share his predilections.'

'And if you prosecute him, he could bring the government down?' suggested Agnes.

'That's a possibility. Macmillan knows that he's only one more cock-up or scandal away from handing the next election to Wilson and his Red friends on the proverbial plate.'

'You said that he likes teenagers. Does that include boys?'

'So it seems.'

'"The girl was buggered after she died," Agnes told him.

'Christ.'

'Was Tobin in Berlin at the end of the war?'

'I'm not sure. Why?'

'I seem to remember that at the end of 1945 seven teenage girls were found dead. All of them had been buggered after they died. The police never caught anyone, did they?'

'No. It was put down to the Russians, I believe.'

'What if it were Tobin and he's been killing ever since?'

'Christ. That *would* bring the Government down. But if I start an investigation, it will be closed down before it begins.'

'I know, so why not let my tame policeman stir the pot for you? If he finds conclusive evidence of Tobin's guilt, I'll let you know and you can take the action required.'

'You know that if Tobin is involved, the case will never go to trial? Other action will have to be taken.'

Agnes hesitated for a moment, then said, 'Yes.'

'And you still want to pursue it?'

'Yes.'

'All right. What do you need?'

'A copy of your file on Tobin and his military service record.'

'Anything else?'

'Yes, whatever you have on Peter Carver, Phillip Morrison, Trevor Kent, Colin Spencer, the dead man Andrew Young and – a bit of a long shot – a disc jockey by the name of Jimmy Ravenal.'

'Very well. However, I do hope you're wrong about this. I've already got a Cabinet Minister sharing a prostitute with a Russian spy to contend with. Is that the lot?'

'I'd like to see your file on Inspector Burgess and—'

'I don't think he's involved. All he cares about is his career and keeping the people who can help him become ACC happy.'

'I'd still like to see his file. Also, any information you have on Eddie Bishop. My policeman seems to think that you might already be investigating him.'

'Why so?'

'Because he came across a Sergeant Richards who seemed far too much like an ex-public school boy to be a mere policeman in Birmingham CID.'

'We do employ people who didn't go to public school, you know. In fact, we have a number of very good grammar school chaps.'

'But not in the top jobs.'

Aubrey smiled thinly, 'Any revolution in Britain takes

time. You know that.'

'I suppose I do. But the files...'

'I never could say no to you, Agnes. You can have a copy of them all, for your eyes only, provided you join me at Simpsons for lunch. I haven't had a good steak and kidney pie for months. Claire's got me on a reduced meat diet, whatever that is. The files will be here by the time we get back.'

'That would be nice. Now, if you give me five minutes, I'll go and powder my nose.'

'Yes and I'll make a few calls.'

After Agnes left, Sir Aubrey flicked the switch on his intercom and asked Miss Florin to connect him with the Home Secretary on the secure line. 'Good afternoon, Home Secretary. I thought you'd like to know that I've just finished my meeting with Mrs Winters. I have agreed to give her Tobin's file along with one or two others.'

'Good. Let's hope that we have not misjudged the tenacity of Constable Collins and the well-attested skills of Constable Clark.'

'Quite so, Sir, but given Constable Clark's apparent willingness to burn down Bishop's house, I don't think we need concern ourselves on that score.'

'Quite so.'

'What about your man, Richards? Has he come up with anything?'

'Nothing that would be of interest to us, but he's made it clear to Clark and Collins that he is willing to help.'

'Good. Keep me informed.'

———

On the train home, Agnes continually reviewed her conversation with Aubrey. Yes, he'd been genuinely pleased to see her, but it was as if he already knew what she was going to request. Indeed, the production of all the files she asked for in under three hours seemed proof of that.

Not for the first time in her dealings with MI5, Agnes had

the feeling that she was being manipulated – but for what purpose, she couldn't tell. If Tobin was involved in Simone's death, it would be disastrous for the Government. Surely MI5 didn't want that. No, MI5 would want to hush it up; to protect the Government at all costs and, perhaps, pressure Tobin to resign quietly. However, as Party Whip, Tobin probably had enough information on government ministers and MPs to ensure that he held onto his job. If he was considered a security threat, it was entirely possible that a suicide or accident could be organised. But MI5 could have done that without risking an investigation by Collins and Clark. Why did they want Collins and Clark investigating Tobin?

When she alighted at Snow Hill, she was no nearer an answer.

Hockley, 12.00hrs.

Collins was impressed, considering that Clark had spent a good part of the previous night breaking into Bishop's house, he was full of energy and looking forward to having a quiet chat with Mr Carver. Standing in a doorway two shops down, Collins and Clark waited until they saw Davy leave on his delivery bike before they crossed the road and entered Carver's shop. Collins closed the door, slipped the bolt and turned the open sign to closed.

Carver emerged from the back at the sound of the door chime. His customer-friendly smile slid from his face when he saw who it was. 'Constable Clark and...'

'Collins.'

'Yes. Collins, of course. I didn't expect to see you again.'

'Well, that's it, Mr Carver. Normally wi don't come back to see someone a second time.'

'Unless we discover they've been lying through their back teeth to us,' said Collins.

'What do you mean lying to you? You asked me if I'd seen a

particular piece of jewellery and I said I hadn't. That was the truth then and it's the truth now.'

'Well, Mr Carver, we find that hard to believe, as we have a witness who saw you talking to Simone Winston on that very doorstep,' said Collins.

'That's right, Mr Carver. They recognised Simone from her photo,' said Clark.

'Now, Mr Carver,' continued Collins. 'I'm new to this job. Just off the boat, in fact. I like to trust people, but when I find a piece of jewellery in a recently murdered girl's bedroom and then discover that a jeweller who buys similar items has been talking to her on his front step, even I can add two and two together.'

'That's right, Mr Carver. Me mate here is real bright for a Paddy.'

'What is this girl supposed to look like? Maybe I've seen her. I see a lot of people in my business. However, I repeat that no one offered me any jewellery like the piece you showed me.'

'We dain't say that there were more than one piece, Mr Carver. Where did yow get the idea that there were more?'

'I just assumed there was. Look here, it was just a figure of speech.'

'You need to be careful there, Mr Carver. An assumption like that could get you hanged,' said Collins.

'Let me see this girl's photo.'

Collins passed Carver the snapshot of Simone that Mrs Winston had given him. Carver looked at the picture for several moments. Then, like a poor actor in a second-rate amateur production, a look of surprised recognition spread across his face. 'Oh, her! Yes, I think I do remember her now. She came in here one afternoon asking for directions. That's probably why you have a witness who says they saw me on the step with her. I was trying to direct her to the nearest number 8 bus stop.'

'That would explain it, except for one thing, Mr Carver. I think yow are a lying toe rag,' said Clark.

'How dare you take that tone with me. I shall report you.'

'I'm sure you will, Mr Carver,' said Collins, 'but it won't be the Superintendent you ring. It will be Bishop or the Major, won't it?'

Clark circled around Carver, sizing him up. From behind, he stretched upwards and whispered in his ear, 'Yow need to understand summut Mr Carver, me and my mate are going to cut the balls off you and your friends.' With that, Clark delivered a right jab into Carver's kidneys, which sent him slumping to his knees. Grabbing him by the hair, Clark pulled Carver's head back and said, 'I've had enough of yow, yow lying little sod. Yow've got until Sunday to tell us every-thing if yow want to avoid conspiracy to murder and aiding and abetting a murder charges. 'Cos on Monday, wi are going public with everything wi got.'

Picking up one of Carver's receipt forms from the counter, Collins wrote Clark's number on it. Turning, he said, 'We'll be expecting your call,' and stuffed the number into Carver's top pocket.

Outside, the two men raised their collars. The wind was blowing straight down the road, hitting their backs and pushing them forward. Even the heavy duty police coats were struggling to keep the wind out and both men needed to hold their helmets in place.

'Do you think he'll call?'

'It depends who he's more scared of, us or the Major. If I were a betting man, I think he'll call the Major – but he may call us. Either way, the one thing I can guarantee is that this lot will be over by Monday. Get your box on.'

Collins nodded. He understood exactly what Clark meant, but his only response was, 'What the feck is a box?'

Handsworth, 14.05hrs.

Leaving the station after Parade, Collins and Clark rehearsed some of the actions that Bishop or the Major might take and their likely response. After an hour and a half, both men felt that they needed a rest from trying to predict the actions of a psychopath and a child molester. The only thing they had agreed was that Collins would stay at Clark's house until this was all over.

They stopped off at Mitchell's Greengrocers for a cuppa and quickly found themselves sitting in the storeroom behind the shop, with a cup of tea and a round of toast each. 'What happened to that lad you pinched here?' asked Bert.

Collins quickly brought him up to date with Jamie's fortunes since they had found him in the storage shed two weeks earlier and Agnes' plans for his future education.

'Well, it sounds like he landed on his feet. Listen, you tell him that if he wants a Saturday job to come and see me. It's 8 until 6, and a quid a day. You heading up to the Hawthorns now?'

'Me favourite part of any day,' said Clark, with Collins shaking his head in pity.

Twenty minutes later, as they approached the New Inns, they spotted an old friend outside the Albion Cinema. Upright Freddie was still limping from his unfortunate accident, which had quickly entered into station folklore. Drawing closer, they could see that he'd nailed a couple of boards to an old orange box and painted the whole thing white. On the front, he'd drawn a reasonable representation of the crucifixion and written under it: "Repent and return to the Lord".

'Now I've seen everything. The wanker has gone and caught religion,' said Clark.

'What's going on, Freddie?' asked Collins.

Looking up, Freddie's face broke into a huge smile. 'Constables Clark and Collins, how wonderful to see you on today of all days. The Lord has blessed me with your presence.'

'That's sounds very nice, Freddie, but what are you doing here?'

'I've been saved, Constable Collins. You and Constable Clark were the tools that God used to deliver me from my wicked ways. For the Lord has said: "If your foot leads you into sin, cut it off. If your eye causes you to stumble, pluck it out. For it's better to enter heaven as a blind cripple than be cast into hell". My accident has removed the cause of my sins and I have you to thank for saving me from the eternal fires of damnation. Your presence here today is a sign that the Lord has blessed my mission.'

Collins and Clark exchanged looks, each desperate not to start laughing.

'I know what you're thinking, officers, but I will show you by my actions that I have become a true disciple of Our Lord Jesus Christ.'

'Well, it will be grand if you can turn over a new leaf. What about your court case, though? When's that due?'

'Next week and I fully expect to be sent to the Godless pit that is Winson Green. I welcome the chance to be punished for my sins. It will provide me with the opportunity to reach out to the lost souls who live in that loathsome place and show them what can be done when they embrace the Lord.'

'Well,' said Clark, 'yow will let me know how you get on with that after they release yow from the prison hospital.'

'Laugh if you will, Constable Clark, but the Lord will protect me.'

Collins noticed for the first time that a small knot of people had formed around them. Nudging Clark, he said, 'We'll be on our way, but we'll be watching you. Just in case old Satan pulls you back to his side.'

'Never. Never will I betray my new calling.'

As they moved away, Collins could hear Freddie start to engage with those watching. At least two of the small crowd recognised Freddie from before his conversion and intimated that if he turned up in their road he'd get his head kicked in.

'What do you think of that?' asked Collins.

'I dain't like being called a tool!'

Hockley, 17.35hrs.

Carver had resisted the temptation to call either Bishop or the Major from the shop. Nor did he leave the building to make the call, just in case he was being watched. Instead, he carried on as normal. He served his customers, spoke to suppliers, and waited. He waited until his usual closing time and five minutes later he put the Mk 2 Jag in gear and pulled smoothly away from the curb. He drove through Digbeth, turned left at the strip club on the corner and passed the Birmingham City Football Ground – all the time checking in his rear-view mirror to see if he was being followed. Satisfied at last that he wasn't being tailed, he took the A45 for Elmdon Airport and pulled over at the first phone box he saw.

Finding he was short of change, he bought twenty Senior Service from a newsagent before returning to the familiar red box. He was still worried that he was being followed, but he could see no suspicious cars or anyone who might be a copper. He dialled the Major's home first. The Major's wife answered and, after the usual pleasantries, she passed the phone over to her husband.

'Sorry to disturb you at home, but I thought you should know that our competitors are looking to close down our operation by Monday. I think we need to talk.'

As always, the Major took the news calmly. 'Thank you for letting me know. I think we should have a meeting with the other members at the Club tonight. Can you make nine?'

'I'll be there.'

Handsworth, 18.30hrs.

Agnes sat with her head in her hands. She had spent a fruitless four hours working through the MI5 files, first on the train and then here at home. She felt tired and dispirited. Pushing the files away, she stood up and paced the study, reflecting on what she'd learnt.

Tobin's file was the most extensive. *Nothing odd in that*, she thought. It's what you'd expect for a party whip who was privy to the secrets of the most powerful politicians in the country. Yes, it contained hints and allegations concerning his private life, but Agnes had to agree with Aubrey's conclusion that speculation wasn't proof.

She had been convinced that she would find something in his service file, and her hopes had soared when she read that he had been promoted from the rank of sergeant following the recommendation of his commanding officer. Picking up the phone, Agnes had immediately called Sir Aubrey for clarification. He listened and said he'd get back to her. Thirty minutes later, Miss Florin called back and, in the frostiest of tones, reported that, 'Sir Aubrey has been called to the Minister's Office and he's asked me to tell you that Sir Marcus was not a Sergeant-Major at the time of his promotion. He was a Sergeant.' Agnes could almost hear the pleasure in the secretary's voice as she delivered the disappointing news.

However, the file had confirmed the link between Tobin and Bishop, and had added an interesting detail that Victor's Colonel had not mentioned. Shortly before Bishop was shipped back to England to be demobbed, and just before a stock audit, there had been a fire in the stores that had destroyed a significant amount of stock and nearly all the records. *How very convenient*, she thought.

Agnes found two details of great interest as they revealed how strategic Tobin had been in creating his new persona after the war. Firstly, Tobin had changed his name from Mark Tobin to Marcus Tobin before he left the army, which meant that his discharge papers read Marcus. This supplied Marcus Tobin with a creditable war record on which to build his new life and invited all the right people to assume that Marcus was one of them and had been commissioned at the start of the war.

Secondly, following Tobin's election as an MP in 1952, Special Branch had dug into his background and found that when discharged from the army in 1946 his personal wealth amounted to £102,000. This indicated that his marriage had not been about money, but breeding, class and connections. The Burgess file was slimmer. He'd joined the police in 1939 and had remained in the force throughout the war. His record was one of a plodder who every now and then seemed to have a flash of inspiration that enabled him to tie up a big case. One of his early bosses had noted that "Constable Burgess is a very conscientious police officer who I would recommend for promotion to Sergeant, but no further. My reason for saying this is that his greatest weakness is a desire to please those in authority."

The idea that Burgess was a plodder yet able to land big cases intrigued Agnes. It was contradictory enough for her to spend the time it took to make and drink a cup of coffee thinking about it. By the time she resumed her seat, she was certain that Burgess either purposely hid his talents from view, which she accepted was the sign of a great police officer – to be underestimated by your enemies always gives the hunter an advantage over his prey – or he had outside help. Agnes' mind had turned to who benefited from the convictions that Burgess secured. Was it Bishop? Was Burgess removing Bishop's competitors? There was no proof, but Agnes made a note to check the relationship between Bishop's enemies and Burgess' arrest record.

Kent's early file spoke of an exemplary officer who clearly had a bright future ahead of him. In the Malaysian Emergency, he'd been mentioned in despatches for his work in defeating a heavily armed band of insurgents and capturing the leader, who unfortunately had been wounded and later died under questioning. Other actions were also highlighted by his commanding officer. There was only one blemish on his Malay record. A father had complained that Lieutenant Kent had raped his thirteen-year-old son while the boy had been in custody. The claim had been investigated and Kent exonerated.

Unfortunately for Kent, the case of the young girl screaming rape at midnight on the parade ground was not so easy to dismiss – even when she later retracted her story. By mutual consent, Kent and the Army had parted company. Since then, he'd made a very comfortable living as an estate agent selling expensive houses to people who only wanted the best.

Agnes had expected that there would be little of interest on Carver, Morrison and Young, but she was still disappointed at the dearth of information. All three were mentioned as contacts of Tobin, but that was not unusual given his prominence in the Conservative Party. None of them had a criminal record and the only official document about each was their National Service Record. It appeared that all three had done their compulsory two years and left without leaving an impression on the Army or a stain on their character.

Agnes looked at her watch. It was nearly seven. She closed her eyes and rotated her head to relieve the stiffness in her neck and shoulders. She was just about to switch on the radio for her daily appointment with *The Archers* on the Home Service when her Quaker sense of duty stopped her.

With a sigh, she picked up Tobin's file again. Although she'd read it three times she remained convinced that it contained the answer to the problem. She must have missed something. She decided that she'd use an old trick, learnt at Bletchley Park, and read the file from back to front. Placing the information in a different order might throw something up, jog in her mind or help her make a connection between two discrete pieces of information. Even if it didn't, it would at least keep her awake.

She turned to the last page of the file. It was the second page of Tobin's Initial Army Assessment. She started to turn over and read the report from the start, when she saw the pocket attached to the back cover of the manila folder. She'd noticed it before, but had ignored it on the grounds that it was clearly empty. On impulse, she pulled the pocket open and peered in. Lying at the bottom was a single sheet of copy paper folded in half.

Normally so calm, her heart fluttered as she withdrew the folded document. Opening it, she saw why it had been placed in the pocket. The flimsy paper had been torn at the punch holes and become loose. Instead of putting it back in the correct place, some clerk had stuffed it in the pocket.

There were just three lines of writing on the paper, but that was sufficient to tell Agnes who The Major was.

Birmingham, 21.00 hrs.

The Major, accompanied by Trevor, arrived at Bishop's office just before 9 pm. They had spent the journey from Warwick discussing their options and knew what had to be done. Bishop, Benny, Brian, Morrison, Carver and Spencer were already there when the two men walked in.

It was obvious to the Major that Carver was still nervous as he paced the floor. He'd already told his story to the group twice as if it would somehow relieve his fears. It hadn't. The glass of Scotch in his hand, and the three he had downed earlier in the evening, hadn't done the job either.

If Carver was scared, the others were concerned. Each, in their own way, had come to the same conclusion. Collins and Clark had to be killed, but Birmingham in the sixties wasn't Chicago in the twenties. You couldn't kill two coppers and expect to get away with it. The whole country would be after them.

Not that Bishop was worried about that. He was too busy

fantasising about how he'd kill that bastard Clark, who had defiled his home and burnt his book collection. He was looking forward to pulling the trigger. He'd already rehearsed the shooting in his mind several times. He'd start with the knees. One shot in each from behind, to cause maximum pain. Then he'd wait ten minutes, that would give Clark time to think about the pain he was in and what was yet to come. Then he'd shoot out Clarks' elbows. Again he'd take his time, before blowing the little fucker's balls off. To round things off, he'd put a hole in Clark's head. The more he thought about it, the more excited he became.

'Right,' said the Major. 'It would seem that Collins and Clark have become more than a nuisance. They've been warned off several times, but all that's produced is a small fire in Eddie's library and three idiots in hospital. They now pose a threat to the organisation and to every person in this room. They can't be frightened off and I very much doubt that they can be bought off. It only leaves us with one option. We kill them.'

'If we do that, we'll be arse deep in coppers,' said Carver.

'Possibly, but not if they disappear for good – along with, say, £50,000,' said Trevor.

'I think they have to be taken out,' said Bishop, 'but no one is going to believe that Clark pinched £50,000. Not with his record.'

'What they believe doesn't matter. The evidence will say they took it,' said the Major.

'And you can arrange this?' asked Morrison.

'Yes.'

'How?'

'The less you know, the safer you'll be if the plod do come calling after the event,' said Trevor.

'Trevor's right,' said the Major. 'I'll handle the details and I'll make sure that none of it can be traced back to any of us. Are we all agreed that they disappear?'

Everyone in the room nodded – even Carver, although he was the last to agree.

'While I get a drink, Trevor will outline what we discussed on the journey in.'

'Before they die it's essential that we find out what they know and who they've told in that order,' said Trevor.

'That's all well and good, but Clark isn't going to tell us anything and he's a dangerous little fucker. I say kill Clark and take Collins,' Bishop said.

'You're forgetting that we need them to disappear simultaneously. We can't have any evidence or witnesses fucking that up. The best and safest way to do that is to get them both on our turf. When we've finished with them, they can go in the crusher with a couple of cars.'

'Clark's not stupid. He won't just turn up at the scrap for a meet,' said Morrison. 'He'll smell a rat.'

'Of course he will,' said the Major. 'The trick will be to give him no choice.'

'And how are you going to do that?' asked Morrison.

'I'll tell you how,' said the Major.'

———

Handsworth, 22.20hrs.

Shift over, Collins and Clark headed for Agnes' house. Ignoring the bitter wind and the swirling eddies of snow that were being thrown up from the large front gardens they continued to speculate on how Bishop and the Major would react to their recent provocation and plotted a response to each possible scenario.

When Collins opened the front door he was confronted by Agnes standing in the hall.

Without any preamble, she said, 'I know who the Major is.'

Collins stopped dead and Clark bumped into him. 'You do?'

'Yes.'

'Well, who the hell is it?' asked Clark.

'It's your Superintendent Hollis.'

Clark shook his head, 'Na. It can't be. I don't believe it. I've known him years. He's as straight as they come.'

'That's probably why he's never been caught. Everyone believed he was above suspicion.'

'Where's your proof?' asked Collins.

'I'll show you.' Agnes led the men into the lounge. Laid out on the table were the files from MI5. 'My proof may not be sufficient to stand up in court. A good lawyer would argue that at best it's circumstantial, but unless you believe in coincidences, I think you'll find it compelling.'

Walking to the table, Agnes picked up two carbon copies. 'I found this,' she said, handing the copies to Clark. 'It's a copy of the report that Tobin's commanding officer sent to his Colonel recommending that Tobin's field commission be confirmed, It's signed by Major W. Hollis.'

Clark placed the report on the table. 'Hollis, good God. The devious cunning bastard. Yow know what this means, don't yow, Mickey?'

'Yeah, we can't trust anyone at the nick. He's bound to have others on his payroll.' Collins stopped, then, looking at Clark, said, 'Oh God, Richards.'

Clark immediately went to his breast pocket and pulled out the paper with Richard's number. 'I'll call him.'

'Why don't we go in the kitchen and make some coffee? I'm sure we could all do with it.' Collins followed Agnes, all the time straining to hear what Clark was saying to Richards.

Moments later, Clark joined them. 'He's coming round and he's bringing someone with him. He didn't say who.'

***

Agnes was still outlining the other information she'd found in the files when the doorbell rang. Taking no chances, Clark took up position behind the door as Collins opened it.

'You!' said Collins.

'Me,' said Hicks, stepping into the hall and taking his coat off.

Clark stepped out from behind the door, looked Hicks up and down, and said, 'Bloody hell. Is he working with yow?'

'It's a long story. I think we all need to sit down and put our cards on the table,' said Richards.

'Suits me,' said Clark.

'I think this could be a long night,' said Collins.

A few minutes later, and comfortably ensconced in the lounge, Clark said, 'Yow show me yowrs first, then I'll show yow mine.'

'I don't blame you for being suspicious of me,' said Hicks, 'but the truth is, we're all after the same bastard. However, we've been searching for him for different reasons.'

'Explain please,' said Agnes.

'Mrs Winters, Sir Aubrey sends his best wishes and apologises for not being entirely frank with you when you met earlier today. He told me to mention Hut 6 as proof of my bona fides.'

'You're MI5?'

'No. Until I saw Richards at the Station on Monday, I had no idea that MI5 was interested in the case. I'm on secondment from the Met's Anti-Corruption Squad. You see, ACC Morris has had his suspicions for some time about Hollis. Nothing specific and nothing concrete, but big cases were being lost because evidence disappeared or witnesses were reluctant to give evidence. He thought that Hollis might be taking backhanders, so he asked the Met for the loan of an officer. I was selected and the story about me being under a black cloud because of missing evidence was cooked up. We thought it might encourage Hollis to make an approach, but he didn't. I think he was suspicious of me from the start.

'My inquiry was going nowhere, but then you pair of reprobates found Simone's body. Hollis had to assign me to the case, but he demanded daily reports and wanted to know about every line of enquiry that we were following. Now that might be a bit odd, but for a Superintendent to let another force take the credit for solving a murder case is unheard of. I asked myself why he would do that. However, that was the wrong question. The real question was why the body was dumped in Handsworth and not in the middle of nowhere?'

'He wanted the body to be found under his jurisdiction,' said Agnes.

'Precisely. He wanted to control the investigation.'

'But when it led back to Stratford, he unloaded it to Burgess – someone he could trust to close it down,' said Collins.

'Exactly. I couldn't continue investigating the case. He was watching every move I made. It would have aroused his suspicions, but fortunately this pair were daft enough to take the risk and go on digging.'

'Like I said, Sir, strong in arm and weak in head.'

'All right. I'm a bit clearer about your role in all this, Sir,' said Collins, 'but how did you two link up?'

'Well, that was sheer luck,' said Richards. 'There were rumours circulating in London that certain influential people – politicians, civil service bods, police officers, councillors and others – were involved with a group working out of Birmingham. The word was that they could find you whatever you wanted, whether boy or girl, young or old, blonde or darkie. Well, that presents all kinds of security risks and lays the participants open to blackmail. We were concerned. Then, a promising junior minister committed suicide. He'd opposed the building of a new hotel in his constituency. When we went through his belongings, we found some pictures and a blackmail note. We were worried. If criminals had gained access to such photos, how long would it be before Russia or East Germany became involved?'

'So you weren't looking for the Major,' said Agnes. 'You were after a blackmail gang.'

'Correct. We thought it was Bishop who ran things, but slowly I heard things, hints and nudges about another top man. By the time you two burst into Bishop's office, I knew he was called The Major, but that was all.

'When I reported back to Wise that Bishop was battening the hatches down because of your visit, he was furious and insisted on reporting you. I didn't see any harm in it because I had no idea that Hollis was under investigation by the Anti-Corruption Squad. If I had, I may have put two and two together. Fortunately, Inspector Hicks saw me in the station and recognised me as MI5 and caught up with me in the lavatory – which, considering my cover, was somewhat appropriate. We arranged to meet outside the nick, but he suggested that I hang around and speak to you two. I couldn't tell you who I or Hicks were because there was a very slight risk that you, Constable Clark, were part of it. And obviously I didn't return to Bishop's, just in case he was connected with Hollis.'

'Yow know, Britain is well known for having the best spies in the world. Given how well wi manage to confuse and bugger up our friends, it's no wonder our enemies don't know what the hell we're up to.'

'So where do we go from here? Arrest the lot of them?' asked Collins.

'Unfortunately, it's not as simple as that,' said Richards. 'Somewhere, there is a stash of dirty photos – maybe even cine films – lying about. We should find that before we move on Hollis and his friends. Otherwise, they'll barter their way out of it.'

'So what are we going to do?' asked Collins.

'You're our best hope. You pair have really pissed them off. They're bound to respond and when they do, we grab them in the act. Then, we hope that one of them does a deal and tells us where the pictures are.'

'So we're the bait?' said Collins.

'The poor sods at the bottom of the heap are always the bait Mickey, but wi can't complain. Wi asked for it. At least this way, we'll have some cavalry to rescue us when wi fall in the smelly stuff.'

'Nothing is going to happen tonight, so I suggest that we all get a good night's sleep,' said Hicks. 'I'll get some lads down from London tomorrow to discreetly guard you pair. Until then, stay out of trouble and don't go into work tomorrow.'

'I'm staying the night at Clark's, just in case,' said Collins.

'Good idea,' said Hicks. 'I'll give you pair a lift.'

Thursday 28th February 1963.
Handsworth, 10.30hrs.

It was nearly 2am before Collins stumbled into bed in Clark's spare room. Oblivion came the moment he closed his eyes, but his sleep was restless. He dreamed of Ireland, of black doors he couldn't open and a banshee wailing as a headless man drove a taxi down O'Connell Street and a man who shot people on bus platforms with his finger and laughed when they pretended to be hit. On waking, the dream was vivid in his mind, but by the time he'd stretched, yawned and checked that it was nearly 10.30 on his watch, he'd forgotten it entirely.

He could hear Clark moving about in the kitchen and, finding his shaving gear, headed for the bathroom. Twenty minutes later, he was downstairs.

'The tea in the pot is fresh and I've left yow out an egg and a couple of rashers.'

'So what's our plan for the day?' Collins asked, laying the bacon in the pan and cracking his egg.

'I disagree with Hicks. I think wi should carry on as normal, but make sure wi have each other's backs covered every minute of the day. They'll have to come at us soon. I told 'em Monday would be the day of reckoning, so they don't have much time.'

'Aren't you afraid?' Collins asked.

'Scared? No. Nervous? Yam damn right I am. I'd be a fool not to be. Nerves keep yow on your toes and the adrenalin pumping. Them yowr friend. They keep yow alive as long as yow don't let them control you.'

'The only way I could be more on me toes would be to slip on a pair of stiletto heels.'

'I could imagine yow in a pair of stilettos. You've got the calves for them.'

'It's nice of you to notice. So few men do,' said Collins. Smiling, he relaxed a little and returned to the pan.

The phone rang and Clark went to answer it. 'It's probably Ruth. She can't go a day without hearing me dulcet tones, you know.' Picking the phone up, he said, 'Hello my lovely. What yow been up to?' His tone quickly changed. 'Sorry, Dad, I thought it were Ruth.'

He listened for fifteen seconds or so and then shouted to Collins. The cry sent Collins running into the hallway. He was shocked by the look on Clark's face. 'They've taken my Ruth.'

'How? When?'

Still holding the phone, Clark held up his finger for silence. 'No, Dad, I don't want yow to call the police. I'm not sure who wi can trust. I'll deal with it.' Collins could hear the sound of Mr Clark's voice, but couldn't make out what he was saying. Finally, Clark said, 'Don't worry, Dad, I'll get her back. And there ain't a snowball's chance in hell that I'm going to go off half-cocked on this. I'll ring you as soon as I have news. Tell Mom not to worry. Tarrar.'

'What happened?'

'She went to get the paper. The shop's only 100 yards from the house. When she came out, a big burly bloke took her arm and led her to a black car by the curb. The newsagent saw it all, but he reckoned that the bloke was one of me mates, another copper and he were taking her somewhere.'

'But how did they know where she was?'

'It's my fault. In all the excitement last night I never thought about Ruth. Everyone in the nick knows that I've got an Auntie Dianne. I've told hundreds of stories about her. It wouldn't have taken much for Hollis to find Di's address and check if Ruth were there.'

'Bastards,' said Collins, with feeling.

Both men were silent, reflecting on what this meant. When

Collins spoke, his voice was unsteady, 'You do know that they will kill her, don't you?'

'Yep. They won't even exchange her for me. Next to murder and treason, kidnap carries the longest sentence. No, them going to use her as bait and then kill us all.'

'In that case, you'd better work out a plan for how we're going to get Ruth out and kill every last one of those fuckers.'

Even in the midst of his concern for Ruth, Clark had to smile. It was the first time he'd ever heard Collins really swear in anger.

For the next twenty minutes, Clark sat writing at the dining room table. He wrote quickly and precisely. Every minute or so, another note or list would be laid on the table.

Collins remained quiet and ate his breakfast – not because he wanted to, but because he had a feeling it would be a long time before he ate again. Finishing up, he made two fresh cups of tea and added a shot of whisky to Clark's. He left it on the table without saying a word. Automatically, Clark picked the cup up and took a long swig. He didn't seem to notice the spirits.

When Clark stopped writing, he looked up and smiled. The smile sent a shiver down Collins' back. It was the cold smile of a man doing what he was best at and what he had been trained for. It was the smile of a killer on the trail of his prey. At that moment, Collins was certain that whatever Hollis, Bishop and the rest did to him or Ruth, Clark would find a way to kill every last one of them – even if it meant he had to die in the process.

'Mickey, I promised I'd get yow through your first months' probation if yow did everything I said. Well, lad, what's going to happen today or tonight is way beyond what yow signed up for. So take my advice and piss off. I won't think any the worst of you.'

Collins raised his head and looked into Clark's eyes. 'Bollocks. Show me what you've done.'

'Well, at least yow picking up the lingo. That's sommut,

I suppose. There's nothing here worth talking about yet. Them's just notes, lists and reminders to meself,' Clark said indicating the notes he'd made. 'Once we know where they want us to go, I'll be able to put different pieces together and make a plan.'

'Oh I get it. They're like building blocks. You've summarised everything you might need and then when you know where Ruth is being held you'll select the bits you need for your rescue plan. I suppose you learnt that in the Commandos as well.'

'No, it was summut I taught them. Of course, some other wanker tried to take the credit for it. I can't stand bastards who try that on.'

'So all we can do is wait?'

'No. There's a couple of things wi need to do. First we're going to have a drink with an old army mate. You'll like him. He's another mad Celt but from this side of the water, Jock Cronin. Then we'll pay a visit to Mr Bishop's offices. I doubt we'll find anyone there. They'll all have gone to ground until this thing is finished. However, wi might find something useful. First, I need to phone Jock.'

Clark went into the hall and Collins started to read the various notes and lists, trying to work out their individual and combined significance.

Once connected, Clark put on his poshest accent. 'Good morning. I'd like to speak to Mr Cronin, please. Yes, the Chief Engineer. Yes, I know he's a busy man, but if you tell him it's Mr Clive Clark calling he'll take my call.' There was a pause of about forty seconds before Clark heard the familiar Scottish burr. 'Well, if it isn't the wee shite from the Black Country. How are they hanging?'

Clark gave the expected response, 'Around me ankles,' and heard Jock give a high-pitched giggle in response – a giggle that was totally out of keeping with the look, sound and temperament of the man, and which had landed him, Clark and other assorted members of the unit into more than one punch-up.

'To what do I owe this great honour?'

'I need your help. It's Ruth and it's serious.'

The response was instantaneous. During the war, the unit had developed its own code for describing events and situations. Serious meant life or death. No one used it unless they meant it. 'Tell me what you need.'

'Thanks, Jock.'

'Fuck that, laddie. Just tell me what you want.'

'Four sticks of explosives. Anything you've got will do. I can cut them in half if it's a problem, but I want to make as big a bang as I can. Detonators for each stick, plus a few spares and some sort of timing device for each.'

'Anything else?'

'Not unless you've got some spare ammo lying about that I could throw on the fire.'

'OK. It's 11.20 now. I'll see you in the Garden Gate at 13.00hrs. Is that soon enough?'

'That's fine,' said Clark, and hung up.

Hamstead, 13.00hrs.

Jock was not difficult to pick out in a crowd. He stood a full head taller than anyone else in the Garden Gate bar, and his wild red hair and bushy beard marked him out as a Scot from 100 yards.

When he shook Collins' hand, the grip was vice-like but surprisingly gentle. This was a man with nothing to prove, least of all to himself. Collins liked him on sight. Picking up the four drinks he'd already bought, Jock led the way to the small lounge behind the bar. Closing the door, he slipped the bolt. 'Barry will see that we're no disturbed. So, who's this?'

'That's me mate, Michael Collins. Wem in this together.'

'Fair enough, but what is *this*?'

'Wi don't have time to explain everything, but me and

Mickey have been investigating the death of that little half-caste girl found on Hill Top.'

'I read about that in the *Mail*.'

'It turns out that a lot of important people were involved in her killing one way or another. Some of 'em are coppers and they've been trying to close us down.'

'But you'd na backed-off and now they've taken Ruth. Is that it?'

'That's about it.'

'When do you think they'll call you?'

'Probably late tonight. They'll want to do it under cover of darkness and get rid of us before first light. That's how I'd do it.'

Jock took a sip of his pint. 'Well, you can count me in. In fact, I can probably get one or two of the lads to join us by six.'

'I appreciate the offer, Jock, but these fuckers are going home in a box. As coppers on the case, wi stand some chance of claiming that wi got involved in an unexpected fight and I were able to grab a gun. That wouldn't hold water if half me old unit were there backing me up.'

'OK. How many do you reckon will be there?'

'Maybe seven or eight,' said Collins.

'Seven or eight! Are you out your fucking minds? There's no way you can get them and get Ruth out of there unharmed. I'm coming.'

'Jock, I can't ask—'

'Ask? You're not asking. I'm telling you. I'll play guardian angel.'

Clark considered what Jock had just said. He was right. With an angel on board, Ruth's chances of getting out of there unharmed had just soared to 50/50. 'OK. Wi can use you.'

'Right, now that's settled, let's have a pint. Here, lad, have one of Clark's. I did na know he was bringing a friend.'

'He doesn't drink.'

'A name like Michael Collins and he doesn't drink?'

Collins shrugged his shoulders and smiled. 'What can I say? I'm the black sheep of the family.'

Even without Collins' help, the four pints disappeared within twenty minutes. Clark wanted to keep a clear head, so Jock was forced to consume three. He didn't seem to mind.

Before they left the pub, Jock called his secretary and told her he was taking the rest of the day off. Outside, they climbed into Jock's new Land Rover and drove to Clark's house. Jock lifted a wooden crate from the back and strode up the path. Inside, he placed the box gently on the kitchen floor. Removing the straw on top, he started to unpack the contents.

Collins had trouble keeping his mouth from falling open as Jock placed a dozen sticks of dynamite, detonators and timers on the table. There was also a carton of .303 shells, one Sten gun with five ammunition clips, two .455 Webley handguns and a pair of limpet mines.

It was all too much for Collins, 'How the feck did you manage to get all this stuff together in less than two hours?'

With a straight face, Jock replied, 'Did I no mention it? I'm the Chief Engineer at Hamstead Colliery. It means I'm in charge of all explosives.'

'Since when did coal miners need Sten guns and limpet mines?'

'Them? Simple. Me and a few lads do a bit of charity work in Africa every now and then you'd be surprised what you need in the bush.' With that, he winked at Collins.

'This stuff is bostin. Just what wi need. Me and Mickey need to go and check out Eddie Bishop's Office. Wi won't be long. Can yow sort this stuff out and have a quick decca at me lists and ideas. Yow'll find them on the dining room table. See what I've missed?'

Collins was still thinking about African charities and limpet mines when he and Clark pulled away in the Land Rover.

Clark had been right. Bishop's office was deserted and was locked up as tight as a miser's last pound note. Every door and window seemed to be locked and bolted. Working their way to the rear of the building, Collins drew his baton and broke a small window, which provided light to the ground floor corridor. Reaching in he released the clasp and climbed through.

Once inside, both men stood and listened to the building. There was plenty of noise from outside and the structure itself creaked, groaned and whispered incessantly. But, there was no one in the building. Collins was sure of that. However, that didn't mean that there wouldn't be any nasty surprises.

'OK, we'll start with Bishop's office and work our way down,' said Clark.

The secretary's office was exactly as Collins remembered it. Nothing seemed out of place and the filing cabinets were still full. Bishop's office was different. There wasn't a single sheet of paper on or in his desk. Even the few reference books that had sat behind his desk were gone.

'Mickey, see if you can find a safe.'

A quick but through search of both the walls and floor failed to reveal any safe.

'He's got to have a safe somewhere.'

'I don't think it's here,' said Collins.

'OK, let's try downstairs.'

This time, neither man worried about picking the locks to the bedrooms or bar. They just kicked the doors in. It was the first time Collins had ever actually kicked his way into a room and it gave him a momentary sense of power and pleasure as he did what he'd previously only seen his heroes do on screen. He smiled at his own childishness and laid into the door to the blue room with real enthusiasm. The door gave way on the second kick and there was a satisfying bang as it bounced off the wall. The room was exactly as Collins remembered it. He started in the most obvious place and checked behind the picture. Nothing. The floor also revealed nothing. He sat on the bed. Somewhere in this building, there had to be a safe. His thoughts were interrupted by a shout from Clark. 'I think I've got something, Mickey.'

Collins joined Clark at the open door to the storeroom. 'Do you see what I see?'

Collins scanned the room. 'Fresh scuffmarks on the floor. Someone's been in here recently. It looks like they were moving that filing cabinet.'

'Yows know, Mickey, I'm beginning to think yow ain't just another ugly face. Come on, give us a hand.'

Rocking the cabinet to and fro, they were able to pitch it onto one corner and walk it away from the wall to reveal an unlocked safe. Collins - started to pull the door wide open when Clark grabbed his hand. 'Steady lad.' Taking his torch, Clark wriggled behind the cabinet until he was lying flat on the floor. Shining his torch through the 2-inch gap, he was able to confirm that there were no wires attached to the door or any object sitting on either of its shelves. The safe's only contents was a brown paper envelope, which was identical to the one he'd received on Tuesday night.

Clark ripped the envelope open. There was a single sheet of paper and a picture of Ruth. She was sitting on a chair with her hands tied behind her back and her ankles tied to the chair legs. Her skirt had been rolled up to reveal the top of her stocking and panties. Clark felt the blood rush to his face. Anger rising he fought for control and handed the picture to Collins and started reading the note.

Surprise, you little piece of shit,

Not a bad piece of pussy, your missus. Nice legs and I like her pink knickers. She wouldn't be out of place in Spick and Span. Mind you I don't think I could shag it. I mean, my standards would have to be below rock bottom to fuck a kike. Pity Hitler didn't finish the job he started.

Nothing has happened to your little Jew bitch yet and nothing will as long as you play ball. We'll exchange her for you and that Irish fucker. Be at H & T Scrap Metal Merchants, off

Kirby Road tonight at 11.

Don't bring any friends or she dies.

'Are you all right?'

Clark took a deep breath and let it out slowly. The tension and anger visibly drained from his face as he did so – or so it seemed to Collins. 'I'm fine. Bishop's just trying to wind me up. Hoping it will throw me off me game and I'll make a mistake.'

'Do you think she's still alive?'

'Oh yeah. She's too valuable to harm just yet.'

'How do you mean?'

'They need to find out what wi know and who we've told before they kill us all. The best way to do that is tie me to a chair and make me watch as they do you and Ruth. They'll want her looking her best for me. That way, when Bishop, or one of the brothers, punches her in the face for the first time, the results will have maximum effect on me.'

'How the hell do you know all this?'

'Cos that's what I'd do.' Clark looked down at his boots and, keeping his eyes averted, said, 'They'll soften me up by starting with yow and, if what I have in mind is going to work, yow'll have to take a beating.'

'For how long?'

'I can't be certain. Maybe five or ten minutes.'

'I'd be grateful if you could make it five.'

'I'll do me best.'

'Good enough. Let's get out of here. With my skin and bones on the line, I think you need to discuss your master plan with Jock. You do have a master plan, don't you?'

'Oh yeah, I got a great plan. Trouble is it'll probably fall apart in the first five minutes.'

'Now he tells me.'

As they drove home, Clark took a quick detour and drove slowly past H & T Scrap Merchants. It was locked up and looked deserted. Collins couldn't help but think it was a great place to commit a murder.

By the time Collins and Clark returned, the six o'clock news was on, and Jock had attached a detonator and timer to every stick of dynamite, stripped and cleaned each gun and checked that the handcuffs Clark had left on the table were working properly. He'd also found time to review Clark's ideas and add a few thoughts of his own.

'How did it go?'

Clark handed him the note and said, 'There were a picture of Ruth with it.'

Jock didn't ask to see the photo. Instead, he said, 'OK. Now that you know where the bun fight is going to be, we can firm up your plan. What do you have in mind?'

Clark told him and, for the next three hours, the men went over each detail. Checking, assessing, changing. All agreed that Bishop would draft in some additional heavies to protect the office and that these would have to be taken out before any rescue could be made.

'How many do you think he'll use?' asked Jock.

'Can't say for sure. Outside, he'll probably go for three or four. Inside, he'll want Benny and Brian for the dirty work and I'd be surprised if Hollis wasn't there. Wi may also have Kent to contend with.'

'Why him and not Carver or Spencer?' asked Collins.

'He's got experience of this. It ain't going to worry him. Carver and Morrison have probably never seen it before.'

'Right.'

'If there are four goons outside that will slow things down a bit' said Jock.

'Yeah, I know. How long will yow need to deal with 'em?'

'Difficult to say. Five or ten minutes. It'll depend on how dispersed they are.'

Collins tried to imagine what it would be like if he had to take a ten-minute beating. He wasn't sure he would be able to resist for that length of time. He wasn't even sure if he could survive such a beating – not if Benny and Brian were set loose on him. He tried to put such thoughts out of his head and concentrate on what Clark and Jock were saying.

As the discussion went on, Collins realised that a lot of what was being said was for his benefit. Both men in their own way were trying to prepare him mentally for what was to come. However, he accepted that he would never know how he'd react until the firing actually started. He offered up a silent prayer to St Michael that he wouldn't freeze.

Jock used the last half-hour to show Collins how to use the Sten gun. 'OK, Mickey. If you forget everything else, what are the four things you have to remember about the Sten?'

'Safety off, point and fire, and additional clips will be near your cap.'

'Yow forgot one thing,' said Clark.

'What?'

'Don't shoot me.'

At 9.15pm, Clark looked at Collins and Jock. 'Ready?'

'Yep.'

'Then let's go.'

At 9.45 pm Jock parked the Land Rover in the Ice Rink's half-empty car park. Another 45 minutes and the kids would be streaming out heading for a quick fumble up some alleyway and then home before the last bus went.

From the top of the hill the three men were able to look down on the huge mounds of metal that were H & T Scrap Merchants. The yard was bordered on two sides by darkened factories. No nightshift – good. To the rear, the frozen canal ran the full length of the yard. With travel on the canals impossible, there were no barges in sight. The only road in and out of the yard reminded Collins of a hangman's noose. Drivers had to loop around the yard's office before heading back to the gate. Collins hoped it was a good sign. He wanted it to say: "We're going to close the noose on you". But he realised it might also be saying: "You're going to be strung up by your balls".

Clark broke into his reflection. 'OK, me and Mickey will do a quick recce of the place and sort out the canal fence. Jock?'

'I'll do a full recce and try and identify the number and location of all the guards. You'll know when I've taken them out.' Turning to Collins, he held his hand out, 'I'm going to do me best to keep the time down. You hang in there for as long as you can, laddie, but don't be a hero. Drip-feed them stuff if you have to, OK?'

Collins remained silent and just nodded, afraid that if he spoke both men would hear the fear in his voice.

A t 11 pm exactly, Collins and Clark walked up to the locked junkyard gates. A single floodlight illuminated the men and gates, throwing the area beyond its glow into total darkness. Almost immediately, Collins heard the footsteps of two men approaching from off to his left. As they stepped into the light, he could see they each carried a sawn-off shotgun.

Without speaking, the shorter of the two guards placed his gun on the floor. The second guard moved to his friend's left to ensure that his field of fire remained clear. As he approached the gates, the shorter man said, 'Stand back. Hands up where I can see them.' Only when Collins and Clark had complied did he open the gates. Backing off, he said, 'Come in, close the gate and place your hands on it, legs spread. No messing or I'll have you.'

Collins and Clark did as they were told. The man started with Clark and immediately found his baton, which he lobbed into the darkness. Seconds later, he found his handcuffs. He dropped them on the floor, but his mate said, 'Use the cuffs. It'll save tying the bastards up.' After cuffing Clark, hands behind his back, he spun him around and tried to knee him in the groin. But he was only partially successful, as Clark had seen it coming and had moved his thigh just enough to block the worst of the attack. Even so, he collapsed on the ground, giving a very good impression of a man in desperate pain.

'That's for Tony. You damn near bust every tooth in his head.'

Turning to Collins, he repeated the process – but instead of trying to knee him, he pushed Collins in the direction of the office. 'Move.'

After retrieving the shotgun, the guards marched their prisoners down the 70 yards or so to the office. Both kept a safe distance from Clark. Neither wanted to join Shepard and Co in the hospital.

On each side of the road were huge mounds of junk. Several of the largest piles were made up of old cars. Other mounds were comprised entirely of copper boilers, rods and wires. Two huge piles were given over to yesterday's household appliances, including boilers, zinc baths, mangles and pre-war mowers. One low-lying but widespread pile was made up of gigantic factory presses and pumps that would have taken days to move.

As his eyes adjusted to the darkness, Collins thought he'd seen a movement off to his right but he wasn't sure. He hoped to God it had been Jock. In one clearing, a long hydraulic crusher lay open. A tall crane, used exclusively to feed its cavernous jaws, stood sentry beside it. For a fear-filled instant, he wondered if that was where he and his friends would end up. However, a quick look at the little man beside him was all the reassurance he needed. He was going to get out of this alive.

Much of the scrap was covered with a thin layer of fresh snow from that afternoon's flurry. Underfoot, the snow had long since become mixed with the black cinder track to make a filthy slush. Collins stumbled and nearly fell as he stepped in a pothole. 'Feck,' he said, as his boot filled with freezing black muck and water.

The guard who'd hung back at the gate laughed, 'Don't worry about it, mate. A wet foot's the least of your problems.'

As they drew close to the office, the road opened out into an apron around which four cars were parked. Collins recognised Hollis' Ford Cortina. They stopped and one of the guards shouted 'I got 'em, Boss', as if he personally had hunted and captured the two men single-handedly.

Another guard appeared from the back of the shed to have a look at the coppers who'd put Shepard in hospital. They didn't look so tough now.

Only three, thought Collins. *Good.*

The door of the brick shed opened and Tobin and Hollis emerged. *No Benny or Brian*, thought Collins. *Maybe I will get out of here in one piece.* However, no sooner had his hopes been raised than the brothers appeared from the darkness. *Feck, this is not going at all well.*

'Inside,' said Benny, a revolver aimed at Clark's spine.

'Where's me wife?'

'Inside,' said Brian.

Collins wasn't sure if it was an answer to Clark's question or an order. Either way he stepped forward.

The shed consisted of two rooms. The first was used as an office; a glass hatch with a sliding window had been cut into the gable end, so that men could present their chits and get paid for their deliveries without the need to traipse into the office. On the right was a second room. Brian opened it and pushed Clark in.

The room was used for brewing up. There were a couple of small tables and several cheap chairs. Bishop was waiting for them, his hand resting on Ruth's shoulder. Kent sat in the corner, cleaning his fingernails with a Swiss Army knife.

Ruth was still tied to the same chair that Clark had seen in the photo. Whether to humiliate her or to enrage Clark, her dress had been pushed up to her waist.

'Yow all right, love?'

Ruth just had time to say 'Yes,' before Benny smashed his forearm into the back of Clark's head.

'Naughty, naughty,' said Bishop. 'No talking unless I say so.'

Bending down, he ran the back of his hand along the inside of Ruth's exposed thigh. His fingers lingered on the naked flesh between the top of her stockings and panties. All the time, he held Clark's eyes. If he'd expected threats and curses from the little man, he was disappointed. Clark was silent. Impassive. Waiting. Disappointed by the lack of a reaction Bishop said, 'String 'em up.'

Ruth reacted automatically to the command, 'No, please.'

Bishop laughed, 'Don't worry, you little Jewish bitch. I didn't mean it that way. Anyway, what did I say about talking without permission?' The slap across Ruth's face wasn't particularly hard, but the sound bounced off the concrete floor and brick walls like the ricochet of a rifle bullet.

Brian gave Bishop the revolver before undoing one of Clark's cuffs. 'Raise your arms, short arse.' Clark did as he was told and Brian looped the handcuffs over a pipe that ran the width of the room, before snapping the cuff over Clark's wrist for the second time. After checking Clark was secure, he did the same with Collins.

Moments later, Hollis and Tobin entered. It was the first time that Collins had seen Tobin in the flesh. He was exactly as you'd expect a successful politician to look. A little under six feet tall, he was solidly built with well-defined features, neatly trimmed hair and moustache, and brown eyes that proclaimed he was a man you could trust. His trustworthy image was enhanced by a dark blue Crombie overcoat and a grey, three-piece suit from Savile Row that screamed good taste and dependability. In his hand, he carried a large pilot's briefcase.

'I warned you pair to lay off, didn't I? But you had to play the bloody heroes,' said Hollis. 'Well, from here on in, it's going to get really painful for the three of you.' Hollis nodded and, without warning, Benny hit Collins with a sharp right just below the ribcage.

Unprepared, Collins had no time to tense his stomach muscles before the blow landed. He doubled over as far as the handcuffs would allow and tried desperately to suck some air into his empty lungs.

Ruth cried out. 'No.'

Before Ruth's cry had died out, Brian hit Collins with a straight jab to the kidneys. This was worse for Collins. He felt his back arch and a sick, nauseating pain spread swiftly across his stomach. *Feck*, he thought, *I'll be pissing blood for a week.*

Holding his hand up, Hollis walked over to Clark. Standing just inches from his face, he said, 'Now that we understand each other, Constable Clark, I want you to tell me who you've discussed this case with and what you told them? If I don't like your answers, Benny and Brian are going to keep hitting that sack of Irish shit until he's either a vegetable or dead. Then we'll start on that pretty little wife of yours. Understand? You know that you're going to talk in the end. You've seen enough of these things to know that people always do. So, save your friends and yourself a whole load of pain and talk now.'

'And then what? Yow'll let us go?'

'You know I can't do that. You knew it when you walked in here. However, I'll make sure it's quick and painless and that Eddie and his friends don't get to enjoy the undoubted pleasures of Mrs Clark.'

'Yows going to swear that on your honour as a police officer?'

'Don't get smart with me, Clark. It'll only make things worse for you.'

Collins had regained his breath by now and said, 'I don't see how they can get much worse from where I'm hanging. '

'The brave little soldier willing to risk his life for his friend's wife. Is it friendship, honour, loyalty or the chance to get into Mrs Clark's knickers down the line that motivates you, Constable Collins?' asked Hollis.

'Fuck you,' said Collins and he spat at Hollis, the saliva coming to rest on his shoe.

Hollis' open backhand caught Collins flush on the cheek-bone. Collins felt his head snap back and a light show suddenly erupted in his brain with reds, pinks and yellows projecting onto his closed eyelids. A buzzing sound set up home in his left ear, liked it's new accommodation and decided to stay. Returning to Clark, Hollis asked, 'What's it going to be – more pain or quick oblivion?'

Clark looked past Hollis and latched onto Ruth's terrified face. 'It'll be all right, love. Just remember the first time we met.'

Hollis stepped back and nodded for Benny and Brian to go to work on Collins.

Watching from behind a huge copper urn, Jock saw Clark and Collins disappear into the office. As expected, the outside guards had all appeared to see the men who had taken out Shepard and friends. Jock was pleased to note that there were only three of them.

As soon as the door was closed, the two guards who'd escorted Clark and Collins headed back to the front gate. The other one returned to his position at the side of the office, from where he could see most of the front and back of the building.

Jock worked his way around to a position where he was behind the side guard. Unfortunately, the guard was standing with his back to an old Ford Popular. There was no way that Jock could take him from behind. Stepping into the path that separated cars from household junk, Jock looked for a place to hide. He found it behind a metal cabinet.

Finding a wheel rim, he threw it at a household junk pile that was two or three yards away. The guard heard it, stepped out of his improvised sentry box and looked down the path. Seeing and hearing nothing more, he returned to his cubby-hole, content that it had been a stray cat or a fox.

Lazy bastard, thought Jock, before flinging a nearby tyre

high up into the mound of household junk. It landed with a soft thud and started to roll down the mound, creating a series of satisfying noises in its wake. This time, the guard did investigate. Two yards past Jock, he stopped and shone his torch down the path. Nothing. As he began to turn, a huge arm caught him around the neck and squeezed. Even before the man's brain could register what had happened, Jock drove his knife into his back in an upward motion and then pulled it sideways, rupturing his heart and lungs. Unable to breathe or cry out, the man's death was quick and silent.

Checking his watch, Jock saw that three minutes had elapsed since Collins and Clark had entered the office. He must hurry.

B rian and Benny were working Collins over slowly and methodically, with a professional care to detail. They knew it was no good concentrating on just one area at a time. The pain had to be spread around with a brief respite between each blow, so as to allow Collins time to experience the hurt and for Clark to reflect on the harm his silence was doing to his friend.

Ruth was crying softly. Her head rested on her chest as she tried to blot out the dull thud as fist met stomach or face.

Collins tried to pray. To beg for help, for the strength to hold out, but the only image that came to his semi-conscious mind was one of Agnes standing in the garden. It was the day of the snowball fight and she was laughing as Collins and Clark were rolled in the snow by Jamie and the women. The weak winter sun had bathe her in a golden glow that had taken Collins' breath away. Unable to smile, Collins concentrated on remembering every tiny detail of the image.

Holding his hand up, Hollis waved Benny and Brian aside and approached Collins. 'Listen, lad, I admire your courage, but you're wasting your time and your looks. Once we start in on his missus, your mate is going to tell us everything. So why not save yourself a whole load of grief and tell us what we want to know?'

Collins raised his head. He wasn't sure how much of this he could take, but he was damned if he was going to show any weakness in front of Hollis. 'Sure, Superintendent, what's the point of being the best looking corpse in the graveyard?'

'OK, have it your way.' Stepping back Hollis nodded at Trevor. 'Start with the left hand.'

Trevor smiled and, stepping forward, took a pair of electrical pliers from his inside pocket. Waving them in front of Collins' eyes, he said, 'I brought these with me as I thought they might come in handy.'

Bishop laughed and Tobin said, 'Get on with it; we don't have all night.'

Reaching up, Trevor took the little finger on Collins' left hand. The nail had been cut short and it took several seconds for him to work the pliers far enough under the nail to give him the purchase required. Leaning into Collins, he said, 'Shall we count? Five, four...'

Collins' scream was deafening in the enclosed space. His whole body shook with pain and he wriggled on his handcuffs like a pike on a hook as the nail was pulled off.

'You fucking bastard. I'm going to kill yow for that, so help me God,' shouted Clark.

'Save me the histrionics. If you truly cared about your friend, you'd tell us what we want to know,' said Hollis.

Jock found the remaining two guards easily enough. They were enjoying a cigarette out of the wind and out of sight of anyone passing the front gates. At a little over 20 yards, with the tops of their cigarettes burning brightly, he couldn't miss them. The difficulty was in getting both of them before the second target dived for cover. He'd have to be quick.

Jock moved closer. With each step, he checked that there was nothing on the floor between him and his targets. If he did miss the second man, he wanted to be on him as quickly as possible.

Raising his silenced revolver Jock lined up his first shot. There was only a yard gap between the two men. He was confident that he could get both men. Taking aim, he took a deep breath and let it out slowly. As the last of the air left his body, he fired. Without looking to see if the first man was down, he adjusted slightly and fired again. He heard both bodies hit the ground, followed by a low moan. One of the guards was still alive. He approached the figures on the floor cautiously. The man was keening softly, holding what was left of his shattered jaw in his hands, blood and teeth slipping through his fingers. He saw Jock at the last moment and there was just enough time for a pleading, beseeching look to appear in his eyes before Jock put him out of his misery.

Jock checked his watch. Five and half minutes had elapsed. He had to hurry. Unhooking his backpack, he selected three sticks of dynamite. They were already set to go off. Flicking the switch on the first, he left it beside the bodies and inches from the bottom of a pile of household junk. He threw the second stick on top of another junk pile fifty yards on and positioned the final one just outside the pool of light provided by the office lights.

Keeping in the shadows, he ran around to the back of the office. The quarter stick of dynamite he had hidden earlier was still in the overturned zinc bucket. From his very quick survey of the office earlier, he estimated that it should be enough to do the job and hopefully not kill everyone in the building. He had no way of being sure, but there was no turning back now.

⬥

Benny hit Collins with another right jab to the face. Collins felt his head snap back and heard his nose break. Blood, snot and mucus spread across his face.

Tobin approached him and said gently, 'Constable Collins,

it seems your friend doesn't give a fiddler's fuck about you. Why not save yourself any more pain? Who have you talked to?'

With blood and sweat in his eyes, and the buzzing in his ears getting worse, Collins was unsure who was talking. His head fell backwards and he mumbled something. Tobin moved in closer, 'What was that?'

Collins' head snapped forward and caught the MP flush on the nose with his forehead. 'Up yours...' said Collins, before Benny landed a combination of head punches. A straight right closed his left eye and a left hook broke a back molar, which he promptly swallowed. Another punch in the stomach made his head sink to his chest. He was exhausted. He was finished and he knew it. Although, if he could just give Jock another thirty seconds...

'Stop it,' screamed Ruth.

'You heard the lady, lads. Step back.' Bishop stood up and casually placed his hands on Ruth's shoulders. Bending down he cupped Ruth's right breast in his hand and grinned at Clark before he said, 'You know, Michael – can I call you Michael? – you're a good-looking lad, but another few minutes of this and no woman is ever going to look at you again.' Releasing Ruth's breast he produced a flick knife from his pocket and snapped it open. 'Especially when I slice off your dick and shove it down this bitch's throat.'

Bishop's laugh was cut short when a loud explosion seemed to lift the office off the ground, shake it and then drop it back in place. The initial sound was followed by an avalanche of metal tumbling to the ground. Two more explosions quickly followed before the wall behind Bishop billowed inwards, exploding in a shower of bricks, dust and rubble over the gangster. Half-conscious, Bishop fell against Ruth, protecting her from the worst of the blast.

Swirling smoke and dust filled the room. In those few precious seconds of confusion, Clark pressed the barrel of the lock on one cuff and they snapped open. He twisted the cuff and released a curved 3-inch piece of steel with a sharpened spike. It fitted snugly into his clenched fist, the spike extending out between his first and second fingers.

Clark lunged at the closest brother in the chaos, stabbing him four times in the neck within two seconds. Benny or Brian was dead before he hit the ground. Clark really didn't care which it was.

The second brother lunged for Clark, but was cut down by a short burst of Sten gun fire before he had moved four feet. Jock appeared through the hole in the wall and fired into the ceiling, sending anyone with any sense running for the door. Tobin grabbed his briefcase while Hollis pushed Bishop out the door.

Jock tossed the Sten and a revolver to Clark, picked up Ruth and disappeared into the night. Even in his pain, Collins grinned. Jock might not look like it, but he made one hell of a guardian angel. Clark checked for the cuff keys in Collins' breast pocket and undid the lock. Once released, Collins started to slip to the floor. Clark caught him and held him upright.

Two more explosions went off down the road, followed by the sound of more falling metal. No one would be leaving by the front door, which meant that Hollis, Tobin, Bishop and Kent were all somewhere in the yard.

'Are you all right, Mickey?'

'We got Ruth?'

'That we did.'

'That's all that matters. I reckon we've got them bottled up.'

'Oh yes, wi got the bastards.'

'OK then. Give me the Sten and I'll go and play sentry.'

'Are yow sure you're OK?'

'I'm fine.'

'OK, but after this wi get yow to a hospital.'

'Fine, but for now will you go and get the bastards for me?'

'It'll be my pleasure, but don't shoot me. Got it?'

'I think so.'

Collins left the office by the hole that Jock had created. Seeing the black beret resting on the upturned bucket, he bent down and picked up the spare clips and pushed them into his pockets. Looking at his watch, he calculated that it had been less than three minutes since the first explosion. The police wouldn't be here for at least seven minutes. Twelve, if they were lucky.

Stumbling forward on unsteady legs, Collins looked around for something he could use to steady himself and found part of Ruth's shattered chair. Jock clearly hadn't wasted any time untying her. Despite the pain, he smiled when he realised that with luck Ruth and Jock were already well on their way to the Land Rover and safety.

The freezing night air helped to clear his head, but with clarity came pain. Every bone in his body hurt and each step was a study in exquisite agony, as was each breath that allowed the cold air to attack the exposed nerves of his broken and missing teeth and three nails on his left hand.

He desperately wanted to lie down in a warm safe bed and go to sleep, but he couldn't let Clark and Jock down. It was his job to close the back door. He plodded on, the pain in his side growing worse with each step.

After the longest three minutes of his life, Collins found the spot in the fence where he and Clark had removed three rails earlier. A nightlight burning in the warehouse across the canal illuminated the gap and provided an irresistible lure to those desperate to get the hell out of here before the place was crawling with police. All he had to do now was find a place to hole up and wait for the scum who were deserting the sinking ship.

He found his spot behind an industrial water tank and slumped to the ground exhausted. Once seated, Collins found it difficult to keep his eyes open despite the pain and cold that had invaded his body and was making him shake uncontrollably. It was only the sound of Kent slipping on the ice and landing hard against a half full barrel of nickel offcuts that alerted him to his presence. Breathing hard and swearing under his breath, Kent hauled himself to his feet. Looking around, he saw the gap in the fence and headed for it.

Collins waited until the killer drew level with where he was standing, before he said, 'That's far enough. Hands in the air and I won't blow your fucking head off.'

Kent stopped and turned towards where the voice had come from. 'Well, if it isn't Constable Collins. It seems we underestimated you and Clark.'

'You've been underestimating us for centuries.'

'What's that supposed to mean?'

'Nothing. Put it down to a concussed brain.'

Three shots rang out to the right of where Collins was standing and both men jumped.

'I assume that your gun is real, which is interesting. If it was your friend Constable Clark holding that gun, I'd be dead by now. Concussed brain or not, I don't think you have it in you to kill a man in cold blood, so I'm going to leave now. You can't stop me because you won't shoot and you're too weak to fight me.'

'I am too weak to fight. And as for killing a man, you may be right. I don't think I could kill a man in cold blood, but I could wound one. So, stand still.'

'So what are we going to do? Stand here until you collapse or the police arrive?'

'Maybe. Tell you what. I'll let you go if you answer two questions.'

'Fire away,' said Kent. 'No pun intended.'

'Why did you kill the girl with Young? It was you, wasn't it?'

'Yes, it was me,' said Kent. 'As for why, I would have thought that was obvious. She was in the wrong place at the wrong time.'

'For God's sake, she was only a kid. Didn't that bother you?'

'No. Go to Africa or the Middle East and you'll soon see

how cheap life is. In a lot of places I've been to, a life is worth no more than the price of a bullet. Can I go now?'

'You haven't answered my second question. What was her name?'

'Bishop told me it was Janet Crosby. Now can I go?'

'Just one more thing.'

'What?'

'How much do you think your life is worth? Is it worth half-a-crown?'

What?

'That's the price of a Sten gun bullet, according to Clark or did he say it was 1/6d? I'm not at me best just now. Either way I think your life is worth more than 2/6d,' said Collins.

Kent smiled in relief and moved towards the fence. As his hand grasped the fence, Collins said, 'Don't you want to know how much I think your life is worth?'

Kent turned, 'What?'

'I think it's worth seven and six.' There was just enough time for fear and understanding to register before Collins shot Kent three times in the chest. The force of the short burst propelled him though the gap in the fence and across the narrow towpath. Falling backwards, he landed on the ice. His body lay spread-eagled on the ice. Motionless. Then, much to Collins' surprise, there was a loud crack as the ice gave way and tilted. Slowly Kent's body slid into the filthy, black canal. Collins felt his legs start to tremble and sank to the ground, his back resting against the rust-ravaged water tank. He tried but it was no use. He had to close his eyes.

Clark had followed Hollis, Bishop and Tobin out of the door. There was no sign of Tobin, but from the porch he saw Hollis and Bishop disappear down the path towards the canal. Instead of following them, Clark turned right. If he was correct, they would come out about fifty yards from where Collins was standing guard. He needed to get there first and set off at a fast jog.

With no torch, Clark stumbled on the uneven track and nearly tripped twice over junk that had become dislodged from their mounds by the shock of the explosions. When he reached the spot where he thought Hollis and Bishop would emerge, he took three deep breaths, letting the air out slowly. By the time he'd finished, his breathing had returned to normal. All he had to do now was wait quietly. It wasn't long before he heard the sound of footsteps and heavy breathing to his right, he stepped further back into the shadows.

The two men emerged from behind the last mound of junk and started across the 16 or so yards of snow-covered grass that separated them from the canal fence. Clark waited until they were up to their knees in the soft drifts before shouting, 'That's far enough. Turn around slowly. Hands in the air.'

Reluctantly, both men complied. 'Now, come back. Keep yowr hands where I can see them.'

As he retraced his steps, Hollis asked, 'So, what now? Are you going to arrest us?'

'That's the general idea.'

'Good. You and I both know that this case is never going to come to trial. At most, I'll be forced to resign and lose my pension. Far better if you let us go now and early next week you'll get a nice little parcel in the post containing £25,000. What do you say?'

'I'd say, stuff it.' As he spoke, Hollis stumbled. Bishop immediately grabbed him under the arms and tried to pull him up.

'Hands,' screamed Clark. 'Show me yowr hands.'

Regaining his feet, Hollis pushed Bishop aside and levelled a .38 revolver at Clark. He managed to get off one shot before Clark hit him with two bullets in the stomach. The revolver dropped from Hollis' hand and he sank to the ground. Clark saw the shock register in the Superintendent's face as he realised for the first time that he might die on this non-descript piece of waste ground behind a scrap yard.

Before Hollis hit the snow, Bishop launched himself at

Clark. Keeping low, he caught the smaller man in the midriff with a rugby tackle and both went sprawling on the cinder track. The impact of landing with Bishop on top of him drove the breath out of Clark's body and his gun went spinning into the darkness.

With his knee pinning Clark's right arm, Bishop's hands encircled Clark's throat and he squeezed. Clark looked up. Bishop's eyes were bulging with effort and spittle was forming in his mouth, 'I'm going to kill you, you fucking bastard, and then I'm going to find that fucking bitch of yours and kill her too.' As he spoke his fingers dug deeper into Clark's neck.

Clark responded by trying to break Bishop's grip with his free hand while smashing his knee into the middle of the gangster's back. The periphery of Clark's vision was starting to go black. Another few seconds and he'd be unconscious. "Think," his mind screamed.

Clark's attempts to break Bishop's hold became weaker. His knee thrusts feeble. His eyes turned up. His entire body jerked in unison and then he lay still. A smile appeared on Bishop's face and he loosened his grip imperceptibly. That's all Clark needed. He threw a left hook that landed high on Bishop's head and simultaneously drove his right knee into his back. Bishop's body weight shifted and that momentary loss of balance allowed Clark to pull his right arm free and smash a right hook into Bishop's face. This time he connected with the nose and felt it implode under his fist. Bishop fell off him and Clark rolled to his right.

Both men regained their feet at the same time. Slowly, they circled each other, looking for an opening or a weapon they could use. Bishop found his on the floor half hidden by a bin of metal offcuts – a two pound lump hammer. Kicking the bin over, he grabbed it.

Grinning, he started to advance on Clark – all the time swinging the hammer in a wide arc. 'Come and get it, copper. What's the matter? Scared of a little hammer? I thought you were a hero or sommut.'

Each swing forced Clark to back up further. Soon he would be pinned against a pile of washing machines and mangles, and there was nothing there that he could use. Despite the situation Clark's mind was clear, calm and cold. While part of it monitored what Bishop was doing, the rest looked for a way to kill the man who just minutes earlier had put his hands on Ruth. Clark had no doubts that Bishop was going to die in the next few minutes. The question was how.

Then Clark saw his chance. In his anger Bishop was swinging wildly and at the end of each swing he was off balance for an instant. It might just be enough time. Behind Bishop, Clark could see the spilt bin of metal offcuts and decided it was worth a try

He waited for Bishop to swing, then threw himself into a forward roll beneath the hammer and passed Bishop on the right. Coming out of the roll, he made a grab for a bar of metal, but Bishop was too quick and Clark was forced to back up. Almost tripping on a length of copper wire in the process, he scooped it up.

Bishop swung again and this time the hammer only just missed Clark's head. His mind made up, Clark waited for the next swing. Instead of backing up he stepped into the swing. Bishop's arm hit Clark in the back. As it did so, Clark elbowed him in the face. There was the satisfying sound of a cheekbone breaking.

Distracted by the pain, Bishop failed to withdraw his arm. Clark pirouetting 180 degrees, and grabbed Bishop's wrist with his left hand. Simultaneously he brought his right forearm up with as much force as he could generate and struck the elbow. Clark's scissor blow broke Bishop's elbow joint and sent a sliver of shattered bone though his arm. He screamed and dropped the hammer.

Clark released Bishop's broken right arm and elbowed him in the face again. Bone and gristle gave way and Bishop's broken nose exploded for a second time in a fountain of blood. Stepping back, Clark opened his hand and using the thenar space, between his thumb and index finger, rammed his hand into Bishop's windpipe. Bishop sank to his knees, his one good hand scrabbling at his throat. Unable to breath or move. Not sure if the blow was fatal, fear and panic gripped him and he felt warm urine spread down his leg.

Powerless, unable to move, Bishop watched Clark wind the copper wire around his gloved hands. Somehow, in one last desperate attempt to live, he staggered to his feet and tried to run. But all he could manage was a drunken stumble and after a couple of steps he fell to his knees. He felt Clark loop the wire around his neck and tried to get his hand in the way of the deadly noose. Clark slapped it away and brought his elbow down on the top of Bishop's head. Black lights swam before his eyes and he almost passed out. But unfortunately his luck had run out.

Clark placed his knee in Bishop's back and pulled the wire tight. The thin strand of copper bit deep into Bishop's neck. His left hand scrabbling at Clark's wrists, his head jerking from side to side, eyes and tongue protruding and shoulders moving, Bishop tried to throw himself onto the floor. But Clark had him and pulled his head back further. For an instant Bishop's eyes met Clark's. It was in that moment, staring into Clark's calm, grey, cold eyes that held no emotion or hatred, that he finally realised how much he'd underestimated the little man. Clark wasn't a copper or even a soldier, he was an expert killer. A professional who took no pleasure or excitement from the act, only a grim satisfaction from exercising his deadly skills.

Bishop's body slumped forward, his arms moving like two pendulums across his body. The blood from his hands and nose mixed with the black slush of the cinder track. Clark gave one final tug on the wire, then released it. Bishop fell face down in the black slush and lay still.

The wire had cut through Clark's gloves, and the palms and fingers of his hands were bleeding. But he felt no pain. That would come later.

Slowly, he became aware of Hollis moaning and crying, 'Help me.'

Clark looked around for his Webley and found it. Only then did he walk over to the wounded man. 'Please help me. Call an ambulance.'

Clark sank down onto his haunches. Lifting Hollis' hands away from the wound, he opened the policeman's coat and saw dark blood oozing through his shirt and jacket.

'I got lucky. Two in the liver. I reckon yow've got ten minutes provided yow just lie there and keep pressure on it, or five if yow move about. It's up to you, Boss.'

'Please call an ambulance. You can't let me die like this.'

'Well, that's where yow're wrong. You were willing to kill me, me wife and me friend. You can be damn sure I can let yow die.'

***

Collins could hear the faraway sound of police bells. They'd be here in a few minutes. Where the feck was Clark? They needed to get out of here. Peering around the edge of the tank, he was just able to make out a figure of a man about 35 yards away. He was carrying something. It took Collins a couple of seconds to realise that it was Tobin and that he still had his briefcase with him.

Suddenly, Tobin stopped and listened. The police bells were nearer. He seemed to be thinking and started to look around. Mind made up, he clambered up a pile of household scarp for about 6 feet and pulled open a door. Quickly, he manhandled the briefcase into the space and shut the door. Dropping back to the ground, he looked around and found a large stone which he placed on the ground beneath the stored briefcase.

Standing still, he listened again for the bells, then hurried over to the fence. Collins raised the Sten gun, but his hands, arm and entire body were now shaking so much that he couldn't keep the gun still. Shock was starting to take over. He took a deep breath and let it out slowly, just as Jock had told him, trying desperately to steady his hands.

For a man his age, Tobin was remarkably agile. He clambered up the fence and dropped to the ground before Collins was able to get off two shots. Both went wide of their mark and Tobin didn't wait around for a third. He set off at a sprint, following the canal towards Five Ways.

Collins resumed his place behind the water tank and waited for Clark to arrive. He didn't have long to wait. Clark announced his arrival with a hissed, 'Mickey, yow there?'

Collins stepped forward and nearly stumbled. 'Mickey, lad, you look terrible. Come on, let's get you to hospital'

'Not yet. Tobin was here a minute ago. He stashed his briefcase in that pile of junk over there. He marked the spot with a rock and shoved it into something about 6 feet off the ground.'

'OK, I'll take a dekko. You wait here.'

'I didn't plan on going anywhere.'

Collins slumped against the tank as his friend went to retrieve the case. Minutes later, he returned with the briefcase and a smile bigger than the Cheshire Cat's. 'I could almost kiss you, Mickey lad. He stuffed it in an old cooker and wi got it. You hear me? Wi got the lot. Photos, cine films, diaries, everything. This is his blackmail stash. Without it, he's dead in the water. He must have emptied Bishop's safe, thinking the police might find it if they came looking for us.'

Collins gave the best impression he could of a smile and said, 'OK then. Let's go and finish this.'

'Mickey, we've got to get you to hospital. Tobin can wait.'

'Fuck that. We end this tonight. Wasn't that what you said?'

'Yes but--'

'No buts. Get to a phone and tell Victor we'll meet him at the paper. He needs to copy everything in that case. Then, we pay Sir Marcus-bloody-Tobin a visit. I reckon he'll head for home and call his protection officer. What do you think?'

'It's as good a place as any to start.'

Leaning on Clark, Collins managed to make it back to the

Ice Rink. The Land Rover, Jock and Ruth were gone, and in their place were Agnes and her Rover 100. She was shocked at the sight of Collins, and demanded that they drive directly to the Accident Hospital. It was only when Collins opened the door and started to get out that Agnes relented and agreed to drive the men to Stratford.

On the way, Clark gave her an abridged and sanitised version of events, but it was easy for Agnes to fill in the details given the state Collins was in. Clark provided even fewer details of what had happened after he had caught up with Bishop and Hollis.

Collins adopted the same approach and said nothing about shooting Kent. He just described how the man had tried to cross the canal and had fallen as the ice broke beneath him.

Agnes knew enough not to challenge the stories. She'd learn the truth soon enough. Right now, she wanted to get Collins to a hospital as quickly as possible and that meant going to Stratford first. On the near empty roads, she drove as fast as the ice-covered roads would allow.

Friday 1st March 1963.

Stratford-upon-Avon, 01.30hrs.

Victor was waiting for them when they drew up outside the delivery bay at the back of the paper. He was shocked when he saw the state Collins was in and helped Clark half carry, half drag him into the boardroom. 'My God, what have they done to you, poor lad?'

'It looks worse than it is,' said Collins.

'No it fucking doesn't. Stay there while I get a bowl and some painkillers.' Victor brushed past Clark and gave him a withering look, which seemed to ask how he could have let Collins take such a beating.

When he returned, he had a bowl of hot water with added Dettol, soap and two face towels. 'Here,' he said, 'take these before we start. They'll help the pain.' Collins took the pills and looked around for something to drink. Agnes went to the sideboard, picked up the soda syphon and squirted a couple of fingers of sparkling water into a cut-glass tumbler.

By the time Victor had gently cleaned the blood off Collins' face and hands, the pills had started to work and he was having a hard time staying awake.

'What did you give him?' asked Agnes.

'A couple of my painkillers.'

'Opiates?'

'Yes, but he really does need to see a doctor.'

'I know, but he won't go until we've seen Tobin,' said Clark. 'He's the last of them.'

Victor didn't need to ask what Clark meant by "the last". 'Very well. What have you brought me to copy?'

'The best present yow've ever had,' said Clark, and pushed the briefcase across the floor with his foot.

Victor opened the case and a fire ignited in his eyes. 'As the

Yanks say, it's the mother lode.'

'That it is, but can yow get it copied quick? I want Tobin before he does a deal and disappears.'

'Do either of you know anything about photography?'

'I do,' said Agnes.

'Fine, you come with me while Mr Clark here keeps an eye on his friend.'

Clark looked at Collins, who was asleep in the chair. The concern in Clark's eyes was obvious. Victor read his thoughts and said, 'He'll be fine.'

Forty minutes later, Victor and Agnes returned to the boardroom to find Collins awake but groggy. 'Victor, I've no idea what you gave me, but I feel grand. Even the pain feels grand,' said Collins, smiling like a hideous idiot.

Victor exchanged looks with Clark and said, 'You'd best be going. The pills will work for about three hours. You need to get him to a hospital before they wear off.'

Clark held out his hand, 'Thanks, Victor, for everything. It's probably best that we don't meet again. Things will go barmy after yow write your story.'

Victor took Clark's hand in his, 'It's been an honour and a privilege to have worked with you and Michael. Make sure you tell him that when he recovers.'

'I will. Good luck.'

'You too.'

'Goodbye Victor,' said Agnes, and kissed the old man on the cheek. 'I'll pray for you.'

'Come on, Mickey, wi have one last toe rag to sort out,' said Clark, pulling Collins to his feet. 'Then yow can sleep.'

It was nearly 3 am when Agnes pulled up outside Tobin's house. Clark insisted that she remain in the car just in case Tobin was armed. There was one light on and the front door was ajar. Collins grasped the briefcase in his left hand as Clark helped him out of the car. His steps were unsteady, but supported by Clark he made it to the front door. The light came from the first floor. Collins could hear the sound of muffled voices. Tobin had company. Clark withdrew his .455 Webley and, holding the gun in his right hand and supporting Collins with his left arm, the two men moved up the stairs.

Clark propped Collins against the wall and opened the door. Tobin was seated at his desk, finishing a telephone conversation. He hung up and said, 'Come in, Constable Clark, and bring your young friend. I've been expecting you.'

Clark stepped into the room. Collins remained against the wall, with just his face showing around the door jam.

'This gentleman on my right is from MI5. I think you know him.'

Clark nodded at Richards.

'He's been sent to look after me. He's just finished talking to the Cabinet Office. You see, I've done a deal.'

'I'm sorry, Clark, but you've had a wasted journey. The PM has agreed that in return for not divulging certain material, Sir Marcus is to be allowed to resign before the next election and live out his life in peace and seclusion.'

'Is that right?'

'Yes it is, Constable Clark. The material I have could destroy the Party and even make it difficult for Labour to form the next Government. The PM won't allow such information to fall into the wrong hands. So you and your Mick Irish friend can fuck off out of my house. In future, remember that when you play against the big boys, you need a few aces up your sleeve.'

'You mean like this,' said Collins, stumbling into the room and flinging the briefcase across the room. Landing on its side, the case popped open, spilling pictures and cine films across the carpet.

Tobin's face drained of colour and he slumped back in his chair. Rallying, he said, 'That means nothing, even without it I know enough to cause one almighty stink. And, as the

PM knows, in politics the accusation can be just as damaging as the proof. The Government will never risk putting me on trial.'

'I'm afraid that's true, gentlemen,' said Richards. 'The Government can't allow this matter to become public knowledge.'

'So he gets away with it?' asked Collins.

Tobin laughed at the expression on Collins' face. 'You have a lot to learn, officer. We always get away with it.'

'Who's we?' asked Collins.

'Your betters, my bog-dwelling friend.'

'Is that the way it works in England?' asked Collins, his head spinning. It seemed to him he'd asked this question before, but he couldn't be sure. Everything was becoming fuzzy and the room was spinning.

'I'm afraid so,' said Richards. 'Money, power, position and family connections can buy you a lot of protection in this country. Unfortunately, for Sir Marcus, he has no real family connections to talk of.'

Tobin's head snapped up, his face clouding with confusion.

'He just married into an old family. That makes a world of difference. Also, his power has just been greatly depleted thanks to you, Constable Collins. You may be an upstart, but I must admit I admire your persistence and I'm sure the PM will be grateful.' Drawing his gun, Richards held it against the side of Tobin's head.

A look of shock, followed by bewildered realisation and fear flashed across Tobin's face. Then, the gun exploded and a bullet sliced through his brain.

The noise was deafening in the small room and Collins jumped at the explosion. Clark caught him as he started to slip to the floor.

'Constable Clark, I suggest that you take your friend to a hospital. I'll stay here and arrange matters so as to make it look like a suicide, which Superintendent Burgess will be only too pleased to rubber stamp. Off you go now.'

Clark moved to pick up the contents of the briefcase. 'Sorry, gents, but you'll have to leave the briefcase here.'

Clark laid the half empty case on the table, slipped his arm under Collins' arm pit and lifted him up. Turning, the two men left the room. Unseen by Richards, Clark was smiling. *Underestimated us again*, he thought. *They always do.*

Sunday 3rd March 1963.
Handsworth, 21.00hrs.

Dudley Road Hospital discharged Collins after two days of extensive treatment. The doctors had wanted to keep him in for at least another forty-eight hours, but he'd managed to annoy, beg and cajole every nurse and doctor he spoke to until they had finally relented and agreed to release him.

On admission, he'd been treated for four broken ribs, a broken little finger, three missing nails, a broken nose, seven chipped, broken or missing teeth; multiple and severe bruising and contusions and a serious case of concussion. He would be off work for at least three weeks.

Doctors, nurses and dentists had worked on his injuries for nearly eight hours and every time one of them had left the treatment room, they were accosted by either Agnes or Clark who wanted to know how he was. Later, they were joined by Ruth, and instead of two anxious friends making a nuisance of themselves the medics now had three.

By 1 pm on Saturday, Collins had been tucked up in bed with enough painkillers to re-float the Titanic. He had slept for nearly twelve hours straight, with Clark, Ruth and Agnes keeping a constant vigil throughout. None of them had wanted him to wake up without seeing a friendly face.

As Clark pushed Collins to the waiting car, he asked, 'How are you feeling, Mickey?'

Collins twisted in his seat, grimaced with the pain and said, 'How the feck do you think I feel? I feel like I've done ten rounds with Sonny bloody Liston and then been run over by a bus. That's how I feel. Just get me home, you mad yam yam.'

'Yam yam? Where the hell did that come from?'

'I've decided to learn a foreign language. I'm hoping to get some free lessons from me mate.'

'Strewth, yowr concussion must be really bad.'

—◆—

Between them, Agnes, Ruth and Clark helped Collins up the stairs. Sheba didn't want to be left out but only managed to get under everyone's feet. Although Gloria and her fellow guests did not know the full story, they knew that Collins had saved a woman's life. It was enough for them to greet him like a returning hero and Gloria threatened him with "a free one" when he felt better.

Despite the warm welcome, each step was an exercise in pain. His newly set nose throbbed and his ribs screamed in agony with every breath. He wondered when the painkillers he'd taken before leaving the hospital would kick in. But, he was alive and he'd be better in a week or two, which was more than could be said for Hollis, Tobin or Bishop.

'We can put him in my room. It has its own shower and toilet,' said Agnes, pushing the door open.

Clark manoeuvred Collins through the door and gently sat him down on the bed. A low moan escaped his bruised lips. 'Sorry, kidda; soon have you in bed. Then you can sleep until morning, when the stiffness will make it ten times worse.'

'Up yours,' mumbled Collins.

'Whatever yow say, Mickey. Whatever yow say. Now I'm going to lie yow down and get yowr legs on the bed. OK?' Throwing the eiderdown to one side, Clark slowly eased Collins down and swung his legs onto the bed. 'Right, I'm off. I draw the line at taking any man's trousers off, so I'll leave Agnes to tuck yow in. See yow tomorrow.'

Ruth approached the bed and, laying her hand gently on Collins' cheek, kissed his forehead. 'Thank you,' she said and smiled.

Collins couldn't lift his head to return her kiss, so instead he squeezed her hand and said, 'My pleasure.'

At the front door, Clark turned to Agnes. 'Look after him, yow hear. Yow don't find his kind more than once in a lifetime.'

'I know,' said Agnes and kissed Clark on the cheek, before embracing Ruth.

Returning to the bedroom, Agnes found Collins asleep. She slipped in beside him and pulled the eiderdown over them both. At first, she held him like a child. Later, as he drifted in and out of sleep, she held him like a friend. Then, as the first weak rays of sunlight cast shadows on the wall, she held him like a lover.

———•———

Epilogue

In the immediate aftermath of the events of Friday 1st March, very little appeared to happen. Collins was visited by Inspector Hicks and ACC Morris. Neither mentioned how he had sustained his injuries, but both wished him a speedy recovery.

Despite a careful survey of *The Birmingham Post, The Birmingham Mail* and *The Express & Star*, not a single story appeared about what had taken place at H & T Scrap Merchants – even Agnes was impressed at how the Government had been able to impose a total news blackout of the whole affair. 'Clearly,' she suggested, 'the power of the D Notice has not diminished since the war.'

It was only on the following Thursday that all hell broke loose. For the first time in its 148-year history, *The Stratford Bugle* published a special edition. The six-page special had been written entirely by Victor Begley under great secrecy, and printed and distributed by himself and four trusted employees. The paper was distributed free to residents of Stratford-upon-Avon and a copy was sent to every national paper in Fleet Street, along with Reuters, The Press Association, and the London representatives of *Le Figaro* and *The Washington Post*. Victor's reasoning was simple: even if the Government stopped publication of the story in Britain, the news agencies would ensure that it was published abroad. Each outlet contacted was given permission to reproduce any or all of the contents free of charge, provided that Victor Begley's byline appeared above the story.

In great detail, along with numerous pictures of the guilty, the paper outlined the story of how – starting with fraudulent misappropriation of funds at the end of World War Two – Chief Superintendent Hollis, Sir Marcus Tobin MP and Edward Bishop, a notorious gangland leader and others had colluded to take over the illicit trade in sex, gambling, protection and blackmail in Birmingham. Police officers had been used to ensure that any attempts by London gangs to move into the City were repulsed.

The paper explained how the whole criminal enterprise had been brought to its knees by the dogged investigation of a small number of concerned citizens who had carried out an informal investigation into the death of Simone Winston (14) and Janet Crosby (15), both of whom had appeared to have died following sexual exploitation by one or more men associated with the gang.

During their investigation, the citizens had gained evidence that proved the gang had used photographic evidence of senior public figures engaged in illicit sexual activities with young boys and girls to extort money, gain power and protect themselves from police action.

A vivid description was given of the final "shoot out", as Victor described it, at H & T Scrap Merchants, when factions of the gang fell out and violence erupted.

The story attracted national and international attention and, despite intense pressure, Victor refused to reveal who the "concerned citizens" were or who had provided the material for his expose. Strangely, neither the Birmingham nor Warwickshire Police interviewed Victor in the days that followed publication, although MI5 did take tea with him at his home.

It was only in April when the full extent of the *Profumo Scandal* became apparent that the *Babes in the Wood Affair* was pushed off the pages of the Sunday papers.

Simone Winston was buried on the 11th of March. Collins, Clark, Agnes, Hicks and several other police officers from Thornhill Road attended the service. When Mrs Winston went to the funeral home to settle her bill, she found that it had been paid in full by a well-wisher who wished to express their profoundest sympathies.

Collins returned to work on the 1st April 1963. No one

asked him how he had been injured or what had happened at the H & T Yard. They didn't need to. The grapevine had manufactured a story that was part *Gunfight at the OK Corral*, part St Valentine's Massacre and all Jimmy Cagney and Humphrey Bogart in *The Roaring Twenties*.

At the end of May, Jimmy Ravenal cut short a gig in Birmingham when he fell down two flights of stairs and suffered severe bruising to his face and body along with two cracked ribs. Although he occasionally visited Birmingham in the following years, he never established the same contacts and support that he developed later in the UK.

On the 4th October 1963, Victor Begley was laid to rest. The service was held at the Holy Trinity Church, Stratford-upon-Avon where Shakespeare had been baptised and buried. Local dignitaries were out in force, as were a number of hacks from Fleet Street who had come to salute one of their own. Dressed in civilian clothes and tucked away in a corner of the packed church, Collins, Agnes, Clark and Ruth each prayed for the old man in their own way. All of them hoped that he'd found satisfaction in breaking a story that had been headline news around the world.

A week later, Collins and Clark received identical brown paper packages about the size of a house brick. Inside was a letter from Victor Begley.

Dear Michael,

If you're reading this, then I'm in the ground. I just wanted you to know that I died happy. It was wonderful to land the biggest story of my career at the end of my life – a true crowning glory you might say.

I loved every minute of working with you, writing the story and the madness that followed publication. I even enjoyed being interviewed by MI5. They were actually very decent to me. No thumb screws or truth serums. In fact, I had the feeling they were glad to see the end of Sir Marcus – sodding – Tobin.

It's sometimes difficult for a good man to stand up for what he believes, especially if it puts his livelihood, and that of his family, at risk. You did that and to help you do it again, if need be, here's a small gift from my Fuck You Fund. I got the idea from Humphrey Bogart who didn't always get on with his producers and directors, so he saved enough money to enable him to tell them, "Fuck off, I'm leaving" should he want to. I hope the cash will give you the financial freedom you need to always do the right thing.

The cash has been in a floor safe at home for years. So don't think you have to reveal it to my executors or pay tax on it. It can't be traced. Talk to Michael Griffiths at Griffiths and Collins Accountants about how to invest the money without anyone knowing about it. He'll be expecting you.

With great respect,

Your friend,

Victor.

Beneath the letter was £7,000 in twenty pound notes. It was enough to buy a large four-bedroom house in Sutton Coldfield and still have change left over.

The End
... until
A Death in Summer: 1965

A Death in Summer: 1965

Prologue

The small man in the corner of the storeroom was immersed in his work. What he was doing was not complicated but he found enormous satisfaction in completing the work perfectly. He knew how lucky he was. Most men had a job which they endured. He had a career, a calling a vocation. How fortunate it was that he'd discovered his life's work when he was just twelve years old.

As he wound the lint around the cardboard his mind went back to his twelfth birthday. The August night had been hot, moist and sticky. Thunder was in the air but the storm had yet to break. The birthday boy lay on top of the bed sheet. The bed clothes crumpled at his feet. He was naked accept for his underpants which he'd pulled down to his knees. He was gently massaging his limp penis. He'd been doing this for the last twenty minutes but nothing had happened.

Just that afternoon his only friend, George, had bundled him into the boy's toilets after school and said that he wanted to show him something which would change his life forever. Locking the cubicle door, George unzipped his flies and pulled out his semi-erect penis. 'You're twelve. It's time you learned how to wank,' he said with all the confidence of someone who had discovered how to do it just three weeks earlier. It only took a couple of pulls on the lamb's tail for George's cock to grow long and hard. The man remembered how the crown of his friend's cock had been blue and shiny. A couple more tugs and George doubled over and gave a low moan as if in agony. A thick, white fluid splashed against the cubicle wall and dripped onto the floor.

Grabbing a fist full of toilet paper, George wiped himself dry. Embarrassed now, he said, 'That's how you wank off. Try it tonight and you'll thank me tomorrow.'

Well he'd tried but nothing had happened. He was about to turn over and go to sleep when he heard screaming from outside. Pulling his pants up he rushed to the window and peeked out onto the street below from behind the curtains. Mrs Sims, the pretty young blonde housewife from across the road, was standing in front of her house screaming. Thick black smoke billowed out of the open front door and flames were visible in the front room and the bedrooms.

The young boy's gaze shifted from Mrs Sims to the licks of flame he could see and back again. Both fascinated him. Mrs Sims was nearly naked. She was wearing a pair of white nylon knickers, a white bra and a red suspender belt with a white rose in the middle of the waist. One stocking had become detached and lay crumpled around her left ankle. She was the most beautiful sight he'd ever seen. The tears on her face glinted in the light from the flames. Her glistening face contorted in pain as she screamed for someone, anyone, to help her children trapped inside the burning house.

The road was starting to fill with people and the boy saw his father rush out. Pushing the window up he stuck his head out and smelt for the first time the heady mix of burning leather, carpet, cloth, wood and paint. As people gathered around Mrs Sims, a man carrying his jacket and tie, his shirt tail outside his trousers, slipped out of the side entry to the Sims' house and hurried away towards the main road. The boy knew it wasn't Mr. Sims. He worked nights at the hospital.

People were now shouting and running about as if noise and movement would do some good. Over the din he heard his father shout, 'Someone get up to Mrs Smith's at 23 and call 999 we need an ambulance and the fire brigade.' A young man in his twenties sprinted away from the group and headed for the only phone in the road. As he left, two men wearing busmen's uniforms ran around the corner, the back of their cream and blue bus blocking the bottom of the street.

The boy immediately recognised the conductor. He was a regular on the Number 70. A small but well-muscled Pole who was happy to give any boy who misbehaved or annoyed other passengers 'a clip round the ear'. Both men ignored the crowd and looked around for something they could use as a ladder. The driver grabbed the three-foot high iron railings that separated Mrs Sims' house from her neighbour's and with the conductor's help yanked it free from its moorings and placed it against the wall. The makeshift ladder reached almost to the bedroom window.

The conductor went up first. As the driver started to follow, the boy's father grabbed the bottom of makeshift ladder and held it steady. Reaching the window, the conductor smashed a pane of glass with his elbow. A sheet of yellow, blue and red flame engulfed his head momentarily. He screamed out and patted at the flames that were dancing in his hair and trying to set fire to his heavy serge uniform. Satisfied that he wasn't alight, he reached through the broken glass, released the catch and pushed the window up. Then he slithered through the opening into the darkness beyond.

Silence enveloped the crowd as he disappeared into the smoke-filled room. Twenty, forty, sixty seconds had elapsed since the Pole had disappeared into the blackness. People were becoming fearful. The driver moved to follow his friend when a figure appeared at the window grasping a baby in one arm and a screaming, bawling toddler in the other. Passing both children to his friend, he struggled out of the window. Wracked with coughing, he was unable to move. His face black with smoke, eyes blinded, he sat on the window ledge. His chest heaved as he tried to drag in the oxygen he so badly needed. A crash sounded behind him and the remaining panes of glass shattered into a myriad of needle sharp projectiles. He arched his back and cursed in Polish as they lacerated his neck and head. Still blinded, he eased forward and was about to jump when the boy's father rushed up the ladder, grabbed him by the arm and led him down.

The fire burned freely for a further five minutes before the sound of bells announced the arrival of the fire brigade who quickly doused the flames. Disappointed that the flames had gone, the boy returned to his bed and relived what he had seen. He thought of Mrs Sims and what she'd looked like in the firelight. Her white underwear, the dark patch between her legs, her face beautiful in its fear and agony. The surprise on the conductor's face when he broke the window and was momentarily engulfed in flames. The smell of smoke and the taste of burning carried by the gentle shifting breeze. Each fragment of memory etched on his mind in Technicolor. For the first time he realised that he had an erection. Rock hard, hot to the touch, he brushed his cock with the palm of his hand. Suddenly his body convulsed in a spasm of exquisite agony that spewed sperm over his stomach and hand. It took all his self-control not to cry out in painful ecstasy. When it was over he smiled, the tip of his tongue, sticking lizard like, from between his lips. *George was right*, he thought, *this will change my life.*

Three more times that night he played with his very own lamb's tail. Each time he embroidered the events he'd seen. The image that released his fourth and final orgasm of the night was of Mrs Sims trapped in the bedroom, her body pressed against the window, flames licking at her face and hair, screaming as her underwear caught fire revealing her breasts and the dark 'v' between her legs.

Stepping back from his work, the man took a penknife from his inside pocket and walked to the end of the storeroom where he scratched the initials HT inside a heart on the doorframe. He knew that his signature would not survive the fire but he was an artist and *every artist should sign his work*, he reasoned. Feeling in his breast pocket, he took out a packet of Senior Service cigarettes and lit up. After taking four drags, he checked the tip of his cigarette to ensure it was burning brightly. Carefully he slipped the unlit end into the book of matches. Then he placed the lint covered matchbook on the bed of tissue paper, cotton wool soaked in lighter fluid and packing material that he had prepared earlier. Most of the cigarette lay outside the nest but when it had burnt to within an inch and a half of the end it would ignite the matches and set the lint and tissue paper alight. Surrounding the nest was the company's own packing material and hidden in it were four small plastic capsules of lighter fluid. They were his insurance policy. Not enough accelerant to show up in tests, but more than enough to ensure that when the thin plastic skins melted, the fluid would spill out and the entire shelf of packing material would burn.

He checked his watch, 10.18pm. It would take three minutes for the cigarette to ignite the book of matches. Within seconds the nest would be aflame. The fire's spread, aided by the lighter fluid and packing material would be rapid. By 10.30 the storeroom would be a blaze and by 10.40 the first flagons and plastic barrels of chemicals would start to explode. The result would be total devastation and the end of another medium sized engineering company in Birmingham which had fallen on hard times.

It was time to go. To call his principal and take up his position across the road and watch his handiwork play out. It was a shame that there were no workers, other than the night watchman, left in the building. He would have liked to see the young typists and sales clerks running from the building in their bright summer skirts and dresses. The image of women screaming as they ran from the building in panic took hold of his mind. Trapped women. Burning clothes. Fear and panic. For thirty seconds he luxuriated in the images that played across his mind. He hadn't put on a show just for himself in a long time. He'd been working so hard. He deserved a reward. He'd start looking for a target tomorrow. But for now, he had to concentre on the job in hand.

Outside, he crossed the deserted street and headed for the two red telephone boxes outside the newsagents. Lifting the receiver, he pushed four pennies into the black coin box and dialled a local number. When his call was answered he pressed Button A, waited for the line to clear, and then said, 'Just calling to say that your package has been delivered.'

'Excellent. The balance of your fee will be paid into your account tomorrow morning.'

Lightning Source UK Ltd.
Milton Keynes UK
UKHW022138131118
332284UK00005B/564/P